Dust We Raised
Channing Turner

Dust We Raised
A Red Adept Publishing Book
Red Adept Publishing, LLC
104 Bugenfield Court
Garner, NC 27529
http://RedAdeptPublishing.com/

First Print Edition: February 2018
Cover Art by Streetlight Graphics

This is a work of fiction. Names, characters, places, and incidents either are the product of the author's imagination or are used fictitiously, and any resemblance to locales, events, business establishments, or actual persons—living or dead—is entirely coincidental.

Chapter One

Billings, Montana
March

With Crabby, one of my best mounts, under me, I waited quietly for Jake to come busting out of number four. Tony Garza had drawn him that round. Tony could ride, but I knew he'd crossed himself a couple of extra times before climbing down into that chute. It was the first night of the weekend rodeo, and I felt nervous about Jake. Crabby could feel it, too. He tried to shuffle sideways, like he always did. That little habit had earned him his name.

Ol' Jake was a really rank bull. His registered name was Jacob's Ladder, but the boys all called him Jake. It wasn't that he was so hard to ride—a number of cowboys had stayed on him for eight seconds—but he was mean, like a barroom fighter who'd kick a man he'd already beaten in the back of the head while he tried to crawl away on the beer-wet floor. Jake had hooked quite a few after they'd hit the ground. Whether or not they lasted the full ride didn't matter to him.

Chip and Dale, the two bullfighters, were bouncing on their toes in front of the chute, flouncing up and down in their silly cutoff overalls like they were in vaudeville. Across the arena, Bugeye Tommy, my pickup partner, was getting ready. I could see his shoulders knotting up with tension. His eyes blinked hard behind those thick glasses, like he was on cocaine. We all stood by while Rex finished up his line of bad jokes with the barrelman. Rex could afford to be funny—he was sitting up in the announcer's booth.

Jake blasted through the open gate, jumping out with his head tucked. His ass pitched high in the air as he left the ground. Tony's head cracked back against the bull's rump, and I winced for him. It would be over in a matter of seconds since Tony wouldn't wear one of those chickenshit helmets the young riders used. Jake spun to the left as Tony's grip faded. Sure enough, he lost it and flailed off, landing hard and flat on his back. Whatever sense he had left got knocked out after that flop.

Jake kept bucking and juking high up in the ozone layer. He always was a showy bull. But then the ton of beef stopped and spun around in the middle of the dirt patch, big black eyes squinting, looking for something to rough up. Tony was still on the ground near the chute, but he rolled to one side and started to push himself up. Chip and Dale, being crazy men, got up close to Jake, prancing around and waving their bandanas in his face. Tony staggered to his feet and stumbled toward the wall. Everyone in the whole Metra arena could see he was out of it... so could Jake.

Ignoring the clowns, the bull lowered his head and scraped the ground with his front feet, his eyes locked on Tony's back as the cowboy tried to stumble away. Tony clearly had no idea what was happening behind him, even though the crowd was screaming. Pandemonium erupted in the stands, and it probably sounded like spectators hollering at the running of the bulls in Spain.

I eased Crabby away from the wall. His ears were up, and he was shuttering air in like a fat man snoring. Tommy and I exchanged a look. My rope was out in my hand. As soon as I twirled it once, Crabby was off. We broke for the bull just as he put his horns down to the ground and lunged. It was a long throw, but the good Lord let me drop the loop over one horn. *Now comes the fun part.*

Two thousand pounds of hamburger could jerk my horse right off his feet if the physics were right. Crabby knew that, too, and he was tensing up. I turned him away just a little and slowed him down as the rope tightened. Saddle leather creaked, and I yanked on the rope. Crabby stutter-stepped a little but stayed upright. Together, we pulled Jake's head to the side, and the bull forgot about Tony.

Crabby backed up to keep the rope tight. New problem: Jake had noticed us. Other bulls would kick and fight the rope, but Jake only locked eyes on Crabby and me then took one step forward. Crabby backed up.

At that second, there was nobody else alive in the arena except that bull, Crabby, and me. I didn't see Chip and Dale pulling Jake's tail. I didn't hear the crowd hollering. Nothing existed but those eyes—as black as hell, and just as mad.

Good old Tommy broke the standoff. He came up on the other side, riding that big buckskin of his and swinging a lariat to beat the band. His eyes bulged out like big white china doorknobs behind Coke-bottle lenses. Tommy didn't know how to quit. He roped both horns and dug in. Dust popped off his chaps when the rope snapped against them.

Jake couldn't fight both of us, so he resorted to bucking and swinging his head, putting on a show while he let us drag him to the exit gate. The gate swung open, and he stopped dead. Then he walked out, as slow and as proud as a king. *Show's over.* Tommy and I dropped our ropes to let him drag them behind the chutes. Someone would bring them out to us later.

Rex was going apeshit on the PA. "Well, how about those bullfighters, ladies and gentlemen? Let's have a hand for our pickup crew, too, Jimmy Lloyd McGowan and Tommy Deutsch. Those cowboys down there really appreciate these men, folks."

Rex always had to lay it on thick, but the crowd loved it. Tony Garza, looking a little woozy, sat high up on the railing nearby. He gave Tommy and me a lopsided grin with a finger to the hat. Cowboys along the rail were hurrahing for us. Tommy and I bumped fists at the gate, got our ropes back, and positioned ourselves for the next ride. Crabby was breathing hard, but I tried not to show it my-self—wouldn't do for the ladies in the crowd to see me looking soft at just thirty-five years of age. *Another night at the rodeo. Welcome to Montana.*

Chapter Two

I got back to work on Monday morning after the weekend shows wrapped up, ending my long string of days off. I would have two twelve-hour day shifts at the refinery before getting off for a couple of days again then going back on nights. The beater Ford pickup I called Ol' Brown rumbled over the railroad tracks in the dark, then I wheeled into a parking space near the change house, feeling stiff all over. A jolt of pain shot up my back when I slid down from the seat and my feet hit the pavement. My boots met with one of the hard-packed little patches of snow and ice scattered around the parking lot, and I grabbed the door to keep from falling. A cold breeze cut through my jacket. Yellowstone country was trying to decide whether it was an early spring or still winter.

In the change house, some of the boys said hello while I started to put on my work gear. "Saw you riding Saturday. Hell of a deal," Jack said. "That gray bull give you some trouble?"

"A little. Wasn't too bad," I answered as I opened my locker. I pulled a blue Nomex jumpsuit over the same Wranglers I'd worn at the rodeo. Then I added steel-toed boots and a white hard hat.

"I heard you was near 'bout jerked off your horse," Ronnie said. "That wasn't a problem?"

"Naw. Tommy Joe came through for me in a big way. The only jerking off was you again in the bathroom."

The others were still guffawing when I left and the door closed behind me. I headed for my post in the pipe still's control room.

I walked across concrete into a labyrinth of steel pipes and pillars. The working refinery was like no natural place on Earth. It throbbed with pressure, heat, and noise while steam hissed from pumps and valves. Big furnaces rumbled with fire in their bellies. The constant roar could turn a man into the walking dead if he had to endure it all day every day. He would end up with a pounding head, not wanting to do anything but sit down on a pail and spit.

I felt the machinery's hot breath as I passed the operating equipment. I could roast meat on the reboilers I tended. Hydrocarbon smells, sweet aromatics and sour sulfur compounds, wafted everywhere. The company always tried to put a cap on emissions, but a hundred thousand barrels coursed through those lines every day. Seals busted. Leaks happened.

The control room had been built to be blast proof, so it was quiet inside. I put my hard hat on the rack and checked in with Terry, the senior operator I was there to relieve. Reading a paperback western, he was sitting in front of a wall of dials and gauges, each one tracking some variable in the process of separating crude into its dozens of components. Refining was a complex thing that we tried to keep contained so we didn't blow ourselves the hell up.

"Morning, Jimmy Lloyd," he grunted.

"Howdy."

He stood up and stretched. "Nothing much to tell you. Flows are steady. Jamie is hearing a chatter in P-33. I've written up a work order for mechanical to look at it." He slapped a hand on the paperwork sitting on the desk.

"Sounds good." I leaned over and initialed the logbook. The pipe stills belonged to me as of right then. "See you tonight, Terry."

He picked up his lunch bucket from the counter then turned back to me before he went out the door. "Heard you had a close one Saturday night. You okay?"

"I'm okay, Terry. I wish people would stop wanting to take my pulse all the time. I'm fine." I sat down and ran both hands through my hair.

"All right, Jim. I'm just asking. That's all."

"I know. I know... and thanks. I appreciate it. Now go home and get some sleep."

"Later."

MY BACK AND SHOULDER were killing me. I felt sure I'd hurt something the other night, pulling cowboys off broncs. By lunch, I had trouble even just sitting down to eat, so I decided to go over to the nurse's office. The carpeted halls in the main office building were even quieter than a control room. I passed by a dozen cubicle offices before I reached Janet's.

"Hi, Jimmy Lloyd."

"Hey, Janet. How's life on the frontiers of medicine?"

She leaned back in her swivel chair. "Just like life on the western frontier, I guess. Nothing much happens for a while, then all of a sudden, here comes Jimmy Lloyd McGowan, and now there's shit splattered all over the fan."

We both laughed, and I watched her eyes crinkle. Nurse Janet had been pushing pills at the refinery for years. Still single at fifty, she was everybody's pal but especially friendly with one of the department heads in the other wing. Most of us liked her all right, though.

"Take a seat. What can I do for you?"

I explained that I needed a few heavy-duty Ibuprofen tablets for my aching body. She rested one arm along the desk as she listened. Her forehead wrinkled, and she shook her head. I stopped talking.

"What?" I asked.

"You didn't just hurt yourself stacking firewood, did you, Jimmy Lloyd?"

"You know I didn't."

"Riding in the rodeo again?"

"I don't compete anymore. I was riding pickup." I'd already been over this with management, and I didn't like talking about it again.

Janet wagged her hand back and forth. "Same, same, Jimmy..." She sat up straight in the chair. "I can give you some stuff, but I have to tell you this. The refinery manager's already directed me to document and report to him any injuries or medications you take because of your 'outside activities.' You're aware of that?"

"Yes, Janet, I'm aware of that. I got the signed piece of paper in my file. Just give me the damn pills, would you?" I was already thinking I should have just bought something over the counter at a drugstore.

She spun around to reach into a cabinet. "Okay, here you go. Just sign here."

I signed and got up, holding the little packet of white tablets. "Thank you, ma'am. Do what you gotta do. No hard feelings."

"Okay, Jimmy Lloyd."

Fuming, I walked back to the pipe stills. Over the past several years, I'd broken a few limbs and once had a separated pelvis. It meant using up all my sick leave then covering a lot more with vacation time and light duty. Management seemed all right with it for a while, but lately they'd decided to lower the hammer on me, especially for missing work due to hazardous "outside activities." They'd warned me: One more rodeo injury and I was out of a job. Dave, my union rep, and I had both signed the warning letter then watched the HR head put it in my folder.

"This is serious, Jimmy," the office geek had said. "Any more missed time because of rodeo, and we have no choice but to terminate you. You understand?" He turned to the rep. "Are we clear?"

"No problem," I'd said when Dave nodded.

Three months later, it looked as though the issue still hadn't gone away. They were keeping tabs on me. I kicked at a rock. *Working rodeo part-time or my job. Rodeo or car-e-e-e-r.*

I stopped to listen. Pump P-33 was for sure chattering. The bearings were about to go out. I decided to call mechanical to speed up getting some millwrights on it before it blew, and I needed to switch the feed to P-33A in the meantime. I decided something else, too. *The hell with them if they can't take a joke. I'm going to keep on rodeoing.*

I chuckled to myself as I started walking again. *This is the very hardheaded, stubborn reason you get yourself in so much hot water, Jimmy—the very reason.* I knew the truth of it, too. I had lost Esther because of that.

BY SHIFT CHANGE, IT was dark again. After shucking the Nomex and boots, I walked out to Ol' Brown. That Ibuprofen seemed to be working; the aches felt better. I traded the hard hat for a Rand's custom cattleman made out of black beaver felt—better than a Stetson. There wasn't much traffic as I headed north up the hill on Billings's Main Street. The busiest thoroughfare in the state was nearly empty at night.

Esther's house was on my way home, so I planned to stop by with her half of the rent money. She had agreed to let me keep the house and land because she knew how much it meant to me. I only had to give her half of the income from the little rental house at the back. I could have just sent it to her in the mail, but I hand delivered it every month for a chance to see her again. Divorce was too easy in Montana. It only took six weeks. From "I need some space" to "Get out, we're done!" had gone by way too quickly for anyone to have second thoughts about it. I'd had plenty of second thoughts since then, though.

My headlights swung across her Toyota in the driveway. I felt relieved that some other cowboy's pickup wasn't sitting next to it. That day would come soon enough, though. Blond and blue-eyed, Esther was a good-looking woman—always had been since we first met at Shepherd High. She could fill out tight jeans like no other female I'd ever seen. I was sure the male patients at Billings General, where she worked as a nurse, had wet dreams about her. God help me, I still did, and I'd never stopped loving her.

I had been a real dick in those days—and still was sometimes. Too much cowboy and not enough man. I did try to rein in that immature brat inside me, but my efforts weren't good enough... or soon enough. After eight years, Esther couldn't take any more, so she'd left. That had happened last September, just six months ago.

I clomped across her porch and rang the bell.

"Hi, Jimmy."

"Hello, Queenie." I stuck the folded check forward between two fingers like I was flipping over an ace of spades. "How you doing?"

Esther took it without looking at it and slipped it into the pocket of her flannel shirt. "Pretty good, I guess. How have you been?" She leaned on the doorjamb, holding her elbows, and staring at me like a judge.

"Can't complain." I shuffled my feet, and my heart throbbed in my throat. "Any chance of me coming in for a spell?"

She smiled sadly, and I almost reached out for her, then she shook her head slowly. "Not tonight, Jimmy. We've been through this before. Let's just leave it where we are. Okay?" She stepped back. The door started to close.

"Sure," I said.

Back in the truck, I cranked up the heater and leaned my head on the steering wheel. I guessed she might never trust me in her heart again.

Chapter Three

Billings
May

The weather had warmed up considerably, and I decided the time had come to check the fence lines for winter damage. After breakfast, I stepped out on the front porch and stared up the highway to see if my hired help was going to show. Chad White Horse worked with the contract night crew the refinery used for janitorial work, and he lived in a dilapidated shack just over the hill, close enough to my place to walk there when he wanted to. I tried to give him odd jobs now and then to help him out a little. Like most troubled young men from the rez, he had a sad backstory, but I didn't ask about it. I had told him I could use him that day, yet I didn't see him coming.

I sighed and slapped my gloves together. *I'll just do it by myself.* Sweet Ginger still needed to work anyway. The little gal hadn't been ridden much since the first snows flew last October because she was bred a little too light bodied for rodeo jobs. Her dam was a local dandy of a mare, and the sire had been a high-priced Arab stud from Bozeman. I didn't usually keep Arabians—an AQHA quarter horse suited me for what I did most of the time—but Esther loved them.

Sweet fidgeted in the stall as I brushed her coat and raked off a basketball-sized wad of brown hair. She knew we were going out.

"Easy, girl..." Along with the saddlebags, I hung gear on the saddle for any wire pulling I might have to do.

The excited mare practically bounced out of the barn. She would've burst into a run if I'd let her. The midmorning turned out beautiful and sunny. Bunchgrass and little wildflowers pushed up everywhere. The air smelled fresh like the snowcapped Beartooth Mountains I could see clearly fifty miles off to the south. A grand day.

My place was a couple of miles north of Billings, up on high ground called the Rims. At forty acres, the property was easy to ride around in an hour. There were no farms and not many profitable ranches around me. The land was good for nothing much except raising livestock, and it wasn't even so great for that. The Yellowstone River valley below had some good acreage, but up around my place was mostly sandstone and sagebrush.

At night, over the edge of the Rims, I could see the glow of lights in the sky from the largest city in Montana. The refinery also lit up, and when the wind was still, I could hear it rumbling. Mostly, I shared all that with coyotes and the occasional mountain lion. I was pretty sure I'd seen a wolf last fall, too.

Right away, I found loose wire in the fence. I dismounted and hammered in a staple, taking care not to scratch myself on the barbed wire. Then it was on to the next spot. I enjoyed the work and didn't mind being alone to do it. There weren't many wire breaks, so in forty-five minutes I was at the back edge of the fence line, not too far from the rental house. On a wild hair, I turned Sweet in that direction to drop in on Kamal.

I'd never thought I would be renting my place to a college student from Saudi Arabia's sandbox, but seven months ago, Kamal al Dossari had answered the ad with two months' rent in advance, plus a deposit. He seemed like a nice enough kid who kept to himself, and he paid his rent on time, something I've found to be highly desirable since the cowboys that Esther and I rented to before weren't so reliable. He always paid in cash, too. I'd wondered at first if that was drug money until I realized he never had visitors and rarely went out himself. The gravel drive to the back house went right by my kitchen window, so it was no big chore to see who was coming and going. Other than that, I hadn't dealt with him much.

The rental house wasn't a whole lot to look at, with two bedrooms and a bath. The county would probably condemn it if someone ever remembered it was back here. The barn and corral with it were actually in better shape than the house. I found Kamal sitting cross-legged on a car-sized sandstone slab behind the little house, a notebook open in his lap. He spotted me while I was still a ways off, and set the writing tablet aside to watch me ride up.

"Howdy, Kamal."

"Hello, Mr. McGowan."

"Just out checking the fence. Looks like a good day for it." I noticed the notebook beside him was actually a sketchbook. "You an artist?"

"What? Uh, no." He shrugged dismissively and rolled his eyes downward at the sketchbook. "I only like to draw a little bit sometimes. I am not good." Then he stared at Sweet Ginger as though he'd never seen an equine animal before. "Your horse, is she an Arabian?"

"She's an Arab for sure. Comes from your part of the world, doesn't she?"

The kid's eyes widened, and he nodded a little bit. "I thought so. She has excellent conformation. What is her name?" Kamal slid off the sandstone to stand beside Sweet. He stroked her neck.

"She answers to 'Sweet,' but her name's Sweet Ginger... my ex-wife owns her." Another moment passed while he silently patted Sweet. "You have horses yourself?"

He shook his head. "My father has some Arabians. I used to ride them... a long time ago." He bent and blew softly into the mare's nostrils, and she relaxed under me.

On a whim, I swung down and handed over the reins. "You want to ride her?"

He looked at me as if I had just offered him a date with Miss Universe. "Me?"

"Sure, go ahead. She won't buck. How long's it been for you?"

"It has been years. A long time since…" He fingered the reins and looked down. "You mean this? You want me to ride her?"

"I said so, didn't I? Now get on and go."

Kamal gathered the reins and put his left foot in the stirrup. He swung up easily, the mark of a horseman. He and I were about the same height, so the stirrups fit well enough, even though he was wearing running shoes.

"How's that feel?" I asked, rubbing Sweet on the neck.

"It feels good… the saddle is a little strange."

"Never been on a western style?"

"No, never one like this."

"You'll get used to it. Just cluck to her and call her 'Sweet.' She'll do what you want—neck rein and leg pressure. You know what I'm talking about?"

"Yes. I think so." He straightened his shoulders, and I could see he was already getting comfortable. "Where do you want me to ride her?"

"Anywhere you like. How about going down to the far corner of the pasture and back? You can check the fence for me. Look for breaks and loose wire. Sound good?" I pointed at the distant corner of the field where I hadn't been yet. "I'll just wait here till you get back."

"Very well."

Sweet cocked an ear at me, but she seemed just fine with her new rider. Kamal must have felt considerably lighter than me, being slightly built at about one hundred sixty pounds. He made a kissy noise and lightly squeezed with his legs. They moved off toward the fence line at a walk, Kamal grinning like a kid with candy.

I watched them for a minute until it was plain my renter knew what he was doing. Leaning against the sandstone slab didn't seem like much of a thing to do, so I scampered up to where he had been sitting and settled down to pass the time. I could have just lain back and dozed right then, the way the sun warmed up the rock and me together, but when my elbow nudged Kamal's sketchbook, I picked it up to see what he had. He seemed to be about half done with a drawing of the mountains in the distance. It didn't look too bad.

Kamal and Sweet Ginger were just a speck when they reached the far corner of my land, but they were starting back. I flipped through earlier drawings nearer to the front of the pad. He had some cityscapes—the Billings town hall and police headquarters, the federal courthouse, and a couple of bank buildings. His very first sketch surprised me, though.

The detailed drawing of the Excalibur Mountain refinery where I worked had been done from the bluffs overlooking the complex across the Yellowstone River. I could make out the crude unit, cat cracker, light ends—each unit plain as day. Arabic writing had been scribbled all around the margins.

I looked up when I heard hoofbeats. Kamal had kicked Sweet Ginger up to a canter. He looked like a natural, rocking easy in the saddle with a loose hand on the reins, smiling happily. I had to smile myself when I saw him. They pulled up in front of the giant slab, spraying gravel forward. Sweet did her little jiggy two-step and blew to show she could run some more.

"Well, how was it?" I asked, still smiling. "Looks like you know how to ride all right."

"It was very fine. Sweet is a good horse, a very good horse. I like her. My father always liked mares, too." He ran his fingers through her mane before he lifted his right leg over and dropped to the ground. He kept patting her until Sweet nuzzled his shoulder. About that time, he saw that I was holding the sketch pad, and a cloud passed over his face. "You looked at my drawings?" He could have been accusing me of grand theft.

"Well, yeah, I guess I did. Hey, don't be mad. These are pretty good. You an art major or something?" I stood and turned around to climb off the rock and get the reins back.

"No, I don't major in art. This is just a hobby, something I do while I wait."

"Well, that's too bad. It looks like you got a good eye for this stuff. You know, your refinery drawing could have been done by an engineer."

Kamal almost snatched the pad from me when I held it up. "It's just a hobby." He looked at the ground, his broad smile gone.

Then we both just stood there without saying a word.

"Hey, look, I wasn't trying to get in your business, Kamal. Don't take it sideways. I thought your pictures were pretty good, that's all."

His features softened, and he handed me the reins.

"Yes, of course. They are just... private to me." He looked up. "I am sorry I acted rudely."

"No problem." I swung up into the saddle.

Kamal gazed at Sweet again. "This is your wife's horse? You are married?"

"My ex-wife, and no, I'm not anymore." I smiled at him. "Now *that* would have been my turn to get grumpy."

"I am sorry."

"Oh no. No problem. Those're just the facts." Sweet Ginger danced sideways under me as I had a thought. "Say, Kamal, would you like to do me a favor?"

He stared up at me blankly.

"It's nothing big, but how'd you like to come up to the house in the next couple of days and do a picture of this horse? I think you'd do a good job of it. I know my ex would like it. I could pay you—oh, I don't know... twenty dollars, maybe?"

Kamal seemed startled at the idea. "Yes, I could do that. When would you want me to come?"

"I'm off today and tomorrow. How about tomorrow at noon? I can fix us a sandwich. You eat pork?"

Chapter Four

Kamal started stopping by the house fairly often after that. I even hired him and Chad White Horse to paint my barn and corrals, and the two of them seemed to get along pretty well, thick as hibernating bear cubs. Chad started showing up regularly to paint with Kamal. They didn't work more than a couple of hours at a time, but I wasn't in any hurry. They got their cash daily when the job was done. No taxes, and no social security. It worked out fine for everyone.

Kamal finally did a sketch of Sweet Ginger, then I had him do the four horses that belonged to me. The kid could really draw. I framed the one of Sweet and gave it to Esther with the next rent check.

"You didn't do this, Jimmy. Who did?" She held the picture out and studied it with a smile.

"That Arab student, Kamal. The one who's renting the back house."

"Really? Well, he knows horses. That's for sure." She looked at it more closely. "Look here. He even got her topline right. That's hard to do." She lowered the frame. "Kamal? Like the ship of the desert?"

"No. It's more like 'Kay Mall,' I think. Polite young fellow. He draws other stuff, too."

"Have I met him?"

"I'm pretty sure you haven't."

"I'd like to."

"Well, you know where we are. Come on over. I'm home for a couple of days."

Esther sighed. "No tricks, Jimmy Lloyd. Don't be thinking this is something it's not. I just want to see the person that can draw a horse like this."

"No tricks, Queenie. Come meet him. He's drawn Crabby and the others, too. They're all this good."

She blew a strand of hair out of her eyes, considering. "I'm off till three today. You gonna be at the house?"

"No other plans." My palms started to sweat.

"All right. Let me finish up here. I'll be out there in an hour."

"Take your time." My boots barely touched the concrete as I walked back to the truck.

THEY MUST HAVE REALLY lowered the standards at MSU-B, since I'd gone there because, as far as I could see, Kamal hardly ever attended any classes.

I found him at his house, where he met me at the door. "Kamal, come on. I need you up at my house."

"Your house? Is something wrong?" He opened the screen and stepped out.

"No, no. Nothing like that. My ex wants to meet you. She liked your picture of Sweet Ginger and wanted to see who drew it."

"She liked it?"

"I'm telling you. Hop in the truck—she's on her way."

He climbed in, a puzzled look all over him. "She is the one who owns Sweet Ginger?"

"That's right. I just let her keep the horse here." I turned the truck around and started slinging gravel on the way back up to my house. "Now look, Kamal. Her name's Esther, and she's a beauty. So don't you be gawking or winking at her. Understand?" I grinned to show him I was kidding. Partially kidding anyway.

He grinned back. "I understand, Mr. Jimmy Lloyd."

Her car was already bouncing up the long drive when we got back to the house. Esther's beauty bowled Kamal over, just like I knew it would, and he gave me a funny look when she climbed out of her little car.

"Hello, you must be Kamal." She reached out to shake hands, and he took her grip awkwardly, as though it were a squeeze toy made out of shit. His mouth tightened just a bit. I remembered some deal about Arab men not touching females—something about their religion.

"Yes, I am Kamal," he managed to stammer.

Esther didn't seem to notice a thing, and inside of five minutes talking with him there on the porch, she had Kamal eating out of that poop hand.

"I love that picture you did of my horse," she said. "You are a very talented young man. Jimmy Lloyd tells me you have some others, too. I'd *love* to see them!" She gushed about the drawing enough to beat Old Faithful, but that was just Esther. She never faked it when she liked something. I stood off to the side and watched her do her magic.

Kamal blushed at the attention, and it occurred to me that maybe he hadn't talked to very many American gals in the few months he'd been here.

"Esther, there's more inside. Kamal's done Crabby, Feedbag, and the others. Come on in and take a look," I said, trying to make it sound casual. She hadn't been back inside the house since driving away that fine autumn afternoon the year before.

"Sure," she answered. She tried to pretend there was no big deal about the whole thing, too, but I saw the hesitation.

I led the way up onto the porch and held open the door. Kamal walked in ahead of Esther, not being familiar with Western chivalry, I guess. She shot me a quizzical glance. I shrugged, and she grinned.

"Have a seat," I said. "I'll go get the pictures in a minute. You want anything, Esther? Kamal? A beer?"

Without meaning to, I had put both of them to the test. Esther might not be so happy about having a beer with me again, and I had no idea what my renter's views on alcohol were. He looked quickly at her, waiting for her reaction.

"Yeah, I'll have one. You still have Bud Light?" she answered.

"You know it... Kamal?"

He sat beside Esther on my couch, his hands on his knees, studying her profile before he answered. "Yes, uh, I will have the same, please."

"Sure thing."

I grabbed three cold cans from the fridge and returned to the living room. I handed two of them over then sat and put mine down on a side table. I hadn't changed anything about the place since Esther had left. It looked messier, of course, but the furniture hadn't moved. She didn't seem to notice. A short, uncomfortable silence hung there before I slapped my knees and stood up.

"Let me go get the drawings," I said. "I'll be right back."

In the bedroom closet, I dug around until I found the large folder that Kamal had presented to me. I heard the fizz-pop of a can being tabbed open in the living room, then another a few seconds later. I stopped to listen for a minute. Hearing Esther's voice again in what used to be our house made me feel funny. When I heard her laugh, I made my way back to where they sat.

"You found them? Oh, good! Let me see," Esther said, reaching out for the pictures. She began to look through the stack. "Oh, Kamal, these are *good*."

He blushed some more, staring at her and hanging on every word she said.

"There's some more stuff in there," I said. "He's done landscapes and buildings and all sorts of pictures."

"I see that. Oh wow. These are *sooo* good." Esther was holding out a drawing at arm's length. It looked like the picture Kamal had been doing the day I'd let him ride Sweet. She took a long pull from her can and set it down.

His expression deadpan, Kamal sipped his beer. I didn't think he'd ever tasted beer before that afternoon. It was turning into quite a day for him.

The three of us talked for almost an hour, just sitting there shooting the breeze and laughing. Esther asked if she could buy the mountain picture, and he gave it to her. Apparently, they'd both forgotten it was my picture first.

"So, Kamal, tell me about Saudi Arabia," Esther said. "I'd love to know about your family."

"Uh. It is different from here. It is desert mostly." He went silent and stared at the floor.

"Oh..." She laughed. "That's not so different. Sometimes when it doesn't rain in Montana for a spell, it seems like a desert here, too." There was an awkward pause, then she asked, "What about your family? Do you have any brothers and sisters?"

Kamal looked up. "I am the youngest son of six, and I have five sisters."

"Really? That's a big family. Are any of them here in the United States, too?"

"No."

Esther clearly wanted to ask him more, but she could see that Kamal didn't want to say much more about where he came from.

I turned the talk to horses. "Kamal here is a pretty good rider. He got on Sweet the other day and rode like a pro."

"Yes, you told me," she answered brightly and turned to Kamal. "So you can ride, too? How did you like Sweet Ginger?"

The young man's eyes lit up. "She is a very nice horse. I liked her very much." He looked down at his hands in his lap before he turned his whole body toward Esther and met her eyes for the first time. "Would you sell her to me? I can pay you what she is worth." His words came out in a nervous torrent.

It took a lot to rock Esther back on her heels, but that did it for her. Her eyes flew open, and she drew in a quick breath. Esther loved that horse. "Why, Kamal... I'm so pleased that you like Sweet that much, but no, I can't sell her. She's like my child. I'll always have her. I only keep her here because Jimmy is good enough to take care of her for me until I get a place I can do it myself." She turned her face to me, and her eyes softened.

Kamal nodded and hung his head. "Yes, I understand. My father would not sell any of his favorites, either—not for any price."

Esther laid a hand on his knee, and Kamal stiffened at the touch. She noticed and took the hand back. "But, Kamal, there is something we could arrange. I'll let you ride Sweet anytime you like as long as you're staying here at the back house. You just have to be gentle with her. I can't have anyone mistreating her." She looked over at me again. "And Jimmy Lloyd here will tell me if you do." She smiled, and I raised my beer in a toast to both of them.

"Will do," I said.

Kamal looked puzzled. "You would just allow me to ride her for nothing? That is very kind, but no, no. I must pay you. I would buy her if I could, but I must at least pay you something, Miss Esther."

"Just Esther."

"Excuse me?"

"You can just call me Esther. We're not living down south, and I'm not that old yet. Don't call me 'Queenie,' either." She smiled in my direction again. "Only Jimmy calls me Queenie."

I met her gaze and smiled back.

"Very well, Esther, but I still feel that you should take a payment for your kindness."

She leaned forward and patted that knee again. "Kamal, if we all got paid for being kind, then it wouldn't be a kindness at all, would it? But I tell you what. Why don't you lease her? It's like rent. Just pay me, let's say... seventy-five a month, and you can have exclusive use of her—except for me, of course. What do you say to that?"

I whistled to myself. Seventy-five dollars to lease a horse like Sweet was dirt cheap—too cheap, actually. *Esther must really like this boy.*

He thought for a second. "Yes, I would do that."

"Good." She sat back. "Keep her at the corral at your place if you like. Jimmy can help you with her if you need it." She turned around on the couch to face me. "Won't you, Jimmy? You know that horse as well as I do."

I raised the beer again. "You bet."

I hadn't felt so relaxed in a long while. Esther had that way about her. It almost felt like old times. And as for Kamal, that kid would have taken her into his harem right there on the spot.

Finally, it started to get late. I offered them each another beer, but Esther politely refused. "Got to get to work in a little while, Jimmy. Can't have booze on my breath, you know. Some other time, though," she said.

That "some other time" made my heart jump. "Okay."

I walked out on the porch with both of them. Esther stopped at the steps to shake hands with Kamal, and this time, he actually gripped hers.

"Thank you for the picture, Kamal—both of them." She held up the mountain-view sketch. "It was nice meeting you." She turned to me. "Thanks for inviting me out, Jimmy. I really enjoyed this. Really."

"I'm glad, Queenie. So did I." We touched hands for a second before she looked away. I watched her skip down the steps and walk to her car.

Kamal and I both waved at Esther turning the Corolla around in the yard. "You want a ride back to your place?" I asked him.

"No thank you. I think it is a good day for a walk." He looked sideways at me. "Esther is a very nice lady. Why are you divorced, Jimmy Lloyd?"

I leaned against a porch post, watching her car drive away on the long gravel driveway. "Long story, Kamal. Maybe someday."

"I understand. Okay, goodbye." He hopped down from the porch and turned back to me. "Thank you for this afternoon. I enjoyed it very much."

"That's good, Kamal. Maybe we'll do it again sometime."

He started down the road to his house, and I stayed on the porch, keeping Esther in sight on the highway until her car disappeared over a little rise. When I went back in the house, I cleaned up the beer cans. Esther had drained hers. Kamal had barely touched his, so I finished it.

Chapter Five

I mowed the grass that afternoon, first time for the year. The new growth had come up in patchy clumps since most of the yard was bare earth. Yellowstone County never had enough rain for a magazine-picture lawn. Afterward, I leaned back on the porch steps with a sweating glass of iced tea. Dunker showed up with his new shiny red truck about then. I had to admit it did sparkle like a ruby ahead of the dust cloud it kicked up. He pulled to a stop in front of where I sat.

"Come over and sit down," I said, not getting up. "If you get out of it quick enough, maybe nobody'll know you drive around in a Dodge. They'll think I'm the dumb one."

"Too late for that. People already know you're dumb. Being crazy's just extra." He eased down from the cab.

I could hear his knees creaking clear across the yard. Dunker was about sixty-four and still as hard as river rocks. His last injury and his first Social Security check had come the same week, so he'd figured that was the time to quit doing the rodeos. In the years before he retired, though, he showed me everything I needed to know about being a pickup man. My dad died just before my fifteenth birthday, so his best friend Dunker had been the next closest thing for me. No longer six feet tall, he carried a little dewlap that hung over his belt, yet I would pity any poor guy who decided to mess with the gray-haired old badger.

"Well, come on anyway. No use standing in the sun, talking to a crazy man. You want something to drink? Beer? Tea?"

He eyed the wet glass in my hand. "That tea looks good. Already sweetened?"

"Sure is. I'll get you some. Sit down." I went inside to pour him a glass from the pitcher in the icebox.

Went I came back, Dunker had sprawled on the wooden steps and pushed his hat back. A strip of white forehead showed between his tan and his hairline.

I handed the glass to him. "What's up, Dunk?"

He stared off at the peaks of the Beartooths then wagged his chin at them. "Ice is starting to come off the lakes. Won't be too long now."

"You think it'll be early this year?" Every summer after the big snow melt, a group of us would go up into the Forest Service mountains to fish and drink beer. For years, Dunker had taken on the job of being the organizer for our bunch of misfits.

He nodded at me. "You betcha. I think in a couple of months or so, we can be up there in God's country." He took a sip. "You got some time coming?"

"I can get it. You got a particular date in mind?"

He shook his head. "Naw, I thought maybe you and me and some of the others could meet down at the Rainbow and maybe do a little calendar scratching."

"Tonight?"

"Well... you got any reason not to? Somewhere else to be?"

"Guess not." I thought for a second. "How about I bring a friend?"

His eyebrows tipped his hat up a little more. "*You* got a friend? That beats all I ever heard." He scratched day-old whiskers and grinned. "A lady friend?"

"No way, funny man. Not tonight. I was thinking about bringing my renter." I jerked my thumb in the direction of the back house. "He doesn't seem to get out much."

Dunker rubbed his chin again, thinking. "That A-rab boy?"

"Yeah. He's all right. Likes to ride."

"Okay then." Dunker drained the rest of his glass, set it down on the steps, and stood up. "I guess about eight o'clock before the band cranks up. I'll have Thor and Brownie there. Maybe some more." He started walking to his truck, which gleamed, despite the light coat of dust. "Thanks for the tea."

I got up. "Wait a minute. That's it? You drove out here to tell me to come to the Rainbow? Jeez, Dunker, why didn't you just call me? You heard of the telephone? This little black thing that used to have a dial on it?" I held up my cell phone. "Yours probably had a crank on it."

He stopped and turned around. "I know. I just like to get out some when the weather turns nice. The tea was good, too. You don't get that over the phone." The truck door slammed as he got in. Within a minute, he was churning up dust again, bouncing on his way back to the highway.

I SAT BACK AND LISTENED to Dunker's tires whining away on the gravel. It was time to haul hay back to Kamal's place for his new horse. As excited as an A student on the first day of school, he had already returned to my house earlier with a halter and rope to lead Sweet Ginger away.

I bucked a couple dozen square bales into Ol' Brown and drove them back to Kamal's place later that evening. He came out to help when I parked next to the barn. He climbed up in the truck bed to heave them down to me, pretty strong for a wiry little guy. Together, we stocked up the pallets in the barn. When we got done, we leaned against the side of the truck, watching Sweet nosing around in her new home corral.

I wiped my face with a handkerchief before I said anything. "Hey, Kamal, I'm going into town tonight. Wanna come?"

"Into Billings?" He looked at me curiously. "Why?"

"Oh, just to see some fellas, friends of mine. You ever been to the Rainbow?"

"The Rainbow?"

"It's a bar. We'll have ourselves a couple of beers. Shoot the bull. Stuff like that."

"I don't know, Jimmy Lloyd," he said. "I am not comfortable in a bar."

"Aw, come on. You've never even been in one, have you? Tell the truth now."

Kamal smiled, looked down, and shook his head. "No, I haven't. But... would I even be welcome?" He shrugged and looked at me.

"Aw hell, boy. You'll be with me and some other buddies. No problem. Just put on some clean jeans and be ready about a quarter to eight. I'll come pick you up." I smacked the side of the pickup as I turned away to get in. I waved out the window when I drove away. "See you in a little while," I yelled. In the mirror, I could see him standing by the gate and watching me all the way up the rise.

KAMAL MUST HAVE BEEN watching for my headlights. He came out his front door before I even rolled to a stop. He had on clean jeans all right—along with a new striped long-sleeved shirt and squeaky new Nikes. A Denver Broncos baseball cap sat squarely on his head. I thought at first that he'd done a pretty fair job of trying to fit in, then he got in the pickup cab, and the smell of aftershave nearly knocked me out.

"Hoo-whee! Do you reckon you put on enough perfume?" I said, holding my nose. "I believe I could scent you when you stepped out of the house."

"Is that a problem?" he answered anxiously.

"No, not really a problem. But, Kamal, there probably won't be many gals there that you'd want to fool with. And you sure don't have to be smelling that good for me. Go easy on the smell stuff after this."

"Okay. I am sorry, Jimmy Lloyd."

"No big deal."

He seemed embarrassed, so I didn't say anything more about it. I just quietly cracked the window about an inch.

The Rainbow Bar was one of those places there always was on the wrong side of town. Constructed long ago of old, weary brown brick, it was the bad boy of Billings's Montana Avenue. Back before the country knew it had a surgeon general, the place would have been thick with blue-gray cigarette smoke curling from its pressed-tin ceiling tiles down to the cracked mirror behind the bar. The stained walls still held some of the odor. Of course, when the smoke left, so had a lot of the atmosphere. The booze stayed on, though. Some serious drinking still went on there.

The last holdout American smokers puffed away outside on the sidewalk around the door. A little Mary Jane perfumed the air, too. I could hear the jukebox inside playing ZZ Top's "Sharp Dressed Man." Nodding at people I knew, I walked in like I owned the place. In a way, I did. The money I had spent there over time probably paid a year's rent for Grady, the owner.

Billiard balls clacked around at the two tables in the far corner. The din of people talking filled the dark interior. A group of middle-aged gals sat at a round table, laughing. I glanced back at Kamal. He looked like a cat at a dog fight, nervous and looking for a place to bolt.

"C'mon, Kamal, let's go see some fellows." I had spotted Brownie leaning over one of the lit pool tables, wearing his trademark brown beaver Stetson and his dark bush of a handlebar.

We walked across the dirty, scuffed wooden floor.

"Well, speaking of friends in low places... how you doing, Jimmy Lloyd?" CK's slow drawl rolled over the green felt at us. He leaned against the wall, as slim as the cue stick he held for the next shot.

I grinned at him. CK worked with me at the refinery. A transfer up from the Deep South ten years ago, he'd come to consider himself a native Montanan. He looked the part all right, with the cowboy hat and vest, but when he opened his mouth, what came out was pure grits and Dixie.

"Doing all right, CK. How about yourself? Ready to go fishing?"

"You betcha he's ready. It's time for all of us to get out and raise some hell." Brownie straightened up after a clean-miss bank shot. His big frame was solid, his hands hard from years of construction work and pipefitting at the local plants. "How's it going, Jimbo?" He eyed Kamal standing behind me like my shadow. "Who's your friend?"

I turned to bring Kamal forward by his arm. "Fellows, meet Kamal al Dossari. He's renting the little house at the back from me. Kamal, this is Brownie. He's ugly, but he won't hurt you. This here's CK. He's even uglier, and he *will* hurt you if you get between him and food. Don't let his skinny little ass fool you."

They leaned forward to shake hands. Kamal used that same limp, cold-fish grip he had first done with Esther. I figured shaking hands wasn't something they did much back in the desert. He mumbled something I couldn't hear over the bar's noise.

I made sure I had pronounced the name right, but sure enough, CK got it wrong anyway. "Camel? You say your name's *Camel*?" He squinted at Kamal.

"No, dipwad. I said 'Kamal'—like 'Kay Mall' with a *K*," I answered, placing my hand on Kamal's shoulder. "Don't pay any mind to him, Kamal. They're still learning to read down in Alabama."

"Don't insult me with that Alabama talk, Jimmy Lloyd. I am a proud *Mississippi* redneck. Thank you very much. We all learn to read by the eleventh grade." He bent to take his shot. "Pleased to meet you, Kamal."

"Thor here?" I asked.

Brownie shook his head, watching as CK missed the shot. None of us could play pool worth a damn. "Not yet. Said he had to drop off his last load of cattle at the stockyard first. Got the auction tomorrow."

"Right. I forgot about that."

Thor Svenson managed a ranch downstream on the Yellowstone for some high-dollar man from the East Coast. The owner showed up about three times a year to bring his girlfriend and pack some guests around for bird hunting and barbecues. Then he headed home and left the ranch to Thor. *What a sweet deal.*

"Here he is," CK said.

Anyone who saw him walk into a bar—or any room—knew right away how Thor had gotten his name. A bushy blond mustache covered and drooped around his mouth, and yellow hair curled over his collar. He looked like a Viking with a cowboy hat. His jeans and Carhartt jacket were filthy with mud and cow hair. "How's it going, fellas?" he asked.

We all shook hands, and I introduced him to Kamal.

"Nice to meet you, young fella," Thor said.

"Hey, we're all here except Dunker," I said. "Let's go ahead and take us a table before it gets too crowded."

"That won't be so easy, Jimmy." Brownie tilted his head at the tables arranged around the small dance floor.

About twenty bikers had come in after me. Some might have just been run-of-the-mill Sturgis-happy riders, but most of them were no doubt hardcore. They were spread out at the bar and at the tables around the group of middle-aged ladies. Pitchers of beer sloshed back and forth on the tabletops. The old gals didn't seem to care that they were in the center of a pack of rowdy leather vests and do-rags. They sure had to notice the sweat smell, though. One table remained un-occupied except for empty beer cans stacked on it.

"This way. Here's one," I said over my shoulder as I headed across the dance floor. I pulled out a chair next to the bandstand. Brownie came right behind me. As he took ahold of his chair, one of the near-by bikers bumped into him with his shoulder. A tattoo of a dagger with a drop of blood at the tip showed on the dude's bare arm.

"That's our table," the man said. "We was gonna sit there." A couple of his buddies stood behind him, looking at us like we were pissing on their kitchen floor.

"Sorry, my man. You shoulda got here sooner," Brownie replied, never having any use for being subtle. He turned back to the table and sat down.

The bikers stayed there for a minute, just glaring at the back of Brownie's head, before they walked away to join up with three more at another table. The six of them looked over at us between swigs of beer. I think I was the only one of us who noticed the exchange, though.

We ordered two pitchers and a few Solo cups. The jukebox played old Doors songs. I laughed at one of CK's elk-hunting lies while tapping my cup to the music. It was all feeling good. Suddenly, Brownie lurched forward over the table, planting his face in his cup and spilling his beer. That same biker from before had walked by and de-liberately run into him. Brownie half rose from his seat, sputtering, "What the hell?"

"Sorry, my man. You shoulda been looking." The biker sneered.

His posse at the next table watched silently. They were poised, ready to jump.

Chapter Six

"What's the headcount, Jimmy Lloyd?" Thor, sitting next to Brownie with his back to the bikers, muttered it just loud enough for me to hear. He pulled Brownie back into his seat.

My eyes darted back and forth. "Looks like about thirteen, fourteen behind you. Half a dozen more at the bar but not looking this way."

He blew out his cheeks. "Three to one, I'd say. Not so good. We have any friends in the place?"

I looked around again. "Big Ted's here. He's with his wife, though. I wouldn't count on him." Chairs started scraping back as more of the leather-clad gang began to stand. The bikers had some of their women with them. The gals stayed seated, sipping beer and watching it all, bright-eyed and grinning.

CK knuckle-tapped me on the arm and leaned toward my ear. "Is your buddy Camel going to back us here?"

I glanced at Kamal on the other side of me. His expression unreadable, he held his cup on the table with both hands while he looked at the wall of unwashed humanity edging closer. "I'm not sure. This isn't his fight," I murmured without taking my eyes off the gang members.

"Hell it isn't," CK whispered fiercely. "That makes it four to one. This is deep shit, partner."

"Okay, boys. We can just back away from this. No harm done. We just get up and go back to shooting pool," I said over the jukebox noise.

"The hell we'll do that. *I'm* not." Brownie wiped beer from his mustache with a napkin.

Thor put a hand on Brownie's forearm. "Don't get up yet. Wait till we need to."

"Okay then, okay. Here's what we do." I held one hand out for attention. "We all get up together then hoof it over to the tables—"

"I said I ain't playing pool!" Brownie interrupted.

"—and then we pick up the sticks," I finished. "It's probably our best chance to get out of here without an ass whoopin.'"

Even Brownie nodded at that.

"All right, Jimmie Lloyd. You say when," CK said.

The bikers had us in a tight semicircle, standing with knuckles dragging at their sides. I got set to do the "one-two-three-go," then suddenly, the timing got decided for us. Someone pulled the plug on the jukebox. Tables overturned around us. The ladies at the girls' table shrieked as they finally realized something bad was about to happen. Brownie and Thor darted sideways, and I flipped our table piled with pitchers and empty beer cans over at the bikers. We ran across the empty dancing area to the pool tables. Elbowing players out of the way, I grabbed the shortest cue stick I saw. In five seconds Brownie, Thor, CK, and I were standing side by side with our backs to the tables, holding cues like baseball bats.

But not Kamal. He stood alone without his cap, facing the bikers in the middle of the brightly lit dance floor. He looked like an orphan meeting the playground bullies.

"Kamal, get back here with us," I shouted.

The gang had gotten over being startled and stepped out on the light maplewood floor.

"You better listen to your friends, Injun. You don't look too good out here by yourself," one of the bikers growled.

I hadn't noticed Jacko until then. A badman son of a bitch who had killed men but never been convicted of it—led the local chapter of the Badlanders. He wore a braided beard, and I knew he had a motorcycle chain wrapped around his waist under his shirt for fights. Everything quieted except for the jabbering folks hurrying out the door. Kamal still hadn't moved. Grady was over in the corner, punching numbers into the phone. The 911 responders would be on the way but probably not soon enough.

I spoke up. "Get back here, Kamal." Then I looked at Jacko. "Let's talk."

He shook his head. "No, no. Too late for that, cowboy. We don't take to being shit on in our own bar. Now we're gonna come over there and stomp your asses into mudholes." He turned and shouted, "Right, boys?"

A round of growls answered him, and I could've sworn I heard one of their chicks giggle.

Jocko turned back and let his eyes bore into Kamal. "But first, we're gonna take care of your little Crow-retard buddy here." He waved one of his members out of the pack. "Come here, Jessie." He smiled. "Break this little turd packer in half for me."

Jessie stepped forward. He had a massive beer belly, and his beefy arms looked bigger than my thighs. The only tattoo I could read on his bicep said "She broke my heart" over a red heart cracked open like an eggshell. He must have been a class favorite because the whole gang cheered for him.

"Go, Jessie! Fuck him over, man!"

It was a chorus from hell.

One of the chicks squealed. "C'mon, baby, show 'em whatcha got! Kill his ass!"

Jessie acknowledged the shouts with a grin that displayed missing teeth.

No way was Kamal going to survive a beating from Jessie, but he acted as if he hadn't heard anything. He took several deep breaths but otherwise became a statue with his arms down by his sides. Lit up under the dance lights, he was the only person clearly visible in the whole place.

"Kamal!" I roared.

Jessie approached Kamal, drawing back a fist the size of a paint can. His swing would have killed Kamal if it had landed, but the kid dropped to the floor ahead of it. He scooted around the burly attacker and pulled Jessie's leg up behind him. Jessie went down like a steer in a slaughterhouse. His belly flop shook the floor. He struggled back to his feet, swearing.

"Whooo... Jessie."

Some of the bikers were laughing. His gal laughed, too, her hand over her mouth.

The biker went into a crouch with his arms outstretched. He padded forward carefully. "I'm gonna squeeze the shit outta you, Pocahontas," he panted.

Kamal crouched, too, backing away from Jessie until I could almost touch him myself. I raised the cue stick. I couldn't do anything else before Kamal ducked again. This time, he rolled to the other side, snatching the biker's ankle, and Jessie crashed heavily once more. He lay almost at my feet.

The gang started laughing at their gladiator again, but before they could catch their wind, Kamal jumped up to his feet. He smashed a kick into the side of the downed man's head that would have been deadly if he'd been wearing my cowboy boots instead of Nikes. The kid spun and drove his foot hard into the biker's kidney then again into his side. The air whooshed out of Jessie, and blood smeared the floor next to his face.

"Holy shit!" CK muttered.

That was too much for the bikers. They started to come across the floor toward us. Kamal finally got beside me as I tightened my grip on the pool cue. I didn't usually pray much, but that night, in a bar in

Billings, Montana, I did a quick one. "Jesus, please help me." Sometimes it was the quick ones that got answered.

"Jacko, what the *hell* is going on?" a familiar voice bellowed over the rumbling in the bar. The gang slowed up and stopped.

Dunker had finally arrived. He pushed his way through the line of gang members and walked up to Jacko, who gaped at him. "Dunker? What're you doing here?"

"Don't act like a dumb shit, Jacko. Me and you's drunk enough beer here together for you not to be surprised to see me." Turning to survey the room, he took in the upended tables, us standing in a line holding up our clubs, and Jessie moaning on the floor. "What the hell is this all about?" He looked at Jacko. "What are you doing? Fighting with my boys?"

Jacko's eyes widened. "These are friends of yours? Damn, Dunker, we didn't know that, but they took one of our tables. You know we can't have that here—"

"Bullshit!" Dunker eyed the five of us against the pool tables. "I know these boys. They didn't start this." He gestured down at Jessie trying to get to his hands and knees. "He one of yours?"

"Yeah, Dunker. Your boys beat him up pretty bad."

"How many did that?"

Jacko dropped his eyes. "One."

"Was it a fair fight?"

"Yeah."

"Good. Then I say it's over." Dunker pulled out his wallet and took out two bills. He gestured at CK. "Take these over to Grady to cover the damage." He paused and raised his voice. "All right, everybody. This party's over. The law is probably already on their way here. I would suggest that we all vamoose. The Wheel Inn is open!"

"He's right. Badlanders, let's go!" Jacko shouted. He shook hands with Dunker and looked at us then at Kamal. "That Injun ride a bike?"

"He's not Indian, and he doesn't ride a motorcycle," I answered.

"That's too bad." Jacko grinned. "See you fuckers around." He waved over his shoulder as he walked away.

We joined the mad exodus for the front door, and once outside on the sidewalk, I could already hear sirens. "My truck's right here. Jump in, and let's get out of this," I said.

My buddies hopped over the sides and hunkered down to hide in the truck bed. Dunker slid into the cab with me. All around us, Harleys fired up and scattered like quail, their headlights sweeping over the truck as they flashed by.

"Don't speed," Dunker said. "Just drive like it's Sunday afternoon."

As I turned the corner onto Twenty-Seventh Street, I saw flashing blue lights in the mirror. The cops were still a couple of blocks away. I turned again at the next block and headed west to put distance between them and me. The guys stayed low in the back. When Dunker slid open the rear window, I could hear them all giggling like schoolboys.

"Damn, Camel, where'd you learn them moves? You a black belt or something?" CK asked.

Brownie chimed in. "Yeah, you can fight, boy. Glad you was on our side."

I swerved to miss a pothole, and they all moaned and groaned as they were slung side to side. Someone banged on the back window.

"Slow down, Jimmy Lloyd. You're killing us back here."

"Kamal's getting sick," Thor yelled.

I sure didn't want puke all over the back of my pickup. I slowed and looked at Dunker. "Red Door?"

He nodded. "Good a place as any, I guess. We'll sort it all out there."

On the way to the Red Door bar, I filled Dunker in about what had happened before he showed up.

"Really? That little A-rab kid did that?" he said in amazement. He looked back through the rear window, where Thor and CK were holding Kamal's head over the side while he tried to vomit. Dunker faced forward again and shook his head slowly. "Well, it just goes to show you," he said softly.

The Red Door represented everything the Rainbow wasn't. Not many cowboy hats in there. The music played lower, and the crowd talked quieter until they got drunk. Yuppies and college kids looked up when we sauntered in, all rumpled, looking like we'd just come off the trail from Texas. We settled around a table, and the waitress delivered two pitchers of beer—with clear plastic cups this time. Everyone raised a cup to Kamal.

"To one hell of a scrawny-assed fighter," I said.

"Cheers," the others echoed.

Kamal smiled back. "Thank you."

Brownie carefully stroked his mustache with a thumb and forefinger while he studied Kamal. "Okay, so where *did* you learn that stuff?" he asked. "Never seen a barroom fight like that."

Kamal stared down at the cup in his hand. "My father had me trained."

"Trained? What? Some kind of A-rab karate?"

"Something like that."

WE SAT AT THAT TABLE for nearly two hours before finally getting around to planning the fishing trip. We decided to pack up the Stillwater River past Lake Sioux Charlie to a spot where we hadn't camped in several years. It was one of the prettiest rides in the state. Everybody agreed that the last week of June would work out fine.

"I'll put in for the vacation time," I said.

"Me, too," CK added.

Kamal sat across from me. Throughout the whole conversation, his eyes kept moving from one of us to the other, but he never said a word. He drank two cups of beer, though.

Finally, Thor looked at him. "That week in June going to work for you, Kamal? You through with school then?"

Kamal jerked. "What? Uh... yes. My finals will be over soon. Why do you ask?"

"Why does he ask? Cause you're going with us, little buddy. Can't leave our main man behind." Brownie clapped a hand on Kamal's shoulder and shook it. "Yessir, you're going with us."

"That's right, young man. I hear you're pretty good at taking on hairy bears. We might need you," Dunker rumbled. He had been eyeing Kamal all evening. That settled it.

Kamal smiled, but shakily.

We figured the cops must have left the Rainbow by then, so we loaded up, and I hauled the guys back across town to their trucks. Brownie couldn't remember where he'd parked, but we found his Ford one street over. Each man shook Kamal's hand before he left the truck bed. When Dunker got out last, Kamal retook his seat in the cab. He had been shivering in the night air. He put his hands over the heater vent to soak in the hot air.

I turned my old truck up Main and headed for home. "The boys like you, Kamal."

"Yes?"

"Yeah, they do. You *are* going fishing with us in June, aren't you?"

He stared ahead, an odd look on his face. "I don't know. I'm not sure... I have never fished."

"That's no problem. We can show you that stuff, but you got to come. They'll be disappointed if you don't."

Looking thoughtful, Kamal rubbed his chin. "Yes, I suppose I will come," he said quietly.

"Good."

He leaned back in the seat and went silent. A minute later, I started to say something then realized he was sleeping.

Chapter Seven

That following Tuesday after our fracas at the Rainbow, CK pulled an overtime twelve on my team's night shift. CK and I didn't normally work together that much. Maybe that was why he liked me.

The night clean-up crew were just leaving the control room when I got there. I high-fived Chad White Horse as I entered the blast-proof building. "How's it hanging, Crow Warrior?"

"Dragging the floor, like always."

"That must hurt. Why don't you throw it over your shoulder like I do?" I couldn't catch his answer over the outside roar of the refinery, then the heavy metal door closed behind me.

I sat at the desk to look over the work orders for the night. Every valve on the unit had to be inspected and tagged before an upcoming turnaround. I paired CK with Joe, and the two of them climbed stairs and ladders until well after midnight. Listening to their radio chatter, I could tell they were getting tired, so I called them in. They came stomping into the control room, peeling off grease-smeared leather gloves before hanging up their hard hats. Big wet rain splotches covered the shoulders and arms on their coveralls. A spring storm was starting to blow through.

"Whew," CK said. "It's really about to come down out there." He shifted his work belt with the radio hanging on it so he could lean back in the swivel chair facing me. "I saw a frog with a snorkel getting ready." He eased his booted feet up onto my desk.

Joe headed straight to the kitchen. He'd eaten Mexican TV dinners every night for the last two weeks, and I didn't doubt that the whole building would smell like enchiladas in a few minutes.

"Glad you made it," I said. "Wouldn't want your candy ass to melt down in the rain."

"Up yours, too, Jimmy Lloyd." CK locked his hands behind his head and looked at me. "Hey, what's the deal with that little Arabian buddy of yours?"

"The deal? There's no deal. He just rents that shack behind me and plays student at MSU-B, as far as I know. Why? You got a problem with him?"

CK flashed his dimpled smile at me. "Now there you go. All you damn Yankees act like every Mississippi boy you know carries a lynch rope in his truck *juuust* in case he meets up with someone tanner than Halle Berry."

"You mean you don't?"

"Naw. All that stuff's long gone. Y'all Yanks are the ones that don't know it yet." He swung his boots off the desk. "Actually, me and the boys was thinking about going to the Drifters this weekend. You wanna come and bring him, too?"

"Kamal? Everybody okay with that?"

He smiled again. "Hell yeah, they're okay with it. That little dude's handy to have around when the fan blades get dirty. We kinda like him."

"Won't be any fights at the Drifters," I replied. A classic country-western bar, the Drifters featured two-steps, waltzes, jitterbugs, and polkas. Bikers generally stayed away. If a fight broke out there, it involved two drunks squabbling over some gal.

"Well, bring him anyway." CK settled back in the chair.

"You got it."

"Hey, Jimmy Lloyd, you think that boy's ever been laid?"

I looked at CK. He had an expression so serious, I had to laugh. A wounded grizzly couldn't have made him frown more. "Now with all due respect, CK, how would I know about that? I don't even know when *you* last dipped your stick. How many years *has* it been anyway?"

"More lately than you, funnyman." He stood and stretched. "I was just wondering, you know. That Camel—"

"Kamal."

"Yeah, Kamal. That's what I said. That Kamal seems like a nice guy, just a little bit off, you know? Looks like he's always thinking about something going on in another room. Maybe he just needs to get his tubes purged."

Joe walked back in, carrying a steaming TV tray of refried beans and rice. "Heard you guys talking about the Drifters. You go there, you'll get laid all right. That place always has the women."

I DROVE BACK TO SEE Kamal the next afternoon after I slept off the night shift. He exercised Sweet Ginger nearly every day after lunch about that time. Sure enough, I found him standing in the center of the round pen, working her without a lunge line. I got out of the truck and leaned on the board fence with one foot on the bottom rail. The mare loped by in front of me, responding to Kamal's hand and arm gestures. He turned with her as she circled. *Lad sure has a knack for this.*

"Hello, Jimmy Lloyd," he called without taking his eyes off Sweet. He lowered his outstretched arm to let her stop and face him. "Come," he said, patting his leg. Sweet lowered her head and approached him until she stopped three feet away, smacking her lips. "Good girl... good." Kamal stepped up to stroke her arched neck. He looked at me and smiled.

"She's looking good, Kamal. Real good."

His smile got even wider. "Thank you." He rubbed her nose softly. "She is a good horse. I am going to send my father a picture of her."

"That's good. I'm sure he'll like that."

"Yes, I hope so..." The smile faded, and he looked down at the dirt between us, making me wonder what sort of dad wouldn't appreciate a picture of his boy's horse. Kamal tapped Sweet lightly on the neck. "Follow," he whispered up at her cocked ear. He walked toward me while the mare followed him, her muzzle at his right elbow. She stopped when he did at the fence where I had my arms resting.

"That's pretty impressive, Kamal. Esther would be pleased to see how you handle her horse."

"Do you think so?" He ran an eye over Sweet. "I truly wish I could buy this mare."

"Well now, who knows? If Esther knew how much you love this horse, she might change her mind. You just got to believe. Give it time."

He stared at the ground again. "Time," he muttered. His lips stretched into a tight straight line.

It seemed like no matter what I said, Kamal took it in a hard way. Before things got uncomfortable, I cleared my throat to speak. "Anyway, the fellows and me are wanting to go out this Friday night. How about you come along with us again?"

He looked genuinely surprised. Then after a second, he shook his head slowly, looking sheepish. "I don't know, Jimmy Lloyd... I don't think I should. If I get into fights... if the police took away my visa—"

"Oh hell, don't worry about that," I interrupted. "We'll be going to a different place this time. No fights. Just dancing and partying with the ladies."

He ran his hand idly up and down Sweet's neck, still not convinced. "I don't know... I shouldn't take risks."

Take risks? What the hell? "Oh, come on, Kamal. This time, I promise it'll be different. Besides, the boys will miss you if you don't come."

"The same men that were with us the other night?"

"More or less. There might be a couple of others. You never know for sure," I answered. Kamal wanted to go. I could feel it.

"There would be girls there?"

I laughed and wagged a finger at him. "Kamal, if you join us this Friday, I guarantee you'll get to see some of our western cowgirls at their finest. Boots and tight jeans, just like the movies."

He grinned. "Like *Urban Cowboy?*"

I smiled back. "Better than that old movie. These will be the real thing. You know Montana gals are every cowboy's dream, don't you?"

"No, I did not know that."

"Well, that settles it, then. You have to come see and find out for yourself." I slapped the fence rail and pushed away, startling Sweet a little. "So I'll be picking you up this Friday night. Agreed?"

Kamal nodded slowly. "Okay. Eight o'clock?"

"That sounds about right. So if I don't see you between now and then, look for me at eight." I went back to the truck and climbed in. Before I cranked up the motor, I leaned out the window. "And, Kamal, go light on the stink water."

"I'll remember, Jimmy Lloyd."

"GOOD LORD, BOY! WHAT have you gone and done?" I hollered out the driver's window.

At eight o'clock Friday night, my truck had just bounced to a stop at Kamal's house when he stepped out, beaming like a lighthouse. I shut off the engine and took a closer look. He had on a silverbelly felt hat with the brim turned up just so, new and expensive looking in the yellow glare of the porch's bug light. His shirt was mostly black with red and yellow lightning bolts zigzagging up and down the sleeves. Pearl buttons gleamed all over the front. When he walked across the wooden porch, I could hear the clump of new cowboy boots.

"What do you think?" He held out his arms, obviously pleased with himself. "The lady at the store helped me pick it out." Actually, the outfit didn't look bad on him. He just needed to dirty it up a bit.

"Looks good, Kamal. Scuff a little dust on your boots and get in the truck."

"Put dust on my boots?"

I sighed. "Kamal, you need to look like you wear those clothes all the time. Clean and shiny like that, your outfit will be screaming 'Talbot's Western Store' all night long."

"Is that bad?"

"Well, it's not good. Anybody can buy a shirt and try to look the part of a horseman, but you show 'em you're for real. Put dust on your boots and toss a little on your hat, and you're good to go. Let 'em know you're a cowboy."

"Okay." Reluctantly, he bent down to scoop up a handful of dust from the driveway.

"That's enough, just sprinkle a little bit on the hat then shake it off. You don't want to get it filthy."

He looked at me, holding dust in one hand and his new hat in the other. "You're sure of this, Jimmy Lloyd?"

"Just do it and get in, Kamal. Time's wasting, and I got to eat before we hit the Drifters."

We stopped at Hardee's once we got into town. Hamburgers, french fries, and chocolate shakes would carry us through the rest of the night. By the time I parked in the potholed lot next to the Drifters, near Brownie's rusted-out Ford, the band had already started inside.

I walked in with an attitude. Having a little swagger always paid. It tickled me to see Kamal hook his thumbs in his belt while he looked around. A chorus of shouts showed me where the rest of them had a table staked out.

"There they are! Hey, Kamal, get your ass over here!" Brownie seemed to be in fine fashion. He and CK had their arms up, waving at us. We joined them and scraped back two chairs just as Thor returned from the john. We shook hands all around. It looked like Kamal was the homecoming king and man of the hour. Everyone pounded him on the back—and said they liked his new outfit. Brownie pushed a beer mug at him.

"Dunker coming?" I asked, hollering over the band.

"Nope. He and Jill are going to the grandson's football game," Brownie answered.

"Football? This is May."

"It's Skyview's spring scrimmage. Danny's probably going to start on the O-line."

"Oh. Well, good for him."

"I talked to Jerry. He said he's going to be here." Thor watched me closely as he said it. Everyone knew Jerry and I didn't always get along. He'd said something about Esther once a long time ago that had started a fight between us. We shook hands later, but I never forgot things like that, and they all knew it.

I hitched one shoulder. "It's a free country."

The waitress brought another pitcher and a mug for me. The band was just finishing up a George Strait song. The lead guitar, a guy I'd known since our college days together at Bozeman, grinned at me with a pick clamped in his teeth. I tipped my hat back at him.

I turned around to the table. "This'll be pretty good music tonight."

"Yeah, these guys play good stuff," Thor said. "Have you ever heard much country music?" he asked Kamal.

My young renter shook his head. "I don't know. I don't think so. Is it like Madonna?"

"Madonna? Oh, *hell* no!" CK pointed toward the bandstand. "This is music you can *dance* to. Tonight, you are gonna hear *Montana* music."

"And you're going to move your ass, too!" Brownie proclaimed.

"All right, fellows," I said. "You guys back off of Kamal for a while. He'll shake it up when he's ready."

They chuckled and nodded at that.

Kamal looked puzzled. "I am to perform?"

That got a real laugh at the table.

"No, Kamal. You don't perform. You just dance with some of the ladies." I stopped as a thought struck me between the eyes. "You don't know how to dance, do you? Can you two-step?"

"Two-step?" he asked, and our whole table moaned.

"We gotta find Alice," Brownie said.

"Best idea you ever had." Thor stood up. "I'll get her over here."

The band started on a Clint Black tune while Thor weaved his way to the bar. Alice would be somewhere around there.

Packed tables emptied around us as pairs got up to hit the lighted dance floor. Dancing to country music could be a lot like NASCAR: Everybody goes around more or less at the same speed in the same direction, but with surprisingly few collisions. Guys went forward, and the gals backed up. Then they switched. Some couples could do fancy; some plowed ahead plain. It was fun to do and fun to watch. Cowboy hats and boots seemed the dominant male attire. Tight jeans were for both sexes.

Kamal watched it all with a hint of distaste. "They are close together," he said in my ear. "Do they always do that?"

I laughed. "Wait till the music slows down. Then you'll see close."

"Jimmy Lloyd! Jimmy Lloyd McGowan! I thought it was you!" I recognized that gal's voice even over the band's attempt to blot out every other sound. Alice's arms came around me from behind, knocking off my hat when she bent down to hug the back of my head against her cashmere sweater and all that was in it. Long, curly brown hair gathered around my ears. I caught the tumbling hat and stood up. A tall gal, Alice met me almost nose to nose before she gave me a peck on the cheek. "How you doing, man? Haven't seen you in here for months."

"Hey, Alice. It *has* been a little while," I said.

Her eyes looked into mine for just the slightest second, and I saw a sadness there before we both turned away. Alice was still a friend to both Esther and me. In fact, our divorce had probably hit her as hard as it had us. Married once herself, she never seemed to have a boyfriend anymore, but everybody knew Alice and liked her. And she had the lightest feet I had ever seen. She'd taught many a left-footed cowboy like me how to dance. Alice could make a walrus look graceful.

Thor must have already told her about Kamal, because she leaned over to him. "And who is this handsome cowboy, Jimmy Lloyd?"

I stood and motioned for him to join me. "Alice, I'd like you to meet Kamal. He's the fellow renting the little house at the back of my spread. He's from Saudi Arabia somewhere, and he doesn't know diddly about two-stepping."

Alice did a mock heart attack with her hands at her chest. "Oh no!" she exclaimed. "We'll have to do something about that."

I chuckled at her antics. Then, while she chatted up Kamal, I looked around the Drifters. Dozens of grinning pairs whirled under the lights as waitresses hustled drinks to their tables and booths in the bar's dimmer reaches. I tapped one foot to the band's music. *This is going to be a pretty good evening. You can't beat a night at a dance hall bar.*

Chapter Eight

Alice always had her wingman, and Jane joined our table less than a minute later. Shorter and buxom with bobbed hair, Jane still wore bling like the Casper County rodeo queen she had been over twenty years ago in Wyoming. She still looked good in it too.

"Jimmy Lloyd! Thor! I haven't seen you guys slumming in here for ages," she squealed. Sliding into the chair next to Thor, she draped an arm over his shoulders and murmured into his ear.

Thor grinned and shook his head. His Nordic skin went sunburn red.

She punched his arm in mock anger and leaned away, giggling. "Okay, cowboy, but one day you will."

I watched Kamal, who hadn't sat back down at the table yet. The whole scene with Alice and Jane had him fascinated, but maybe not in a good way. He scowled at them.

"It's okay, Kamal. They call it 'flirting,' but don't worry about it," I said, waving dismissively at the two gals. "They never follow through on it. Believe me, I've tried. Everybody has."

That got a round of laughs; even the ladies joined in.

"We're just particular, Jimmy Lloyd," Alice answered. "I'm waiting for a stockbroker to come in here."

"Hah!" Brownie laughed. "That'll be the day. C'mon, Alice. Let's do it until he gets here." He reached for her hand and led her away to the dance floor, where a crowd already swirled.

"All right. I'm rolling the dice," CK said. He got up and started to work his way through the tables to the filly he'd spotted, probably another sales girl from the mall. Before long, he and Brownie were both out on the floor, moving with the flow and the music, laughing and smiling with their partners.

"You gotta be a monk not to like this," Thor proclaimed solemnly.

Jane patted the empty chair next to her. "Come set yourself down. I don't bite," she said to Kamal. "Jimmy, tell your friend I don't bite."

"She bites," I said.

Kamal sat down slowly, and Jane smiled at him. "What's your name?" she asked, as bright as sunlight.

"Kamal."

"Kamal. What a nice name. Are you Mexican?"

"No. I am from Saudi Arabia." He frowned. I thought Kamal might have been offended by the question, but he didn't have much time to show it.

"Saudi Arabia! Oh, that's even better!" Jane clapped her hands excitedly and leaned in, putting cleavage right under his nose. "Do you have a girlfriend back there?"

I had forgotten how Jane could work a man. Kamal laughed self-consciously into his lap as he began to talk with her. Her patter had him reeled to the boat and netted before the band even finished that one song. I would have bet my belt buckle that his heart rate jumped up about ten levels when Jane put a hand on his knee. Thor glanced over at me. We both wagged our heads, and I winked.

I got up when Brownie brought Alice back to the table. "All right, Brownie, you've had your shot. Now let me step on her feet." I took her by the elbow. "But stay here, would you? We can't leave Kamal alone with this cougar."

Brownie took it all in and grinned. "Gotcha. I'll watch him." He sat down next to Kamal.

"Oh, shut up, Jimmy Lloyd." Jane turned to Kamal. "Don't you turn into an asshole like these guys."

"I will try not to," he said. Everybody laughed, including Kamal.

"Let's go, Alice." Leading her to the dance floor, I reached back without looking and unintentionally palmed the front of her sweater. "Oops. Sorry."

"Does this mean we're getting married?" She grinned.

I could have loved Alice once, if I hadn't known Esther first. The two of them had been friends since college, and I'd always been comfortable with her. That summed it up though. Esther always had first call on my heart. I knew it, and so did Alice.

The band started an old Eddy Raven waltz, and we stepped out. Dancing with Alice felt like gliding. She tilted her head and smiled at me while moving perfectly with every one of my missteps. "You doing okay, Jimmy?" she asked after our first time around the floor.

I knew what she meant. "I can't lie, Alice. I still miss her. I know I royally screwed up this time."

"That you did, Jimmy. We both know it." She squeezed my hand. "But you're still a good man."

We spun around, and I started stepping backward, checking back over my shoulder every so often.

"I hope it all works out for both of you someday," she said.

"Well, thanks, I guess."

About that time, we bumped into Brownie dancing with one of his many girlfriends.

"Hey, what are you doing here?" I glanced over at our table, where Kamal still sat with Jane. She had his hat on, and they were both laughing. "Dammit, Brownie, I was serious about not leaving that boy alone with Jane. He'll cream his pants in another minute."

Brownie tried to look sorrowful. "I know, but I saw Jackie here..." He grinned at his partner. "And I couldn't resist. Don't you know how *good* she feels?"

I sighed and looked into Jackie's bright eyes. "Yeah, I expect so. Can't say as I blame you." We spun apart, Alice gently guiding me away from another dance-floor collision looming behind me.

"Relax, Jimmy. Jane's not going to hurt him. She never takes it that far," she said as we moved into a side-by-side stroll, Alice following my lead as though she lived in my head.

I had to smile. "Yeah, I know that, but *he* doesn't know that." I looked back at the table again to see Kamal and Jane were still smiling. "It does look like he's getting settled in, though." The song played out when we reached the farthest corner of the floor. "Wait," I said. "Thor told you why he came and got you?"

"Well, a girl just assumes it's because of her sparkling personality and good looks. You mean that wasn't it?" She laughed at my expression. "Yes, he told me that your young Kamal needs a little help tonight. I'll be happy to show him the ropes." She waggled her eyebrows.

"Thanks, Alice. You're the best."

We threaded our way back to the table. CK had brought over his new gal, a pretty blonde whose name I didn't catch. She didn't work at the mall, either; she clerked at Cabela's. I had to shake my head at CK's luck. Every man wants to meet a girl with a Cabela's discount.

Without any foreplay, Alice grabbed Kamal's arm. "Come on, cowboy. Put your hat on. We're going to dance now."

He stood up, looking confused. "I can't dance. I would like to, but..." Kamal could have had wool glued all over him, and he wouldn't have looked any more sheepish than he did at that moment.

"No, Kamal. You mean you can't dance *yet*." Alice plopped his Stetson down over his hair. "Come on."

Pouting, Jane snatched at Kamal's hand. "Alice, I saw him first."

Alice tossed her head. Curly brown hair flounced over her shoulders. "Too bad, girlfriend. He's mine now." She pulled Kamal toward the dance floor. He hung back, protesting weakly. Alice looked like a mother dragging her kid to the dentist.

Jane went off to tinkle, and I sat back and nursed a beer, alone at the table while everybody else took a turn on the floor. Poor Kamal was a newborn foal getting up on legs for the first time. I smiled to myself. Before the night was over, Alice would have him ready to compete on a TV dance show.

"Hello, Jimmy Lloyd."

I looked behind me. Joanne stood at my left shoulder. A weekend regular at the Drifters, she appeared to be between boyfriends that night.

"Hey there, Joanne. Have a seat," I said, pulling out the chair next to me.

"Sure." She sat down, bringing a little whiff of perfume with her. Joanne's long, dark-brown wavy hair bounced up and down like a slinky when she jitterbugged. I had noticed her earlier out on the floor, which accounted for the light sheen of perspiration on her forehead. She set a mixed drink down on the table. "I thought I saw you come in tonight. How's it going?" She made little rings on the table with her glass.

"Same ol', same ol'. Can't complain. How's it going with you?"

"Oh, about the same. You know David and I aren't together anymore. We broke it off the other night." She could have been talking about a spring rain in New York City for all the feeling she showed.

"Oh, I didn't know that. Sorry to hear it, Joanne."

She shrugged. "It happens." She looked sideways at me. "I suppose you know all about it, too, huh?"

"Yeah. I guess I do." I watched the dancers. The band was halfway through a Keith Whitley tune about rain from years ago. *Must have been into golden oldies tonight.* Kamal was starting to look a little less clumsy. Alice smiled and kept him moving along with the crowd.

I cleared my throat. "You wanna dance?"

Joanne looked toward the dancers. "Let's wait for the next song. This one's about over."

"Sure," I agreed.

The song ended, and we got up to work our way against the flow coming the other way. We met Kamal and Alice going back to sit one out. He had a grin on his face that a wire brush couldn't have scrubbed off. "Looks like you're catching on pretty good, Kamal," I said.

"Yes, he's doing sooo good," Alice gushed, and I gave her a high five.

Facing Joanne under the lights, I waited for the music. "I'm a little rusty."

"We'll see about that." She smiled. "I remember you were always a good dancer, Jimmy Lloyd."

When my old college buddy on the bandstand gently strummed the first chord, we started slow dancing to Garth Brooks. I knew I could be in trouble with this one. I put one arm around Joanne's waist. She moved in and laid that scented hair against the side of my face. I tried a little experimental tightening. She responded by melting in closer to polish my belt buckle. I could feel the eyes of everyone at my table watching us, but I didn't care. It had been a long time. A slow burn began in my jeans. Without thinking, I chuckled and broke the mood.

Joanne pulled back. "Is something funny?"

"No." Then I grinned. "Well, yes. I was thinking it's a good thing Alice didn't stay out here with Kamal for this one. I don't think he could have handled this."

She laughed softly. "Is he the Arab student living out at your place?"

"That's him. Word sure gets around."

"Well, I think that's nice that you're bringing him out with you. Maybe he'll go back home and say we're not so bad, after all."

"He's a good kid. Maybe you could give him a dance later."

"Maybe," she answered, her eyes half shut. "But he won't be getting any of this." We smothered the gap between us again, swaying without talking.

I slid a hand down to the top of her ass. "Joanne?"

"Hmm?" She practically purred.

"I'm not so sure *I* can handle this, either."

She reached back to move my hand lower, and whispered, "I think you can."

When the song ended, I followed Joanne back to my seat. She moved her chair over until our thighs touched under the table. My buddies exchanged knowing looks. The only one of them I couldn't stare down was Alice.

"Hi, Joanne," she said. "David not here tonight?"

"We broke up."

"I see." Alice shifted her gaze to me for just a second. Just long enough.

"Well, look what the cat done dragged in." Jerry Erickson's voice boomed over the music. Jerry had the kind of voice that dominated a room or a conversation. He'd swept in from the front door with his black handlebar and two hundred fifty pounds of big and tall. Gloria was back with him for the night. For years, she always came back to him. *Who knows why?*

"Yeah, I see what he dragged in. Sit yourself down, pard," Thor hailed back. He waved at the waitress, signaling for another pitcher.

Jerry sat and pulled himself up to the table while Gloria went to find herself a chair. He looked around, smiling at CK's pretty blonde and raising his eyebrows when he noticed Kamal.

"What's up, guys?" he said, directing his question to me.

"Not much, Jer. How you doing?" I answered.

"Fine as frog's hair," he blared. "Never better."

Gloria came back and set a chair down next to him. He casually laid his arm across the back without looking at her.

"Just thought we'd come down and join you guys to do the *Boot Scootin' Boogie*—whatever the hell that is. Ha, ha!"

People laughed, and I smiled, more at them than him.

The conversation turned to other things, and the night progressed. I danced most of the time with Joanne, her expression promising me more was to come later.

Finally, in the last hour, Alice tapped me on the arm. "Here's one you like, Jimmy. Come dance with me."

Joanne had been rubbing the inside of my leg under the table so I got up a little awkwardly. "Be back in a minute," I said to her.

"I'll be here."

Alice slid into my arms as we started another waltz. "I like your Kamal. He's still a little uncomfortable, but he catches on quick. He could be a really good dancer. He's nice, too."

"Yeah. He's a good kid. He's a good horseman, too."

"Yes, he told me he likes horses. You let him ride Esther's Arab mare?"

"Sure. She doesn't mind. In fact, she leased Sweet to him."

"So he said." A pause passed between us. "You going to take that slut home tonight?"

"Whoa! Where did *that* come from?" I stammered.

"Answer the question, Jimmy Lloyd. You know what I mean." Alice looked right into my eyes, and I couldn't evade her.

"Well, I suppose that is a possibility. Not that it's any of your affair, you know."

"Oh, I know. Jimmy, I know," she answered, never missing a step. "I just hate to see you..."

"See me *what*? I am a single man now, as you know. I don't owe anybody anything. Not Esther. Not you. Not anybody."

She sighed and looked away. "I know, Jimmy. Message received and understood." We did a few more steps. "What about Kamal?" she asked.

"Kamal? What about him?"

"Well, how's he getting home if you're going off to fantasyland with Joanne?"

"I'll get Thor to take him. It's not very far out of his way."

Alice thought for a moment. "Why not let him stay with me?"

"What?" I stopped dead still, causing a logjam on the floor before I started moving again. "Alice, what are you saying?"

"What's sauce for the goose is sauce for the gander." She stuck her tongue out at me. "Relax, Jimmy, I don't intend to deflower your friend. I have a son older than him. He'd be sleeping on the couch. You could swing by and pick him up in the morning. Slut Town isn't that far from my house."

"That's all right, Alice. Could be Kamal's not so innocent. Who'd know?" I said. "Thor can haul him back. I'd feel bad if a nineteen-year-old boy's hormones made him try something because he might misunderstand your offer."

"Oh, so now you have scruples, huh? Don't *you* have plans for yourself later, Jimmy?"

"That's different, and you know it."

We finished the dance in silence, and I kept messing up the steps after that. When we got back to the table, Joanne retook possession of me, leaning into my side. I reached around her and tapped Thor. "Hey, can you take Kamal back to his house tonight?"

He eyed Joanne and me. "I s'pose so. Figured that might be coming up."

Alice gave me a blank look across the table, and Joanne acted like she never heard a thing.

"Kamal," I said, "you're going to be riding with Thor from here. He'll drop you off home."

He looked puzzled. "You're staying here?"

"Not exactly, but sorta. I'll see you tomorrow."

Kamal's eyes went from Thor to me then to Joanne. His disapproval showed as clear as high beams. "I see," he answered. He said to Thor, "Tell me when you are ready, and I will be, too."

"What's the matter, little buddy?" Jerry said, a little too loudly. "You can't get your own date in the US, either? Hell, just slap one on the butt. If she doesn't moo, take her home. If she does moo, take her out back."

Gloria laughed nervously, but a stony silence fell over the rest of the table.

Kamal's face went dark, and he glowered silently at Jerry.

"What?" Jerry continued. "You wouldn't like that? I guess that was wrong what I heard about A-rabs then."

"That's enough," I said.

"Not cool, Jerry. Not cool," CK said, shaking his head.

Jerry took a long pull from his beer. "Fuck it, I was just joking." The mug banged down on the table as he pushed his chair back to stand up. "Come on, Gloria. Let's go."

I put my lips next to Joanne's ear. "You need a ride home tonight?"

Her hand still rested on the inside of my thigh. "No," she cooed. "But you could follow me home."

"I just might do that."

The party was breaking up anyway. The crowd had thinned out after midnight, and people were heading out in groups. The singles who had cast their bait lures all night without any luck walked away alone, the story of every bar at closing time. While Jerry led Gloria to the door, the rest of the guys pulled out wallets to tip our waitress. We pitched dollar bills and fives on the table. Kamal glanced around at us and put a twenty on the pile.

Chapter Nine

I woke up with a start to my cell phone chirping and vibrating on the nightstand. Only it wasn't my nightstand. Bewildered, I bolted upright in the darkness. Then I remembered I hadn't spent the night at home.

"Hmmm, sugar, can you answer that?" Joanne's muffled voice came from beneath the covers she'd pulled over her head. "I think it's yours."

"Huh? Oh, sure." Still emitting obnoxious sounds, the phone shook itself from the stand onto the floor, where it kept vibrating and squawking like an outraged cartoon character. I swung my feet down on the carpet and bent to pick it up. "Hullo?"

The bedside clock showed almost four thirty in the morning.

"McGowan? Is that you?"

I cleared my throat. "Yeah, this is McGowan. Who's this?"

"Jimmy Lloyd, it's Roger. Sorry to wake you up like this, but we need you to come in. There's a big one going on at the tank farm."

"A fire?"

"Yeah, and it's big. Tank 308's going up in a bad way. We're calling out everybody on the fire team."

"What happened?"

"Not sure right now. Just get yourself down here as fast as you can, Jim. We need every man."

"I'll be there. Give me twenty," I said, but Roger had already hung up. I fumbled around in the dark, slipping on my drawers and jeans.

"What's the matter, sugar? Something wrong?" Joanne had turned over to face me, although I couldn't see her very well in the low light coming through the blinds.

"A fire at work. I have to go in. Go on back to sleep, baby," I answered. "Hide your eyes. I got to turn on a light for a minute."

"Go ahead. I have to pee now anyway." The sheets rustled as she rolled out of bed.

I clicked on a lamp and finished dressing before she padded back out of the bathroom, wearing an old T-shirt that barely covered her ass.

She sat next to me on the bed and rubbed my back while I slipped on my boots. "Gonna miss you, honey. I was counting on a rematch this morning."

I tried to grin back. "Yeah, I kinda was, too." But none of this felt right anymore. I just wanted to leave.

"You got time now, though, don'tcha?"

I shook my head reluctantly. "No, not this time. A fire's a big deal."

"So duty calls, huh?" She stuck her lower lip out in a pout.

"Yeah, she can be a bitch, you know."

"I guess." As I stood, she grabbed my hand. "When am I gonna see you again, Jimmy?"

"Can't say, darling. This might take a while." I reached for my hat on the dresser. "I really got to go now, Joanne," I said, starting for the closed bedroom door.

"Wait!" Joanne hopped up from the bed. Her tits jiggled under the T-shirt as she came over. She rose up on her toes and kissed me, her tongue scouring the inside of my mouth. I got an instant jolt of morning breath. "You'll call me, won't you?" she breathed in my ear.

"You bet I will."

"Got my number?"

"I'll get it," I answered. Suddenly, everything was all wrong. I really needed to get out of Joanne's room, out of her house, and away from her in general.

"Wait. I'll write it down." She went to the nightstand and scribbled on a pad, flashing me her backside as she bent over, but I just ached to leave there. "Here." She came back and tucked it in my shirt pocket. "Call me."

"I sure will," I said, already feeling guilty because I knew I wouldn't. I kissed her on the crown of her head. "Got to go now."

Joanne watched me from the front window while I backed out of her driveway. I waved as I sped away then pushed Joanne from my mind.

I DROVE EAST INTO THE graying dawn. Thick, dark hydrocarbon smoke churned up from the other side of the city. An orange glow appeared beneath it as I got closer. Blue lights were flashing where a city cop held up his hand to stop me at a barricade. I jabbed my finger at the refinery sticker on the windshield, and he waved me through. From more than a mile away, I could already hear the fire's roar. *Lord, that's big...* I gripped the steering wheel.

When I stopped at the last stop sign, to my right, the fire blazed in the tank farm near the interstate. I turned left, toward the firehouse, and waved at the scared-looking gate guard as I drove through.

The bunker gear lockers were open at the firehouse when I got there. Equipment lay scattered around the empty parking bays. It looked like a dynamite stick had gone off inside. Kirk, the assistant fire chief, sat at a desk, monitoring the fire channel.

Jack from the mechanical shop stood there, too, already dressed in his fire gear and shrugging a yellow air-pak over his shoulders. "Hey, Jimmy Lloyd."

"What's up, Jack?" I started pulling on my asbestos suit, gloves, and boots.

"Haven't been out there yet. It's still mostly the fire team that was already working tonight. It looks like a bad one, though."

"We're the first ones in?" I asked.

"Looks that way."

Kirk swiveled around in his chair. "Yeah, you two are it for now. I just called for a truck from the operations center to pick you up." He turned back to his radio. "Sounds like they don't have a good handle on this yet."

"So what happened? How'd it start?" Jack asked the questions clamoring in my own head.

Kirk took a deep breath. "Damned if I know. Three-oh-eight was almost full and still mixing, when—*boom!*—it just happened. They heard the blast clear over at the OCC."

I whistled. "Almost full? That's a lot of fuel. It's gonna burn forever."

"I hope not." Kirk pushed his cap back on his forehead. "I've never seen a fire like this one. The whole area inside the berm is hell. I mean it. It's a lake of fire. Somehow, gasoline got out of the tank and covered the ground inside the dam when it blew."

"Anyone hurt?"

"Thank God, no... not so far, at least. No one was out there at the time. I'm afraid it's getting away from us, though. They just called in that the roof collapsed." He stood up and reached for his fire hat. "Fuck this. I'm going out there with you two. Dan's already coming over to babysit this radio."

We waddled to the door in the heavy fire suits. A pickup arrived just as we stepped outside into the early light, and we hitched a ride to Dante's Inferno.

When I got close enough to see the smoke clearly, it boiled up like an angry black god, covering almost the whole sky. Flames a hundred feet high swayed and licked at the smoke. The roar of the fire was overpowering, even inside the closed truck. I slipped earplugs in, and Jack crossed himself.

"You Catholic?" I shouted to him.

"I am today."

"Guess I'm not much of anything. Baptist mostly."

We rode the rest of the way in silence, just staring at the fire as we drove in under the towering fury. Two hundred yards from the burning storage tank, we stopped at a wooden barricade on the graveled road.

"This is as far as I can take you. No vehicles past here," the driver said.

Everybody at a refinery had been trained to fight small fires, but I had volunteered for the fire team to get specialized training on the big stuff. It was an adrenaline rush; plus, it was a week away from work every year at Texas A&M's fire school. Right then, though, I found myself reconsidering the wisdom of this whole deal. I was sure Jack and Kirk were, too.

We climbed out of the truck and into a blast furnace. A wave of heat roasted my face and ears. I quickly ducked my head and lowered the face shield on my helmet. Ahead of us, our three fire trucks were parked in the road. Bundled figures moved around them, staying on the leeward side, away from the flames and heat. Streams of water arced from the trucks and several fire monitors around the fire's perimeter. The water dropped into the inferno and disappeared with no apparent effect. I glanced at Jack and Kirk, then the three of us lumbered ahead to look for the fire chief.

We found James Cartwright hunkered down inside the middle truck with the door open, screaming into his radio. Our chief's name was James, and he wasn't a small man, but everybody called him "Little Joe." Talking over the noise was almost impossible, so he just raised his hand to acknowledge our arrival. He put his head together with Kirk, and they talked and gestured at each other for a minute before Kirk nodded and turned to us.

He cupped his hands and shouted, "We're gonna have to pull back. We're screwed here."

"Why?" I yelled back. Communicating while sitting inside a jet engine would have been easier.

"Can't shut off the flow from the Light Cat Naphtha feed tank. It's still feeding into the fire."

"What? Can't they just close the valve?"

He shook his head. "No can do. The power's out for both the automatic control valve and its backup."

"Turn off the pumps then."

Little Joe held out his gloved hands. "They did that. Didn't work. The flow from that tank is gravity fed now. It's still coming in. They're going to try to plate the line upstream, but that'll take hours—if they can even do it." Sweat ran down his face, and yelling was making him hoarse. He slumped like a weary, beaten prizefighter.

"Wait a minute, Joe. Can't we just stop the flow manually?" Jack asked, straining to make himself heard.

The fire chief shot him a tight-lipped smile. "We could—if we could get to the valve. It's in there." He pointed a thumb back over his shoulder at the blaze, which rumbled even higher, and I could feel the ground's tremor through my boots.

"Oh, *shit*!" I exclaimed. The manual valve for the feed line had been placed inside the earthen berm, which was currently surrounded by flames. "*Shit*! What piece-of-shit engineer designed this crap?"

Little Joe climbed down from the fire truck's cab. "Okay, boys. Go call in the men. Let's get the hoses back to the trucks. We need to back out before something else blows." He started to key his radio mic.

"Wait," I said.

He looked at me hard, the mic held up to his mouth.

"We can do this, Joe," I added.

"What do you mean?" He knew exactly what I meant—and shook his head slowly. "I can't ask you to do that, Jimmy Lloyd."

"You're not asking. I'm volunteering. Just give me two more to go with me, and we'll have this thing whipped."

"I'll go," Jack said.

"I'll do it," Kirk added.

Little Joe looked at the three of us then pointed at his assistant. "No, Kirk. You take charge here. I'll go."

Little Joe called in the hose crews and told them what we were going to try. They stared at him silently, but said they would carry the hose slack and go with us at least as far as the berm.

We tightened up our gear and the breathing air masks. Before I slipped mine down over my face, I leaned in toward Jack. "Better cross yourself again."

His eyes crinkled behind the mask. "Already did."

The air tanks gave us about twenty minutes of air. We needed to hurry, but we could only shuffle because of the bulky protective gear and the turgid hoses we dragged. A line of men helped lug the hoses behind us, though. The chief had assigned Jack the middle spot. He was the biggest man, and if the valve turned out to be stuck, we might need Jack's bulk to move it. He carried a crowfoot wrench for leverage.

As soon as we left the protection of the fire truck, every step ratcheted the heat up until the whole front of my body felt sunburned. I tried to keep looking down but couldn't help stealing a glance ahead. The fire leaped high overhead, whipping back and forth eagerly, as if impatient for us to get there. I heard it talking to me. *Come on, little man. Come on...*

We reached the eight-foot-high berm and knelt. The ground felt hot even through the bunker suit. Noise and heat beat at us so that talking was impossible. Little Joe nodded at Jack and me. We gave him a thumbs-up, and the three of us started crawling up the slope of the berm, dragging the hoses with us. The teams behind fed the hoses up as we moved forward. We paused below the crest. Flames roared ten feet away on the other side. Little Joe pulled the control handle back on his nozzle, and I followed suit. A white curtain of water appeared as we interlocked the two wide sprays in front of us. Keeping the hose steady, I labored to my feet with Jack's help. He turned to assist Little Joe while I looked ahead into hell.

The strong fog spray pushed the fire back but didn't extinguish it. Water vanished into steam where it collided with its mortal enemy. Flames straining like attack dogs on a leash tried to come over our white shield. They licked around its edges but couldn't reach us—yet. Before we'd started out, Little Joe had said that if anyone felt like it was getting too dangerous or wanted to quit, he could tap out, and we would all back up together. I eyed the other two, wondering if one of them would quit soon, before I did.

Little Joe gestured down the inside slope, and we started our descent, walking and sliding carefully on the loose gravel. Jack held the chief and me close together by our elbows. The heat made it hard to breathe, even inside the mask. My lungs felt seared, and I burned all over. I wanted to stop so badly, yet I knew I couldn't. Not if the others kept on.

We got to the bottom inside the tank's containment area. I could see the valve in front of us, about five feet away on a six-inch line, visible in the fine spray from our hoses. A shallow pool of burning liquid about an inch deep covered the whole earthen floor. We could sweep it back temporarily with water to keep the flames from licking at our boots, but it would get in behind us eventually, and we wouldn't even realize it until we were engulfed and dying. Little Joe stepped into the fire-free bare spot we had just cleared. I went in alongside him. I couldn't look up, but I sensed flames closing in over our heads. A hot liquid sensation in my ears felt like my brains were melting, but it was the wax in my ear canals.

Jack released our elbows when we got to the scorched valve. He hooked the crowfoot onto the valve wheel and tugged. Nothing moved. The heat had no doubt caused some of its innards to expand. Jack took another grip with both hands. He leaned back with one leg braced against the pipe. I could have cried with relief when I saw the valve give a little. Little Joe and I rapidly swept the hoses from side to side, keeping back the burning hydrocarbons while Jack strained at the wheel. The fire became more insistent. Keeping it at bay forever would be impossible, and I got too busy to watch Jack's struggle. *Come on, Jack.*

After forever had passed, I felt a tug on my arm. Jack held Joe and me again. He nodded vigorously, bobbing up and down like the village idiot. *It's closed.* I don't know that I'd ever loved Big Jack before, but right then, I did. We started the long, stumbling backward climb up the berm, still spraying. When we made it to the top, we dropped the hoses and half slid, half rolled down to safety. Our asbestos suits smoldered at the edges, and I seriously considered moving to Greenland.

Chapter Ten

A few minutes after we climbed out of the fire, the three of us were sitting on a fire truck running board, drinking bottles of water from an ice chest. I downed a whole liter before I violently barfed it back up alongside last night's beer and fast food. I wiped my mouth with the back of my glove and reached for another bottle.

Kirk came over and dropped a hand on Little Joe's shoulder. He yelled over the noise, "Chief, you guys did a helluva job in there! I think you're batshit crazy, but it was a helluva job."

Little Joe looked around at Jack and me before he nodded. "Yeah, it was, wasn't it?"

The fire would still burn for hours with the fuel it already had, but we could beat it. Our assholes puckered up one more time when the tank wall finally buckled with an explosive boom. Streams of burning liquid poured from the ruptures, and fiery waves billowed around and up inside the leveed containment area. Flames crawled the crumpled metal of 308, scorching it a solid black. I tried not to think about what it would have been like if we'd been in there when that wall broke.

The rest of the fire team reported in, and things got easier. I helped man a hose for the remainder of the morning. By noon, we had control. The flames were noticeably lower, and we could stand on top of the berm to spray directly into the containment area. Kirk relieved me so I could take a ten-minute break for lunch, but food didn't appeal to me right then. I felt as fatigued as I had ever been since army basic training. I sprawled out on the ground in the lee of a fire-truck tire, slipped off my fire helmet, and promptly fell asleep.

"JIMMY LLOYD?" SOMEONE was shaking my arm. "Jim?"

I sat up, instantly awake, and looked around. My ten-minute break must have turned into twenty.

Kirk stood over me, looking like a commando with his soot-streaked face. "You all right, Jim?"

"Uh, yeah. Sorry about that. I must have dozed off." I rolled to my hands and knees and heaved myself up in the heavy suit. Sweat squished in my boots. "I'll get back to it. Thanks, Kirk," I said, strapping on the helmet.

"Naw, that's not it. We got this bear beat now. You get to take another break. The refinery manager wants to see you and Jack."

"Who? The refinery manager? What the hell does *he* want? I haven't been rodeoing." Then I noticed Jack standing behind Kirk. Someone must have given Jack a wedgie, the way he shifted his weight side to side.

Kirk actually laughed. "You got it all wrong, Jimbo. I think he wants to congratulate you."

"Is it my birthday? Congratulate me for what?"

"For walking into hell and shutting off that naphtha feed line, you dumb shit." Kirk shook his head. He pointed to the far-off barricade, where about ten vehicles had parked since early morning. A cluster of people stood behind the wooden barriers. Two news vans from the local television channels had arrived, as well. "He's waiting for you over there. Be sure to smile for the cameras." Kirk looked delighted not to be going with us.

"Fuck you," I answered. Jack and I shrugged at each other. I looked at the fire. It was clearly burning out. The worst really had passed.

"Let's go," Jack said. "We got to do this sooner or later." He looked as tired as I felt. I knew we weren't too dapper as we trudged toward the group of suits waiting for us. I put on my fire helmet.

Alton Lucas beamed at Jack and me as we got closer. A prematurely gray-haired man, he represented the latest in a long line of refinery managers swinging through Billings's revolving door. They were a big deal over in the main office building, but the worker bees out in the pipe jungle generally ignored them. Whenever one left, he was like a bucket of water pulled out of the ocean—the hole filled in and you never missed him.

Ordinarily, Lucas couldn't have picked either one of us out of a lineup, but apparently, he had been briefed that day. Or maybe he'd read our name tags.

"Jim! Jack!" he greeted us, bellowing happily like a favorite uncle at the annual lakeside reunion. He stuck his hand out to shake Jack's while I made a production out of shucking my asbestos gloves. "We owe you a big thanks for what you two did today. I understand you're the ones who went in and cut the light-cat feed to the fire. That was good work, men, and I really appreciate it."

I got the gloves off and shook his hand. A cameraman at his shoulder was getting the whole thing.

"Thanks, but we were just doing our job," Jack said.

"He's right. That's all it was," I added.

"Just doing your job, eh? Well, the chief told me what you did. If everyone did their job like you two, I'd have a lot fewer problems running this refinery. I can tell you that."

You two? "Wait a minute. Did Little Joe tell you it was just Jack and me? You do know he went in with us? He told you that, too, didn't he?"

Lucas's jaw dropped. "No, he didn't. He didn't say anything about that." He looked dumbfounded. "So the chief was in there with you two? Well, I'll be damned." He rubbed his chin.

One of the television reporters came to the barricade, pushing a microphone under Jack's chin. "Could you give us a statement about your experience in this fire?"

"Like I said, just doing my job," Jack answered. He turned away to pinch the bridge of his nose and blow. A nice wad of black mucus splatted on the ground. "That was all."

The reporter shifted the show to me. "How about you, sir? Do you have anything to say?" He lowered his voice. "Sir, would you raise your face shield first? We want our viewers to see a face for this story."

I raised the plastic shield, slightly warped by the heat. "I don't think you really want to see this face," I said. "Jack's right, though. This was just a job. We do what we need to."

The reporter nodded and smiled. I thought maybe I had said something profound. Lucas's smile stayed pasted on his face like he was a first-timer in a beauty pageant. I think he was actually scared shitless one of us would blurt out something about just how screwed up the whole operation had been due to piss-poor pipe engineering.

"All right, ladies and gentlemen, let's step back and allow these men to get back to work. Like they said, they have a job to do." He had a fine PR voice. "Thanks, Jim. Thanks, Jack. We'll get out of your way now." He nodded once, dismissing us, and the crowd followed him away toward the vehicles.

Jack and I started the weary walk back to the fire trucks.

"Nice snot job," I said. "That'll look good on Channel Eight tonight. I know the refinery manager was sure proud."

He laughed. "You think so?" He glanced back. "Just don't stop and take a leak here. That cameraman is still grinding on us."

I got released from the mop-up operation about midafternoon. Peeling off the heavy asbestos suit at the firehouse, I discovered my good shirt and jeans I'd been wearing at the Drifters were soaked through with perspiration. A shower at home with a change into clean, dry undies sounded better than the refinery change house, so I dragged myself out to Ol' Brown, feeling as weak as a wet paper bag. I cranked up the old boy and bumped across the railroad tracks for the millionth time to head for the house. A black column of smoke still rose from 308, but it was nothing like it had been that morning. By nightfall, it should be all over.

My cellphone chirped in my shirt pocket. I checked the number, and my heart skipped. "Hello, Queenie," I answered.

"Jimmy? I've been trying to get you all day. I thought you were off, but I heard about the fire out there, and I saw the smoke. I figured you would go in—are you okay?" Esther sounded anxious.

"Oh, yeah. Right as rain. It wasn't that big a deal. I'm driving home now, as a matter of fact. I did get a little funky in the bunker suit."

"Oh, well, good. Thank God. I was worried about you. You're still on the fire team?"

"Yeah. Still packing the hoses around."

"They called you out from home?"

I felt a pang, remembering where I'd been last night. "Yeah, Roger called me at four thirty this morning."

"Okay then, you must be exhausted. I'll let you go. You're sure you're okay? Did anybody get hurt?"

"I'm fine, and nobody else got hurt that I'm aware of. I told you. It was no big deal." I paused. "So you were worried about me, huh?"

Esther sighed. "I'll always worry about you, Jimmy Lloyd. You know that. You take care now. Goodbye." I held the little phone up to my ear for a bit longer before I put it back in my shirt.

Chapter Eleven

I was surprised to see Kamal's silver Honda parked at my house when I drove up. He sat hunched over on one of the porch chairs with his hands clasped on his knees. Jumping to his feet, he came halfway across the yard before I got the truck door open.

"Jimmy Lloyd! You are okay?" he cried.

I held a hand out the window and turned it over and back, studying it. "Well, I think so. Everything still looks the same anyway. Nails are a little dirty." I slid off the seat and landed heavily on the ground.

Kamal's eyes rounded when he got his first good look at all of me. I had already seen myself in a mirror: hair plastered down and sweat-soaked clothes sticking to me. I looked like warm dogshit smeared with soot.

"*Yo Allah*, you look terrible! Were you in the fire?"

"Yeah, I was there. They called me out," I said. "All the fire team members got called."

"Fire team?"

"Firefighters. We train for that kind of stuff, and we go put out the big fires. It's all volunteers."

"That fire was dangerous!" he said emphatically. "You *asked* to fight it?"

"I told you, Kamal, we're all volunteers."

"Oh... I had no idea." Kamal put a hand to his forehead. "I didn't know..." He slumped against the truck bed and bent over, looking as if he might be sick. He mumbled something in Arabic. It sounded like "Subaru Allah."

I clapped a hand on his shoulder. "Hey, don't go getting all squirrelly on me. I already puked once myself today, and I don't wanna see any more from you, especially in my front yard."

He waved me away and straightened up. "I'm all right." He stopped and peered at me strangely. "You're sure you are unhurt?"

"Yes, I'm fine. I told you already. I just need to get inside and shower off this grime. You sure *you're* okay, Kamal? You're acting awful funny."

"I'm okay. I was just worried. You haven't been home all day, and I was afraid that you might be down there." He sounded really concerned.

I looked to the southern horizon. Smoke still rose from the refinery hidden over the edge of the rims. It climbed high up over the Yellowstone valley before the prevailing northwest breezes shredded it and moved the pieces away in long jagged streams. It didn't look very threatening from here. I spoke gently to Kamal. "Well, I *was* there, but as you can see, I'm all right, and so is everybody else."

He nodded, looking at the ground.

"Now if you'll excuse me, I'm going to go in and clean up." I started walking toward the house. "Why don't you come on back this evening, and we'll have us some barbecue?" I said over my shoulder. "Maybe we'll go out some more later."

"Okay."

I had almost reached the top of the porch steps when Kamal called out, "Jimmy Lloyd?"

I stopped and turned around.

"Is the refinery destroyed?" he asked.

"What?"

"Is the refinery destroyed? Can it still function now?"

Even as tired as I felt, I had to chuckle. "Oh, yeah, it's still operational. It takes more than a tank fire to put a whole refinery out of business. We're going to be hurting for a long time, though. For sure production will be cut back, but losing a storage tank won't take us completely out of the pipeline."

Kamal studied me with an unreadable expression then said softly, "I see. That is... good to hear."

"Okay then. Come on back around five. We can catch it on the TV news while we chow down on steak. I got to shower now. I can hardly stand myself."

DUNKER WAS SITTING on my living room couch when I plodded out from the shower with a bath towel around my waist. He'd already popped himself a beer.

"Thought I heard someone out here," I said. "Why don't you help yourself, Dunker? Maybe get a beer?"

"Well, thanks, I might do that," he answered, crossing an ankle on his knee. "Heard you had a little excitement today."

"A little."

"Tell me about it." Dunker leaned back as if he were settling in for a good long story.

"How about you giving me a minute to get some clothes on? You can make yourself useful and fire up the grill while you're waiting. Take another steak out of the freezer and stay for supper."

"I already saw two thawing in the sink. You expecting more company?" He hitched his eyebrows up suggestively. "I don't want to cramp your style."

"It's Kamal, you dipwad. He's coming over to watch the evening news."

"Kamal, huh? I like that kid. Acts a little funny sometimes." Dunker stroked his mustache. "I think there's some deep water there that nobody's poked a stick in yet."

"Yeah, he's all right. Doesn't talk much."

Dunker grinned. "We all got things deep down we don't want to stir up, even you, Jimmy Lloyd. Now go cover your ass up. I can find the charcoal."

When Kamal arrived an hour later, the briquettes had reached that perfect state of red hot and glowing. I laid the steaks on the grill caveman-style with no seasoning. The three of us stood next to it on the back deck, savoring the smell of cooking meat while I retold my refinery fire story to Kamal, taking care not to pad it too much. Kamal listened carefully, but Dunker only stared at the steaks, having heard it all already.

When I finished, Kamal nodded slowly. "That sounds like a very brave thing you did, Jimmy Lloyd."

"That's what everybody else keeps saying, but it wasn't that big a deal. There were two others with me. Anyone would've done the same."

"I sure as hell wouldn't have," Dunker grumbled, but I knew better.

We sat outside to eat the steaks and foil-wrapped baked potatoes. I soaked up the late afternoon sun. Talk turned to horses for a while then football. Dunker's grandson had distinguished himself in a scrimmage game and gotten some attention in the morning edition of the Billings Gazette.

Dunker acted upset about it. "I told that boy and his father both that the best place to play ball is on the O-line. You play. You do your job. Then, after it's all over, nobody in the stands remembers your name. The team knows. The coaches know. That's all that matters." He shook his head in disgust. "Now he got his name in the paper. You watch. He'll be strutting around like he's some kind of big shot if this keeps up." He scratched his armpit. "I got to go over to his house tonight and tell him how proud I am of him. Then I'll slap him upside the head to remind him he can still get his ass whipped."

"I don't understand this. Don't you want your grandson to be recognized as a good player?" Kamal looked puzzled. "I know my father and grandfather would take great pride in me if I accomplished something like he has."

"Oh, I said I was proud of him, didn't I? I'm real proud," Dunker replied, a little smile playing over his mouth. "But there's no need for *him* to get swelled up over himself. I didn't raise any of my kids to be a glory hound. Grandsons neither. That's no way to go, in my book."

Kamal still looked unconvinced.

"Look," I said, "the offensive line is like being a pickup man at the rodeo. He has to be there on every play, picking up cowboys and hazing critters, but nobody looks at him. They want to see the bull riders. Only his girlfriend and people that really follow rodeo even know the pickup man is there. Unless he screws up. Then everyone knows he's been there."

Dunker and I clinked beer bottles.

"This is what you do?" Kamal asked. "You do the pickup man?"

"Yeah, I do the pickup man," I drawled.

"Wouldn't you like to be applauded, too?"

"We want to be *appreciated*," Dunker interrupted. "And that only comes from folks that know the game. They're the ones that count." He looked at his watch. "Looks like it's time to get inside and check the news."

We went in, and I clicked on the television, switching to the channel that had tried to interview Jack and me. The big fire was their lead story. That same reporter spoke live from the site, and it was clear the fire was just about over. The refinery's media spokesman read a statement saying nothing much. They also ran a clip taken at the fire's peak. Sure enough, there was footage I didn't know they'd taken of Jack and me walking up to the barricade. I had to admit the effect was pretty dramatic with the flames reaching up behind us as we approached the camera. With the fire suits and helmets on, we looked like a couple of downed pilots leaving the burning crash of a very big airplane.

Dunker hooted. "Look at that, pickup man. You're a TV hero!"

I grinned. "Nobody can tell it's me. I'm covered." Thank God they didn't air my ten seconds of interview time.

Kamal said, "I'm glad you could get out of the fire, Jimmy Lloyd. It looked very hot."

"Thanks. It was a bit toasty, for sure."

The coverage switched back to the studio, and an anchorman read news that made us all sit up. "Refinery officials also report that there is evidence indicating this fire could have been deliberately set. A sample spigot on the outer wall of the tank had been opened, allowing its flammable contents to spill out into the area around it. KULR 8 will keep you informed of any other breaking developments."

Dunker looked over at me. "What's he talking about, Jimmy Lloyd? Those tanks got spigots you can open?"

"Yeah, it's to catch lab samples. They collect three to five gallons from every new batch to test before it's shipped."

"Well, why don't you lock them shut?" he asked.

I rubbed my head. "They do—with a chain. But I suppose anyone who would start that fire could cut a chain, too, if they wanted."

"Now who the hell would want to go and do a thing like that?" Dunker asked.

I hitched my shoulders. "Who wouldn't? Oil companies have lots of enemies. I suppose some of them could resort to arson."

"It's terrorists, ain't it?"

"Could be. Who knows? I would think they would be a little smarter than this, though. Taking down 308 just dents us a little bit. They'd want to do more damage than that."

The silence dragged out for several seconds. Dunker and I simultaneously swung our gazes to Kamal, whose eyes remained glued to the television.

"Hey, it's okay, Kamal." Dunker laughed. "We know it wasn't you. From what Brownie's told me, you were having too much of a big time at the Drifters last night to get into any other trouble."

I laughed at Kamal's uncomfortable expression. "That's for sure. Ol' Kamal looked like Fred Astaire out there with all the ladies grabbing at him for a dance."

Dunker looked at me. "Heard you had a big time, too."

I felt myself blush. "Yeah, well. A man's gotta do what a man's gotta do."

"Better get your pecker checked. That gal's been around and back a few times."

Chapter Twelve

Thor called me the following Thursday evening. "When you got a few days off again?"

I was stirring some chopped onions into a pot of chili on the stove. I put the phone on speaker and laid it on the counter. "Well, you just missed these last two. I go back on nights tomorrow. Won't be off again till Monday."

"One day'll be enough."

"What'cha got?"

"I need to move two hundred head up to the Bulls for summer range. You want to come help round 'em and load 'em?"

"Sure. Tuesday works better for me. What time?" I raised the ladle and took a taste. *Needs more salt.*

"I'll tell the truck driver to be there ready to go at nine. I'd like to get the first load on board by then, so we need to get started by six," Thor said. "Say, you got another big fire going there? What's that sizzling noise I hear?"

"Just making chili."

"Chili, huh? How much you got?" Thor was about as subtle as a landslide.

"I got enough," I answered. "You in town right now?"

"Just left the co-op."

"Well, come on over. I'll set a bowl out for you." I added some Tabasco and let the pot simmer.

Thor arrived fifteen minutes later in one of his employer's black ranch trucks, the Rocking RS brand—the Rock 'em Sock 'em—proudly displayed in yellow on the front doors, the pickup bed crammed with metal fenceposts and wire. He let the screen door bang behind him. "Boy, that smells pretty good."

I lifted the lid, and fragrant steam rose to the kitchen ceiling. The chili bubbled softly like a lava pit. I inclined my head toward the refrigerator. "Got some drinks in there. Help yourself. This is about ready. We'll eat on the deck."

"You betcha." Thor opened the icebox door and took out two pops. He put them on the tray I had set out with condiments, crackers, and shredded cheese. He nudged open the back door with his foot and carried it all out onto the deck. I picked up two hot bowls of chili with potholders. When I got outside, Thor was already sitting at the patio table, admiring the oncoming sunset.

He leaned back in the chair. "Peaceful out here, ain't it?"

"No more than your place."

"Yeah, but this is yours. I live on another man's property," he replied.

"It's mine, all right. Mine and Wells Fargo bank's for the next twenty years."

"Yeah, I guess there's no getting around that these days." He blew on the spoon of chili before he tasted it. "This is good, Jimmy Lloyd. You sure got a knack for chili. You put jalapeños in here?"

"Thanks. I did cut one up for it."

"Well, it sure works for me."

We ate in silence for a few minutes. The breeze calmed to nothing, and the sun turned golden near the horizon. Coyotes yipped a mile or so to the north.

Thor got up to refill his bowl. "You want some more?"

"About half full this time. Use the pot holders," I said.

When he came back, he placed an almost-full bowl in front of me.

"This is half full?" I asked.

"This stuff is too good to eat halfway."

I pushed my Montana State cap back on my head. "Thanks for bringing Kamal home the other night."

"No problem," Thor answered as he settled down in his chair. "You looked like you might be getting a little busy." He winked and hoisted his spoon. "This'll even us up."

"Well, thanks again." I sipped my pop. "What time did you get him home?"

"Wasn't that late. I reckon I had him here by two thirty at least." Thor looked at me intently. "Why? You worried about how much sleep he's getting?"

"Maybe... did he say much to you?" I spooned in a mouthful of chili.

"Naw, that boy doesn't talk much at all—hell, you know that. Why you so curious about him anyway? Don't you see him most days yourself?"

"Not really curious... just wondering." Actually, I hadn't seen my renter in several days, not since he'd been at my house on the evening of the refinery fire.

"I reckon you could ask him anything you want in just a minute. Isn't that him coming right now?" Thor pointed out the screen door at the highway where Kamal had stopped his Civic at the mailbox. He drove slowly up the long graveled drive since I had asked him once to hold down the dust.

"Let's see if he's hungry," I said as I stepped off the deck then walked out to where the drive went by my house. I waved my arms in a crisscross pattern, and he coasted to a stop beside me. "Hey, Kamal. Haven't seen you in a while. Me and Thor's eating some of my famous chili. Come on in and have some. I'll have to throw the rest away if you don't."

Kamal stared at his dashboard. "You're certain you have enough?" He glanced up at me quickly before he looked down again. "I don't want to eat all your dinner."

"That's right, Kamal. I asked you to supper because I didn't have enough for all of us. Get out and come on over. You can leave the car right here. You're not blocking anybody." I got all the way back to the deck before I heard his car door open. I went inside, wondering why Kamal was being so pokey. The fridge had more soft drinks, and I took another bowl out of the cabinet. "Come help yourself," I called through the back door.

A couple of minutes later, Kamal slurped his own helping of my forte dish. "This stew is very delicious."

"It's his specialty," Thor said. "He screws up everything else."

"Bite me," I replied.

Kamal looked from me to Thor and back again, his spoon partway to his mouth. He shook his head and grinned. "You Americans are strange."

He loosened up considerably after that, and the evening passed pleasurably. The smell of sagebrush along with Thor laughing at old jokes he'd already heard had me thinking the world could be an all right place. Soft clouds spread over the western sky, glowing orange and pink. The three of us turned our heads to watch at the moment the sun slid quietly under the edge of the earth, the only sound being the same distant coyotes.

"This is beautiful," Kamal said softly. No one else broke the silence.

When our meal ended, Thor asked Kamal if he wanted to come and bring along Sweet Ginger when we gathered up the two hundred head. Kamal hesitated a second before agreeing to it. He didn't seem very enthusiastic, and later, as I washed dishes in hot soapy water up to my elbows, I looked out the kitchen window on the moonlit landscape and wondered what was eating at him.

THE FOLLOWING TUESDAY, I hitched up the slant-load trailer at oh-dark-thirty. I'd decided to take Snuffy, my gray gelding, because he had more go than the other horses and would work all day without complaining. I hoisted my ranch saddle up on him with a loose cinch. Snuffy had fourteen years on him, and he'd seen it all. He walked calmly up into the trailer and was dozing by the time I got behind the wheel to leave.

When I arrived at Kamal's, the headlights caught him coming out of the barn, wearing his new hat and leading Sweet Ginger. She loaded as sweet as her name. We rumbled across the highway cattle guard at five in the morning. Not much spark for conversation that early.

I handed Kamal my thermos of coffee. "It's black, but it'll make your eyes pop open."

"Humph." He unscrewed the top that doubled as a cup and wiped its rim with the cuff of his Carhartt shirt before he poured coffee in. He sniffed the contents then took a swallow. "Ugh! This is terrible," he sputtered.

"It's a little hot, maybe."

"No, that's not it, Jimmy Lloyd. This is really bad coffee." He tried another cautious sip. "Really bad."

"Man, you bitch just like a regular cowboy. Did your eyes pop open?"

"I suppose they did."

"Then you got what I promised you," I said. "I never said it tasted good."

Kamal laughed. He leaned back in the cab and watched hay fields go by while he sipped at the cup. The early light made them look like gray seas. "I have never done anything like this before. Is this what cowboys do to herd cattle?"

"Sort of. Today won't be hard work, though. Thor has cattle in a thousand-acre pasture that's flat and mostly open as a table top," I replied. "All we do is get around behind them and ease them into the loading pens at a walk. The truck takes it from there."

"We don't rope them?"

I snorted. "In this new west, the cattle are docile. We shouldn't have a problem." I thought for a second. "'Course, when we go to get them back this fall, after they've been running wild in the Bull Mountains all summer, *that* might be another story."

"Why are we moving these cows?"

"Say 'cattle' when you talk about a herd—a herd of cattle, not cows. Thor's boss leases acreage up in the hills where there's enough grass there in good summer weather to fatten them up. This way, his lowland pasturage gets a little relief time to grow back."

"We can't herd them there?"

"Too far. The truck can make a couple of round trips in one day and be done with it. On horses, the job would take us a week. Plus, we'd walk all the fat off of them, and half of them would get hit by cars on the highway."

"I see." Kamal continued staring out the side window. He'd been living in my rent house for about five months, but I got the impression he had never gone far out of town. The sight of cattle standing in the fields we passed seemed to fascinate him.

I drummed my fingers on the top of the steering wheel. "You mind if I ask you something?"

Kamal looked at me, his expression blank. "Go ahead."

"Well, I was just wondering. I never see you going to the college much. Or anywhere else, for that matter. So I was wondering... what gives?"

His head swung back to the window. "You have been spying on me?" he said to the glass.

For some reason, that answer struck me the wrong way. "Oh, cut that bullshit out," I fired back. "Hell, your driveway goes by right outside my kitchen window. I'd be a pretty poor lookout if I couldn't see when you go off to school." I paused. "And you don't go that much. So how do you expect to stay in school anyway? What kind of grades are you making?"

He kept looking out the window. The relaxed atmosphere in the cab disappeared in two seconds, replaced by a tense silence. I could see his shoulders tighten up, and he raised his chin. "My grades are none of your business, Jimmy Lloyd. Whether or not I stay at college here is none of your affair, either."

He rolled down the window and threw the remaining contents of the thermos cup into the wind that blasted by. It would be splattered all over my truck, but I didn't say anything. He rolled the glass back up and stared at the road ahead.

I gripped the wheel with both hands. "You're right, Kamal. It's none of my business. It's just that, me and the boys, we've taken a liking to you. I hope you get to stay around Billings for a long while, I guess." I looked sideways at him. "You're certainly welcome to stay at my rent place."

Kamal turned to meet my stare. "I believe you, Jimmy Lloyd."

I held out my right hand. "Friends, again?"

His expression softened. "Of course." He took my hand, and we shook. It was the first time we'd done that.

"Good. So you'll be with us for a long time yet, eh?" I put my hand back on the steering wheel and grinned at him. "There's lots more to show you around here."

"Yes, I will stay here for a long time yet. My grades are good." Kamal said all the words right, but his voice had gone flat again. He studied his hands in his lap.

Chapter Thirteen

We ended up being the last ones to get to the loading pens built alongside the road, and full daylight arrived at the same time. Three men and a woman were standing with horses when I pulled into the graveled parking area. I circled around to stop beside an unfamiliar horse trailer hitched to Thor's truck.

Thor walked over to greet us, grinning like a well-fed possum. "Hello there, Sleeping Beauty."

"You're welcome, bright eyes," I replied, jerking my thumb at the strange trailer. "New rig?"

Thor looked at it, a surprised expression on his face, as though the trailer had just sprung up behind his truck. "That? Oh no, it's hers." He nodded in the direction of the gal.

I glanced over at her.

"Good morning, Jimmy Lloyd! Hi, Kamal! It's so good to see you again." Jane waved at us across the parking area before she trotted over. She wore baggy jeans over a pair of scuffed packer boots. A sweat-stained cowboy hat tilted back on her head, and like everyone else except Kamal, she had tied a silk bandana around her neck. She gave Kamal a full-on hug, which he accepted awkwardly, arms down at his sides. I think he probably had a hard time believing this cowgirl was the same beauty he'd met at the Drifters less than a week ago. She looked pretty hardcore compared to then.

I looked at Thor. "Jane?" I mouthed at him.

Grinning, he barely raised a shoulder.

I popped him on the shoulder and laughed. "You dog, you..."

He lowered his eyes, embarrassed. "It's not all what you think," Thor mumbled. But he raised his gaze again to watch Jane's ass as she walked away to her horse.

Kamal and I backed our horses out of the trailer and tightened up their cinches. I recognized the other two fellows as nearby ranchers who'd traded help with Thor on other occasions. We nodded at each other. Everyone gathered around Thor to wait for his instructions.

"Okay, boys, it's pretty simple today. We'll circle behind them at the river from each side." He made wide sweeping gestures with his arms. "And then we just move 'em slow up to the pens here. They should go in the gates easy. They been fed in these pens often enough."

He made assignments. Kamal and I would sweep around to the right. The two ranchers had the other side. Thor and Jane took drag at the back of the herd.

"Go slow, now," he cautioned. "Don't let your horses spook and scare the cattle. Questions?" He looked around at us. "Glad to have you here, Kamal. Thanks for helping."

Kamal had followed Thor's every word intently. He nodded once, tipping a finger to his hat. He'd worn his Saturday-night felt hat since I'd neglected to tell him about getting a cheaper straw one for this kind of work. "I am happy to."

That new hat will be dirty soon.

"Okay. Let's mount up," Thor called out.

We split and started to go wide around the distant herd. The Rock 'Em Sock 'Em cattle, mostly Angus with straight backs and a solid black color, contrasted sharply against the spring grasses blanketing the pasture. As we approached, the ones still lying down started rising, rear end first. New calves frisked around, hopping awkwardly like windup toys. Some of them butted heads against their mamas' underbellies to get more breakfast. Kamal and I walked our horses side by side.

"This doesn't seem very hard," he said.

"I told you it wouldn't be." Then I pointed at the line of riparian growth along the banks of the Yellowstone River ahead of us. "See those cottonwoods and that brush? That's probably the only place that could cause a problem if some of these cows decide not to leave. We'll have to make 'em leave."

"Say 'cattle,'" Kamal replied.

"What?"

He grinned. "It's a herd of cattle, not a herd of cows."

"Okay. You got me."

We circled quietly until we got between most of the cattle and the river. Thor's plan had been for all six of us to gradually push them away from the water. That whole idea went south in a hurry when a dozen cow-calf pairs broke away and scattered into the tangled vegetation along the riverbank. Big, brown-eyed mama cows stared at us through the brush and chewed their cuds, quite content to stay holed up there in the early-morning shade.

"Oh, crap," I muttered.

Kamal looked at me. "What's the matter?"

"Well, we're gonna have to go in that thicket and flush those cattle out. Shit. I didn't bring my chinks, and you don't have any, either."

"Chinks?"

"Chaps. We're liable to get scratched up in there, but there's nothing much we can do about that now," I answered. "Actually, Kamal, you don't have to ride in there. I think I can do it."

Kamal looked at me as though I had just insulted his mother. "I will go, too. I didn't come here to watch."

I smiled. "I figured you'd say something like that. You ready?"

"Let's go."

We crashed into the brush with arms up to protect against the thorny Russian olive trees and the tall undergrowth that reached out to claw at our legs and faces. Both of us got scratched up in seconds.

The cattle started bolting out of the undergrowth and running to the herd as we worked downstream. I yelled like a banshee to hurry them along. Finally, we met Thor and Jane coming from the other direction. Thor had a fresh red welt across one cheek.

"Did we get them all?" he asked.

"I'm not sure. I think so," I replied.

"Kamal with you?"

I looked around. "Well, he was right behind me a minute ago. He must have hit a tree limb or something. I'll go check." I turned Snuffy's head around to backtrack. "Kamal!" I called.

"Over here, Jimmy Lloyd."

I eased through the vegetation toward his voice until I found him at the edge of the river with Sweet Ginger's front feet in the water. When I saw where he was pointing, I shook my head in disgust. "Damn bovines. They just got no sense at all."

Standing shoulder deep in the ice-cold Yellowstone River was a cow and her young calf. The little guy had only his head showing above the surface. They had run the wrong way from us, and they both looked pretty scared. In most places, the Yellowstone was rocky, but those two had floundered out into a soft muddy area covered by the spring runoff that had overflowed the banks. Ten yards beyond them, though, the river moved quick and deep in its normal bed. If they went any farther out, the calf would never survive that current, and mama cow probably wouldn't, either. I sat there with both hands on the saddle horn, thinking. Sticks cracked behind me as Thor arrived. He stopped next to me.

"Damn it to hell!" he fumed, taking in the situation.

Jane came along on the opposite side of Kamal. The four of us sat there in silence, staring at the pair in the river while they watched us fearfully.

Suddenly, Jane drove her horse into the water, splashing the rest of us. "Yip! Yip! Yip!" she cried.

In all the years I'd known Jane, that big Appaloosa gelding of hers always did whatever she asked, and right then, it plunged stirrup deep into the stream then still deeper as her boots went under. Before the cow knew what had happened, Jane had gotten behind her and between her and the fast-moving main channel of the river. She slapped at the brown flood water with a coiled rope.

"Yip, yip! Yeehaw!" She popped the coil on the cow's rump. It should have worked, but it didn't. The mama cow rolled her eyes and stood there like she had been anchored, and the calf wouldn't move without her. Jane poked at them with her boot.

"Jane, she ain't moving. You better get out of there," Thor called.

Her Appy was starting to get nervous. The whites of his eyes showed as he thrashed against the current.

"Come on, Jane... I mean it. We can rope her." Thor sounded anxious.

Jane may not have heard him with all the water rushing around her. She kept prodding and slapping at the cow. Suddenly, another splashing started.

What the hell?

Kamal took Sweet into the water. The game mare churned right out next to Jane, almost losing her footing in the moving water. He leaned over and grabbed the mama's ear. She bawled when he twisted it. Jane redoubled smacking with the rope. It was nothing but chaos there in the swirling current for about five seconds before the cow couldn't stand any more. She broke for the bank, surging up and down and bellowing until she reached land. She crashed through the brush away from us, and the calf struggled to follow. Jane and Kamal each took an ear and pulled him into shallower water. He shivered when he got out, but Mama called for him out in the pasture, and he left, still shaking.

Jane and Kamal rode out of the river with dirty water streaming from their wet clothes. They were soaked from the belly button down and as happy as a birthday party. The two of them grinned at each other, their faces smeared and their hats flecked with drying mud that looked like bits of cement.

"Good job, lover boy," Jane said, high-fiving him.

"Thank you." Kamal smiled so big that I could see his back molars.

Thor shook his head and grinned. "You two crazy knuckleheads."

THE REST OF THE MORNING passed pretty smoothly. We got the herd into the pens without much trouble, and the cattle hauler backed up to the loading platform. Thor had hired Chad White Horse to work the gates and help run cattle up the ramp. Kamal and I waved, and Chad pointed back at us, too busy to chat. With him hustling around in the pens, loading the first batch went off without a hitch. Thor looked relieved when the trucker finally fired that diesel up to go. He shook hands with us.

"Thanks, fellows. I really appreciate the help," he said. "Jane and I can take 'em from here. Chad's riding with us."

"No problem. Glad to do it," I said.

The rancher neighbors nodded. "You betcha," one of them said. They left for their nearby spreads, riding horseback along the shoulder of the highway.

Kamal and I headed to our horses to loosen tack and load them back into the trailers. His jeans were still damp, and he walked as if they chafed.

"You better get those pants changed as soon as we get back," I said. "Your saddle's wet, too. It needs saddle soap on it right away. There's a whole slew of that stuff and rags, too, in the barn at your house. It's all in the tool room there. I'll show it to you when we get back."

"Yes, I think I have seen it. I will take care of it quickly."

"Good man."

I pulled out onto the highway, heading toward home. Kamal looked tired enough to fall asleep, but he surprised me. He stuck his arm out the open window to let his hand swoop up and down in the wind like a bird, the same way I always played as a kid on long car rides. I started doing it on my side.

"How old is Jane?" he asked abruptly, still flying his hand.

"How old is Jane?" I cocked an eyebrow at him. "Why do you want to know?"

"I noticed for the first time today... she has little lines in her face—around her eyes and mouth." He pulled his hand in. "So she is older than I had thought."

I laughed. "Kamal, *all* the ladies look older in broad daylight. Why do you think they keep barrooms so dark? Even the American dream looks better at night."

"The American dream?" He looked puzzled.

"Oh, you know—a good woman, a home, a good life, all of that stuff. I have to admit, sometimes another thing looks pretty good until you wake up next to it in the morning light. That's when you say, 'What the hell was I thinking?'"

"Is that what happened to you?"

"To me?"

"With you and Esther."

I gripped the wheel and watched the road through the windshield. "No, that wasn't a mistake I made in the dark." I looked over at him. "That really *was* a good woman and a good life. I just fucked it up." I puffed out my cheeks. "But to answer your question, Jane is probably older than your mother, so I wouldn't get any ideas," I said, grinning at him. "You don't want to get Thor mad at you anyway."

"Oh no, I wasn't thinking like that," he answered. "She is just so nimble that I wondered."

"Nimble? Boy, she is gonna love it when she hears that. You sure you're not trying to steal her affections?"

"No, Jimmy Lloyd, I only wondered." Kamal settled back in the seat. "But older than my mother? I doubt that. I am the youngest of her seven children."

"Really? Oh, that's right. You're the baby of the family."

"No, my father has two other wives—young wives, and their children are younger."

I whistled. "Well, my hat's off to him. I couldn't handle just one wife."

"No." Kamal looked at me sharply. "No, you would not like him."

"Really? Why not? I like you okay."

"You just wouldn't. We are different."

WHEN WE GOT BACK TO Kamal's place, he offloaded Sweet Ginger while I walked into the old barn. I went in the little corner room at the front and cracked the lid on a five-gallon plastic bucket where I kept leather-care stuff. Everything looked to be in there, but as I turned to get a saddle stand, I noticed some things out of place. My tools usually hung on a pegboard there, but several of them were scattered haphazardly on the workbench. I rehung them in their rightful spots. A couple had a new sheen of three-in-one oil from the can sitting on the counter. I carried the bucket and stand out into the main area of the barn just as Kamal came in, lugging his damp saddle.

"Hey, Kamal," I said. "You having some plumbing problems?" I unfolded the saddle stand and set it on the dirt floor.

Kamal stopped for a second before he gently set the saddle on the stand and fussed with it, arranging and rearranging the straps, acting for all the world like a kid stalling for time until the recess bell rang. "No. No problems... why do you ask?" He studied the leather.

"Well, I see you've been handling some of the hand tools in there." I indicated the corner room with a jerk of my head. "Try to put them back where you found them next time. It's a pet peeve of mine."

"Oh... okay. I will take better care from now on," he said, looking embarrassed.

"Hey. No harm done. I appreciate you oiling them." I clapped him on the shoulder. "Why did you need to use them anyway?"

Kamal ran his finger along a seam in the leather. "I did not use anything. I was thinking that I could help you with your fencing work, and I wanted to be ready."

"I see. I appreciate that, Kamal. I really do, but I can tell you, you won't be needing much of that stuff for fence work. Pliers are good, though. Tell you what, the next time I ride the fence line, I'll come get you and show you what we need. I think you'll make a good hand, by the way."

He still looked embarrassed, but he met my eyes. "Thank you."

"Okay, no problem." I lifted the plastic bucket. "Here's the stuff in here to oil up your tack. Just put a little dab on and rub it in good. There's rags in there, too." I grinned. "Esther's had this saddle a long time. I remember when she bought it. She'll like you taking care of it." I turned to go. "All right. I'll be seeing you. Gotta go get Snuffy out and unhitch the trailer."

"Do you need help?"

"Naw, I got it. You just do that saddle," I replied, waving over my shoulder as I walked away.

"Jimmy Lloyd?"

I stopped at the barn door. "Yeah?"

"You have been a good friend to me. All of you. I am grateful for that, and I will always remember it."

His tone almost made me choke up. "Well, sure, buddy. I think you're a good guy, too. I think most everybody likes you." I cleared my throat and walked out to the pickup.

Ten minutes later, I was leaning against Snuffy's stall, listening to him crunching on the coffee can of oats I'd put in his feed bucket. I pondered what Kamal had said. It seemed that my young Arab renter must have never had friends before. That was certainly a sorry deal.

Chapter Fourteen

The refinery manager called an all-hands-on-deck meeting on Wednesday morning when I got back to work. Everyone who could be spared for a short while hiked over to the mechanical building and into the open lunchroom area. I settled down on a folding chair near the back, next to CK, who greeted me with a mouthful of chocolate chip cookie. He'd already made a run to the side tables, where the sodas chilled in ice chests next to trays with more cookies. The company always provided that sort of free swag for the masses at these gatherings.

"Hey, Jimmy Lloyd. What's up?" he mumbled around a wad of chewed-up cookie.

"Not much, I guess," I answered. "What's all this about? Do you know?"

CK brushed crumbs off his mustache. "Oh, I reckon Lucas is going to tell us the latest about the fire. 'Thanks for y'all's quick response. Couldn't do it without you fine people. Blah. Blah. Blah.' You know the drill."

"Yeah, probably right. Wish he'd just send a postcard."

"Howdy, boys." Ted Marshall, pushing well past three hundred pounds, eased into the seat next to me. Big Ted headed up the accident prevention program, which meant he mostly walked around with a clipboard and a bad attitude, looking for safety violations. He was using both hands to carry a paper towel loaded with cookies. A soda can was snuggled in the crook of his arm.

"What's up, Big Ted? Looks like you're not doing your job so well these days, huh?" CK said.

"Hell, that fire wasn't on me. That was no accident," Ted snapped back. He shifted in his seat to face both of us. "Hey, I saw you fellows at the Rainbow a couple of weeks ago. That skinny boy can fight, eh? What is he? Arab?" He looked directly at me with slitted eyes.

"He's from Saudi Arabia," I answered. "So yeah, that makes him an Arab."

"Huh. Just wondering. He a good kid?"

"The best."

"Well, that's good if you say so." Big Ted took the toothpick out of his mouth to bite into a cookie. "That's real good," he grunted. Ted's attitude pissed me off.

Kamal is *a good kid.*

Wearing slacks and a polo shirt with the company logo, the refinery manager stepped up to a microphone at the front. "Hello, everybody. Thanks for coming. I know we all have work to do, so I'll try to keep this brief." He paused to look around the room as we quieted. "First of all, I'd like to thank you—all of you—for your superb response to the Tank 308 fire last week. Without the quick action many of you took that night, we might have had an even worse incident on our hands."

CK had another bite of cookie while he bumped me in the shin. "Told you," he whispered.

"We are wounded, but not dead," Lucas said. The refinery would have to cruise at about half-speed capacity until 308 and the related piping got repaired or replaced. It all sounded good, but after a few minutes, I started to count ceiling tiles. That was when Lucas snuck one in on me. "And so, in recognition, I'd like for the fire team members who responded that day to stand up."

What?

People clapped while, here and there, guys rose to their feet. I got up, too, grinning and feeling sheepish. Little Jimmy shot me a thumbs-up from across the room. Lucas announced we were each getting a fifty-dollar gift certificate for Rimrock Mall, and we sat down to more applause.

The refinery manager turned serious. "The fire that took out Tank 308 was deliberately set. We know that much. What we don't know is who set it and why. It could have been ecoterrorists. It could've been kids. We just don't know. But we *will* find out. The state authorities, FBI, and Homeland Security have been working on this day and night since it happened. As you all know, someone cut through the fencing at the tank farm and then opened the sample spigot. Gasoline poured out for maybe an hour before they lit it off."

The room stilled, and I wasn't counting ceiling tiles anymore.

His gaze swept around the room. "We are pretty sure they got in after three in the morning. Security and the pumper on duty both passed through the tank farm about that time."

"Who was the pumper?" I whispered to CK.

"Russ," he whispered back. "Says he didn't see a damn thing."

I nodded. Anybody could have done it. The tank farm sat right next to I-90, and it wouldn't have taken much to get up to the fence in the dark. I had the feeling that it was probably Greenpeace college kids. The fire had already brought out a fresh contingent to picket at the refinery gates this week. They came, driving electric pseudo-cars with petrochemical-based plastic kayaks on roof racks, so they could protest about fossil fuels. This period in their life was their last best chance to fight something without the blowback of consequences. In ten years, they would be making payments on Chevy Suburbans and hauling kids around to karate lessons.

Lucas went on to outline new security measures. Off-duty police-men would man the front gate and do roving patrols again, as they had done for a few months after 9/11. Chains had been installed on the back gates by the river. There didn't seem to be much else to say, but Lucas wanted to finish with a big flourish. "We have taken these steps to prevent another incident like this, but I ask you to stay alert. We need every pair of eyes to be watchful. Report anything—*any-thing*—that looks suspicious or seems out of place. I know I can count on each of you to do your part. Together, we can show whoever did this that they haven't put us out of business. We're not beat and never will be. I thank you all."

Maybe Lucas expected some applause. He stood there, holding the microphone stand with both hands while we groaned to our feet. I grabbed a couple of cookies on my way out.

CK AND I WALKED TOGETHER back to the pipe stills. The refinery seemed especially loud that morning. Steam hissed at us on every side, and the crude oil furnace roared like a space shuttle launching.

"So what do you think, Jimmy Lloyd?" CK asked as we shucked our hard hats inside the control room, where we could hear again.

"About that fire? Hell if I know..." I shook my head. "Probably some Missoula college kids out to save the planet." I opened my lunch pail to put the cookies inside.

"Travis was telling me one of his buddies remembered a parked vehicle sitting near the tank farm just off the frontage road that night." Travis Bender was a Yellowstone County sheriff's deputy who rode the mountains with us sometimes. "He said it looked like a little light-colored four-door."

"He didn't stop and check it out?" I asked.

"Nope. He was hauling ass to a wreck in Lockwood, bells and whistles blowing. Forgot about it after that." He spread his hands wide. "Such is life," he said expansively. "Our firebug gets away with it because some piece of shit runs a stop sign, T-bones an old man, and gets his fourth DUI."

"Yeah, I suppose so. That's too bad, though." I rubbed my neck with the back of my hand. "Couldn't he tell what make it was?"

"No way. He would have forgotten it altogether if it hadn't been for 308." CK shot me a sideways look. "That's not for general distribution. I wasn't supposed to say anything about it myself. Travis could get in big trouble if it comes out he's leaking state secrets. They want to keep that car business quiet while they do some checking."

"That's fine with me. My lips are sealed." I made a motion on my mouth like I held a key. "Say, by the way, is Travis coming with us next month to the Beartooths?"

"That's why I was talking to him. He says he might if he can get off then. He's got some seniority, so I expect he will."

"Good deal." I started checking the gauges on the control room wall. *Time to go to work.*

ROGER CALLED ME ON the phone later just before shift change. "Jimmy Lloyd," he said.

"Hey, boss. What's up?"

"You got a minute to come by and see me before you head home today?"

I looked at the wall clock. "How 'bout I come over in fifteen?"

"Sounds like a plan."

Terry came in as I hung up, and I briefed him on where operations stood. Then I said, "I need to see Roger now before I go, so I'm gonna leave you now if you got it, bro."

"Sure thing. I got it."

CK was passing the desk, gathering up his stuff to go home. He whistled. "Hoo-whee. Going to see the boss man, huh? Got your kneepads?"

I slapped my forehead. "Oh gee, no, I don't. Could you give them back to me please?"

"Sorry, I don't have them anymore. You might have to bend over the desk."

"Why's Roger want to see you?" Terry asked.

I shrugged. "Beats me. Maybe he wants to give me the Employee of the Year award."

"Just better take those kneepads if you can find them," CK called over his shoulder as he went out the door.

I walked over to Roger's office in the Operations Center.

"Come in, Jim," he said when I stuck my head in the doorway. "Go ahead and shut the door."

Uh-oh. I softly closed the door behind me before I sat down. Roger was the best supervisor in the refinery, but the last time he had me in his office for a one-on-one, it had been to warn me about working the rodeo. I didn't want to go through one of those lectures again, not even from him.

I crossed one ankle over my knee and clasped the other knee with both hands. "So you wanted to see me?"

He sat back, tapping a pencil on the glass-topped desk. "Yeah, Jimmy Lloyd, I did. I don't want to waste your time, so let me just tell you up front." He held up a folder. "At the end of the year, we're going to have a shitload of people leaving here. The baby boomers are starting to retire. They're going to be picking up their lump-sum checks and buying motorhomes to see America and the grandkids."

"Can't blame them for that," I said.

"I don't," Roger answered. "Fact is, I'll be doing it myself in a couple of years." He put his elbows on the desk. "But here's where it comes to you." Tapping the folder, he continued, "Some of these retirees are management. There's going to be a lot of personnel shuffling coming up. A lot of promotions." He paused to look at me.

I felt he was waiting for a response. "And?"

"I want to make you a shift supervisor. Brian's retiring in the pipe stills, and I'd like to slide you in on his shift to overlap with him for a couple of months before he goes. Then you take over."

A few seconds of silence ticked by. I uncrossed my legs to put both feet on the floor. "Wow... I did not see this one coming."

Roger smiled. "Why not, Jimmy Lloyd? You know you could handle it."

"Yeah, maybe so, but still, why me?"

"Well, for one thing, you know the unit better than anybody else, and for another, everybody likes you. They'll respond to you."

"Oh hell, Roger. Everybody liked *you*, too, until you stepped up into management. Now you're an asshole."

He laughed. "I suppose you got that right. Sometimes you have to do what you'd rather not do... but I definitely know even you can be an asshole if you have to."

I smiled.

Roger leaned back in his chair. "So what do you say? You want to give it a try?"

"Well... what about outside activities? Where would that stand?"

"The company would expect you to give up the rodeo," he answered, not smiling anymore. "They don't want to risk losing *anyone* to an unnecessary injury, but especially not someone in management. How much longer did you figure you would go on picking up cowboys anyway?"

"I figure I've got about ten more good years in me."

"Ten years?" Roger pursed his lips. "No, they for sure won't go that route, Jim. They might let you finish out the commitments you've already signed on for, but you'll have to phase everything else out before you can become a supervisor."

"Well, that's that, then," I said. "I'd like to keep on being a pickup man if it's all the same to the company." I started to get up. "But thanks for the offer, Roger. I appreciate it, and I do mean that."

"Are you sure about this, Jimmy Lloyd? I wish you'd think about it for a couple of days. The pay raise is pretty substantial." He stood up with me. "Tell you what. Just think on it until you come back on days again next week. Then give me an answer. Will you do that for me?"

Roger had a way of looking a man directly in the eye when he talked to him, and it was hard to deny someone like that.

"Sure, I'll think about it some more," I said. "I'll let you know next week."

"Okay, thanks. Just be open to the idea, Jim. I think you'd be a fine supervisor."

We shook hands, and I walked out of his office. I figured then that I wouldn't give up working the rodeo, but Roger was too good a person to just blow off like he didn't matter. I would take a few days so he would know I considered it really hard before I gave him my official no.

Chapter Fifteen

I showered with deodorant soap at the change house and washed my hair. Esther had a rent check coming, and I meant to take it by her house when I left the refinery. The late-afternoon sun still shone warm when I pulled into her driveway. Her blond hair in a ponytail, she stood in the front yard, in cutoffs and a tank top. Despite the work gloves, her arms were smeared with dirt up to the elbows. When she turned to open the gate, I could see the sweaty wet patch where the cotton top stuck to her back.

"Hello, Queenie. You doing some gardening?" I said as I hopped out of Ol' Brown and shut the door.

"A little. I needed to cut the roses back a little bit. Wrong time of year, but they were starting to look like the Amazon jungle." She gave me that wide grin of hers and brushed away a wisp of hair.

I surveyed the front of her house. Rosebush clippings lay piled all along the flowerbed. An unopened bag of potting soil leaned against the foundation, next to a pair of pruning shears. "Boy, you sure did clean them out. I bet that took a little while, huh?"

She glanced up at the sun. "Not that much. I guess I've been at it about an hour." She kept the gate open.

I took that as an invitation and walked through into the yard.

"I was just about to rest for a minute. You want some lemonade?"

"Sure," I answered. My heart tightened, and I handed her the rent check.

"Sit here on the porch. I'll bring some out," she said, leading the way to the covered front stoop. She had two chairs and a little round table there, like the kind of stuff at sidewalk cafés. "Be right back."

She disappeared into the house, and I sat down to wait. My pulse started hammering again, like it sometimes did around Esther. *Buck up, dammit. You're not fifteen.*

She popped out in less time than I'd expected, juggling a Tupperware pitcher and two filled glasses down onto the table. "Here we go," she said, sitting down. "Pour more if you want." She wiped her face and arms with a damp towel and looked at me.

"Thanks." I took a sip.

"Too sweet, huh?" She crinkled her nose at me. Esther always stirred in too much sugar for my taste, but I wasn't going to say a word about it.

"Nope. Just right."

She threw back her head and laughed. "I know better than that, Jimmy Lloyd, you lying sack of shit."

I chuckled with her. "You got me. It *is* a little sweet."

I told her about Roger's supervisor offer to me. I don't know why I did that—maybe I wanted to impress her.

"I think you should take it, Jimmy," Esther said. Her eyes actually lit up like she was excited. "You deserve it, and you know you could do it."

"Yeah, that's pretty much what Roger said, too. He says I'd have to give up my arena work, though."

"Well, then do it. You got to grow up sometime, you know."

"Just call me Peter Pan," I snapped.

An uneasy silence hung between us.

I took a long swallow from the glass. "You're right, Queenie. Sorry. I shouldn't have said it like that."

"'S okay, Jimmy. We are what we are." The quiet stretched on too long again before Esther finally broke it. "How's Kamal?" she asked brightly. "Jane told me you two went to help Thor move cattle. Said Kamal's a good horseman. She sure likes him. I do, too, actually."

"Yeah, he's a good youngster. A little bit of an odd duck sometimes..."

"How's that?" Esther's eyes narrowed. "You don't get along with him?"

"No, not that... not exactly. We get along pretty good, I'd say, considering our differences and all." I fumbled for words. *Don't screw this up any worse.* "Sometimes he just seems to be off somewhere else in his head. Dunker thinks there's more to Kamal than what we see, and I have to agree. Sometimes the kid acts... well, sad."

She smiled. "Well what do you expect, Jimmy? He's probably a little depressed. He does come from thousands of miles away and, from all I hear, about five centuries back. He misses home. And besides, maybe *you're* the one who's having a hard time with the differences."

A year ago, I might have flashed angry at that, but I grinned and shook my head. "Yeah, maybe you're onto something there." I leaned back in the little chair, wanting to change the subject. "Did Jane tell you she and Thor are getting pretty tight with each other? By the way, Kamal thinks Jane is 'nimble.'" I made quotation marks in the air with my fingers.

Esther giggled. The sound fit in perfectly with the warm afternoon. "Oh, Jane will love hearing that. Of course, she's told me about Thor. You know how Jane and Alice tell me everything. We don't keep secrets."

"I suppose I should have known that. They been doing the big nasty?"

"You know I won't tell you that... How's Sweet Ginger?" Esther could change the subject pretty well herself.

"Oh, she's doing fine. Jane's right about Kamal. He's real good with horses. And he loves that mare. I wouldn't be surprised if one day he tries to buy her from you again."

"Well, I would hate like hell to sell Sweet, but I do like that young man. Do you think he's going to stay here in Montana when he graduates?"

"No idea, but I have a feeling he won't."

"That's too bad. I won't sell her if he's going to take her away."

"I didn't say for sure that he's going anywhere."

"I know, Jimmy Lloyd, but your gut feelings about people are usually right on the mark," she said. "It's only about yourself that you get confused."

I let that go, too. "I believe you're right, though. I think he's lonely. Even with me and the fellows, he doesn't get out too much, but we're going to take him with us up to the mountains next month."

"On your summer fishing trip? Where are you going this year?"

"Past Lake Sioux Charlie. We'll base camp at Sunlight Meadows."

"Sioux Charlie! I love that place." Esther's eyes took on that far-away stare people got when thinking of other times. The camping trip would be the annual guys-only event that I hadn't missed since before I got married. But once, Esther and I had ridden in to Sioux Charlie, just the two of us. We camped in a green army pup tent and watched elk and mulies browsing the woods around us. We saw bear sign and scat, and when we rode out, a big boar grizzly stood up to survey us from the opposite slope of the drainage. The horses danced a little bit, but we moved on without any trouble. It was one of the best weeks of our marriage. I wondered why we'd never done it again. She'd glowed faintly in the mountains.

"I remember you liked it all right," I said.

"I did." Esther held onto her breath for a beat before she let it out slowly. "That *was* a wonderful time, wasn't it?"

"It was indeed." I moved my hand across the table toward her, a pretty clear invitation.

Esther met my eyes for just a second before she took the last sip from her glass. She rattled the ice cubes, and the mood beat away hard like an alarmed covey of quail.

She straightened a little. "That's nice of you guys to take Kamal. It'll be good for him, too."

"Yeah, I guess so. Like I said, he doesn't hang out with anyone else," I said, drawing my hand back. "Never see anyone else at his house. No young ladies, for sure."

"That is sad. Loneliness can be a curse," she said softly.

"Oh, it's a curse all right. I know that now," I answered, looking directly at her.

Esther leaned away and held up one hand. "All right, Jimmy Lloyd. Don't start. Not gonna happen. Not today. Time for you to drink up your lemonade and go, and I got to finish my roses."

"I could help."

Esther laughed like carriage bells, only the coach was leaving me behind. "Yeah, you could help, all right. You could help yourself right into my house, and we both know where you'd try to take *that*." Her face softened, and she touched my forearm. "Jimmy, I do love you. That part is still there. I hope you know that. But it's just not going to work for us to try to start it up again. I'm sorry."

"You got yourself another man then?"

"No, that's not it. You'd know for sure if that ever happens."

"I've changed, Esther. I think I've learned something." It sounded like pleading, and it probably was. I almost grabbed her hand, wanting desperately for her to understand how I felt.

"I know you have, Jimmy. I know you have. But I'm afraid it's not enough yet—not yet." She reached for my glass. "Now go on. I've got more work to do yet. Thanks for the check."

We both stood up, and before I knew how it happened, I was back at Ol' Brown with my hand on the door handle. I got in and closed the door, taking care not to slam it, no matter that I just wanted to break something with my fist right then.

Esther stayed in her yard behind the gate. "Jimmy?"

"Yeah?"

"I'm glad you weren't hurt in that fire."

I gave a little wave as I cranked the motor. "Thanks."

On the way home, it dawned on me. *We don't keep secrets*, Esther had said. I would bet my paycheck that she knew about me taking Joanne home the other night. *Dammit!*

Chapter Sixteen

Early June

Kamal stopped his car when he saw me cutting the brown stubble that passed for lawn grass in a Montana summer.

I killed the Toro mower and walked over. Putting my forearm on the roof, I leaned into the open car window. "Hey, Kamal, how'd you like to go see a rodeo this Saturday?"

Months ago, I had signed to do pickup for an upcoming small-town rodeo. It didn't amount to much, but it was close by, so I could sleep in my own bed every night. Kamal turned off the ignition. "A rodeo?"

"That's what I said. It's about sixty miles from here at Absorakee. Thor and Brownie are going and probably bringing some lady friends. You could ride with them."

He grinned. "Jane is going?"

"I have no doubt about that," I answered, pushing up off the car. "So how about it?"

"You will be doing the pickup man?"

"I sure like how you put that," I said, grinning back at him. "No, I don't 'do' the pickup man. I *am* the pickup man—one of them anyway."

"Yes, I understand. I didn't mean it that way."

I punched him on the shoulder. "I know you didn't. You're just a dumbass. So you want to come?"

"Sure... but why do I not ride there with you?"

"Well, that'd be fine by me, but I have to go early to get ready, and I'll be one of the last ones to leave. I'm talking from about early afternoon to midnight." I thought while I drummed my fingers on his car top. "Tell you what. How about you ride out there with me then come back with Thor and Brownie? That way you won't have to stay so late, too."

Kamal considered it for a second. "Okay, but will they mind bringing me back?"

"Oh, hell no, boy..." I laughed. "You know they won't. Hell, I wish they all liked *me* as much as they do you."

He actually blushed.

We didn't talk much longer before he drove on to the back house. I found the Toro still warm when I restarted it to finish the yard.

ON FRIDAY NIGHT, THE Absorakee rodeo had a pretty good crowd that liked to hoorah and clap along with the loudspeaker music, and the barrelman turned out to be a natural-born entertainer. He even made me laugh. Rodeo clowns had to walk a fine line to keep it all in the family. Not many people realized how hard it was to jack fans up with material rowdy enough for the cowboys but still clean enough for kids. This man in the barrel would be going to the national finals in Vegas one day if he stuck with it. I'd seen it before.

The other pickup man with me was a young fellow working his first season on the Montana circuit. I didn't think he could be much older than Kamal. He looked a little nervous when I introduced myself to him before we got started.

"I know who you are, Mr. McGowan. I've watched you pick up for years, since I was a kid," he said as we shook hands. "You're one of the best."

Damn. How long have I been doing this? "Well, thanks, I think. I didn't know I was that old." I looked at him a little closer. "You're Jay

Hollis, aren't you? I've seen you before, too. National High School finals in Bozeman a few years back, wasn't it?"

He nodded vigorously, pleased that I remembered him. "Yes, sir. You pulled me off of Boo Bear in the second go-round. You remember that?"

I shook my head. "Naw. I can't say that I recall every ride I snatch, but I do seem to remember you being a pretty good bronc buster. How'd you do that night?"

"Seventy-one. It wasn't my best ride." He smiled ruefully. "Guess that's why I'm trying this now. Wasn't making much money riding broncs. I hope this turns out better and steadier." He looked up at me under his hat brim. "How do you like it, Mr. McGowan? Being a pickup man and all?"

That question was the only sort of fan mail we all got. I leaned against the arena wall and hooked my thumbs in my belt. "I suppose if you want to stay in the game, this is better than getting hurt all the time riding rough stock, but it's still a hard way to make a living without having a real job, too. I'll tell you that. People that don't know think it's getting hurt that makes it so tough, but it's not. It's the travel. At least it was for me. Cost me a wife."

"Yes, sir, I hear that sort of stuff all right." He paused and looked across the arena. "So why do you still do it, Mr. McGowan?"

"Well, first of all, that 'mister' shit's gotta stop. We're gonna be working together all weekend, so it's 'Jimmy Lloyd' from here on."

"Oh... sure... sorry, uh, Jimmy Lloyd."

"It's okay, Jay. Mind if I call you 'Jay' instead of Mr. Hollis?" I grinned. "About why I still do this..." I puffed out my cheeks and rolled my eyes. "Fact is, I can't really say why. I just like it. Maybe I like to smell cotton candy. Anyway, the wife wouldn't come back now even if I did drag up and quit."

"I'm sorry for that, Jimmy Lloyd. That must be tough."

You got no idea, Jay. "Aw, don't be sorry. It's just life," I said.

The rest of the night went off pretty much without a hitch. Jay turned out to be a pretty decent hand in the arena. He handled a big, good-looking paint mare that jump-started like a cat. Between the two of us, we pulled off about six cowboys, and they all hit the ground feetfirst. After the last event, we put away our horses.

"Nice job tonight, kid," I said.

"Thanks, Jimmy Lloyd. I appreciate that."

Later, driving home in the dark on I-90, I listened to the tires whine and got to thinking. *Tonight was too easy. Something's bound to go wrong tomorrow.* It usually worked that way.

THE NEXT AFTERNOON, I rolled up to Kamal's house in Ol' Brown. In jeans, boots, a new Wrangler shirt, and his now-dirty hat, he sure looked the part.

"Hello, Jimmy Lloyd," he said cheerily, opening the passenger door and climbing in.

"Afternoon, Kamal. How you doing?"

"Very well today. I am excited to at last see what you do." He actually rubbed his hands together like he expected a steak dinner.

I chuckled. "Hopefully, you won't see much. If everything goes smooth, I'll just be dozing in the saddle."

"And if not?"

I glanced sideways at him. "Well now, that's when my asshole gets puckered up, and I might earn my money."

"Is that what I should hope for then?" Kamal looked puzzled, his forehead wrinkled.

"No, don't ever hope for bad shit. You'll get enough excitement as it is," I said. "That's what good rodeo is all about."

"Okay, I see," he replied.

We got quiet for a minute. Then I noticed Kamal staring at me. "What?" I said.

"Is that what you wear?" he asked.

I had to laugh. I had on running shoes, a frayed work shirt, and my MSU ball cap, not exactly PRCA-approved rodeo attire. "No, this is just driving-to-work clothes. I'll change when I get there."

"You bring other clothes?" Kamal's eyes swept over the truck's empty back seat. "Where are they?"

"Locked away in a storage box next to Crabby's stall."

"I see."

As we drove west on I-90, the flat Yellowstone valley morphed into bigger and bigger hills. The Beartooth Mountains rose in the distance off to the left. I started explaining rodeo events to Kamal, and he seemed to understand them... until I got to barrel racing.

"You mean women compete with men? And in public?" His eyes widened slightly. "I didn't know that."

"Well no, the ladies don't race against men, just against each other. And of course they do it in public. It's not like they'll be dropping their pants down around their ankles."

Kamal shook his head, and his mouth twitched up at the corners. "I have never seen that before. America is different."

"You bet it is, and God bless the USA." I smiled, and he shot me a look that I couldn't quite read—a lopsided grin, not happy, not sad, just quizzical. It reminded me of a dog growling and wagging his tail at the same time. I wouldn't know whether to pet it or pick up a rock. "You like it here, don't you?" I asked.

The grin melted, and Kamal got thoughtful. "Yes, I do," he answered softly. "I actually do." He looked out the side window at a pair of mule deer bounding up a steep hillside, flashing their tan rump patches. "It could be good here." He spoke as if he were surprised by his own words.

"Awesome."

We got off the interstate at Columbus and took a two-lane highway that wound through the Stillwater River valley past collections of small ranches and five-acre country gentlemen spreads. Even with all the humanity that had discovered the place, it remained one of my favorite stretches to drive. I pointed out landmarks to Kamal.

"This here is the river we'll be camping along next month." I waved a hand toward the trees lining its bank. "Of course we'll be about forty miles upstream in the mountains."

"It looks very nice."

"Oh, it is. That's for sure." I pointed ahead to a big log archway at the head of a quarter-mile driveway. "See that there? That ranch used to belong to Mel Gibson, the actor. You ever hear of him?"

"Mel Gibson? Oh, yes. The propagandist. *The Passion of the Christ*." Kamal turned as we passed the gate, peering out the window to study the distant red-painted buildings along the river bank. "He lived there?"

"No, I don't think he ever stayed there much. He just visited it some. Used to come ski at Red Lodge. You know the rich folks don't live like you and me do. They get to have vacation homes wherever they like."

Kamal stayed silent for a minute. "My family has several houses," he said, so quietly that I couldn't be sure I heard him right. He stared back at the ranch until it passed out of sight around a bend in the road. We didn't say anything more the rest of the way.

I pulled into the fairgrounds just beyond the little burg of Absarokee and stopped next to my horse trailer already parked behind the arena where staff and contestants stayed. The place could have been a FEMA trailer park. Campers and horse trailers were scattered around like hay bales thrown off a moving train. The older PRCA pros mostly had their own big camp rigs. They lived like nomads, traveling from show to show with air conditioning and TV. The young ones carpooled in F-350s and big Dodges pulling trailers. They all hunted the next paycheck.

Kamal and I got out and stretched. He looked around at a blur of activity. Cowboys and gals led horses or groomed them beside their trailers. Other horses waited in paddocks. Everywhere someone hurried with buckets or notebooks, depending on whether their job involved livestock or people. A group of cowboys sitting on camp chairs played cards under an awning. The smell of manure and dust permeated the grounds.

"So what do you think, Kamal?" I asked.

He eyed the bustle. "It reminds me of a Bedouin camp."

"A what?"

Kamal smiled. "Bedouins are people of the desert. Many of them still live in the old ways and travel throughout. Borders mean nothing to them." He turned to me. "On television, they are the ones you see with camels and tents." He gestured at the scene in front of us. "Here, there are horses and metal tents on wheels, but it's not so different—just a matter of a hundred years or so, don't you think?"

I gawked at him before I clapped him on the shoulder. "Did you learn all that in philosophy class? C'mon. I got to go get ready."

He walked beside me through all the babble, his head on a swivel. When we got to his barn stall, Crabby had his head out over the door.

"Hello, old fella." I rubbed his nose and dug around in my shirt pocket for a horse treat. He lipped it right out of my palm. Snuffy wanted a little bit of that action, too, so I obliged him with another piece.

"They are happy to see you," Kamal said as he stroked Crabby's neck.

"Naw, they just like these horse candy nuggets," I answered. "Actually, they *are* pretty good boys." I patted Snuffy on the cheek. "Kamal, why don't you stroll around a little, see the sights and all? I'm going to tack these big boys up then get my own gear on." I looked at my watch. "We got two hours before the show starts. How about you meet me back here in about ninety minutes?"

Kamal looked doubtful. "You don't need any help?"

"Oh no. My rigging's set just a certain way for rodeo business. Nobody ever does it right but me. Then if it all turns to mush and I fall off, it's nobody's fault but my own."

Kamal still looked skeptical. "Okay, Jimmy Lloyd, but where do I go? I don't know anyone here."

"What would you do in a Bedouin camp?"

"I would greet them in the name of Allah. Hospitality is required in the desert."

"Well, I'd leave Allah out of it today, but otherwise, it's pretty much the same here. If you do run into a brick wall or something, just tell them you're a friend of Jimmy Lloyd McGowan. That ought to get you out of trouble." I stopped and scratched my chin. "'Course on the other hand, knowing me just might get you in deeper shit. Not everybody loves me, you know."

Kamal smiled. "I doubt that, Jimmy Lloyd."

"Oh, you'd be surprised. Okay then. Go do your walkabout. I'll see you in a little bit. And don't pinch any of these cowgirls on the butt, especially if you mention my name. Some of them, I know their daddies."

"Okay, I will only talk." Kamal walked away, looking left and right. In his hat and boots, he could have passed for any of the dozens of southwest vaqueros traveling the rodeo circuit. He just needed to get his gait right. He still walked and gawked like a tourist.

I smiled to myself. *A couple more months, and he'll be carrying Copenhagen in his back pocket.*

I unlocked the gear box and got the saddles out. Down the aisle, Jay Hollis came in to start doing the same thing. Too far apart to talk, we simply nodded at each other. All over the barn, cowboys had started getting to their business. Ropers and steer wrestlers checked on their horses and tack. Everybody got lost in their own thoughts while they prepped. The horses knew what was coming, too. Crabby and

Snuffy stamped their front feet as I tightened the cinches and fastened the breast straps.

"Good boy," I said, patting each one.

When I'd finished with the horses, I carried my zippered suit bag to the staff lounge under the grandstand. In a bathroom stall, I changed into duds that no straight cowboy would ever wear on a sidewalk in any real cow town: a bright-red-and-black satin shirt, a silver belt buckle the size of a dinner plate, polished boots, and a shiny black leather vest. I knotted a new red silk bandana around my neck. A clean straw hat, which I saved to put on for showtime, would top it off. The only drab piece of clothing I wore were old Wranglers that the Dodge boy chaps covered up. Fashioned out of heavy leather, the chaps, a trademark of the PRCA, were long enough they made walking tough. Short chinks would have been more practical, but the Dodge boys looked good on horseback, and they hid my bulky shin guards.

Kamal was waiting at the stalls when I got back. "Jimmy Lloyd, is that really you?" He eyed me up and down. "I have never seen you in your costume before. I am the ugly duckling next to you."

That touched off an old gripe of mine. "It's an 'outfit,' not a 'costume.' Circus clowns and movie stars wear costumes. Native Americans and cowboys wear outfits."

"Oh, excuse me. I didn't mean to offend you." Kamal looked abashed.

"It's okay, Kamal. Lots of people make that mistake." I let that sink in for a second. "So... did you see anybody you know?"

"Oh, yes!" He brightened. "Brownie and Thor are here. They said to tell you we will be sitting on the right side of the arena from where the bucking chutes are. About halfway up." He looked at me in an odd way, chewing his lip after he said it.

"What else? Thor brought Jane?"

"Yes," he answered. "And Brownie has a woman I do not know. She has puffed-out blond hair." Kamal held up his hands to show just how puffy the strange lady's hair was.

"Big hair, huh? Well, that could be any one of a dozen gals. I bet she has big tits, too. Brownie likes to fool around with big hair and big tits. You better get on back to where they're sitting before it gets too crowded. I'll see you at the arena." I threw Crabby's reins over his neck, put a boot in the stirrup, hopped twice, and swung up into the saddle. When I looked back down, Kamal hadn't moved. He was still gnawing on his bottom lip like he was bringing home a bad report card. "Okay, Kamal, what else? There's something you're not telling me."

"There are others with them," he said.

"Others?"

"Alice came... and Esther also. They will be sitting up there with us."

I soaked that up, tightening my grip on the saddle horn. "They alone?" I asked, trying to sound casual about the whole deal, not sure at all that I really wanted to hear the answer. But Kamal knew my real question.

"Esther is alone, Jimmy Lloyd. No other man came with them."

I let my breath out slowly. "Well, then I sure hope Brownie drove and brought his Suburban. It's going to be a little crowded for you guys riding back, otherwise."

"I could still go with you."

I waved my hand. "No, you better ride with them. I'll be here for hours after this is over. Part of the job, you know."

"Very well, then." He turned to go.

"Hey."

He stopped. "Yes?"

"Thanks, Kamal. I appreciate your letting me know. A pickup man doesn't like to get too many surprises at a rodeo."

He nodded. "Sure thing, Jimmy Lloyd." He patted Crabby on the shoulder and left, headed back to the stands through the maze of stock pens.

Crabby started to do his little stutter step as we entered the darkened runway that led into the arena. The audience was singing the national anthem, and I took the hat off even though I was out of sight of the crowd. My pulse started ramping up. It always got a little faster at the start, but this time, it wasn't just rodeo jitters. I really needed to be good tonight with Esther here. I waited alongside Jay while we listened for the announcer to call us out. If all went well, this would be our only applause all night.

"And now, ladies and gentlemen... here they come. Let's hear it for our Dodge boys pickup men—Jimmy Lloyd McGowan and Jay Hollis."

The gate swung open, and we loped out into the arena under the lights.

Chapter Seventeen

A rodeo pickup man is about as anonymous as a man can get. Still, I knew Kamal and my friends would be watching when I made a pass around the arena. And Esther would watch, too. She hadn't been to any of my rodeos since our big D. As bad as I wanted to, I refused to let my eyes wander up in the stands. No quick glances. No peeks. Nothing. It nearly killed me, but it was time for business.

The job seemed simple in theory. If a bareback or bronc rider managed to finish up with eight seconds of glory, he still had to get off an angry cayuse at the end. A cowboy might try some kind of half-assed dismount where he would jump and try to land pretty, but that was hard to do. So generally, they just held on and sat tight up on that jolting back until the pickup men could get alongside, one of us on each side. Then the rider could lean and dive more than jump onto a pickup's horse. Others just bear-hugged the pickup man at the waist then slid down until his boots hit the ground. When a cowboy froze, I usually had to wrap an arm around him to drag him off. Lucky for me, most rough stock riders were a little on the small side.

I took up a position next to the arena wall across from where they all sat. Crabby blew and fidgeted as I rested my right forearm on the railing of the front-row box seats. I caught a whiff of a gal's perfume. People sitting close liked being next to the show and the cowboys, but they rarely said anything to us. We had to keep our heads in the game. Crabby stamped a front foot.

"Easy... easy." I patted his neck and checked that Jay had found his spot on the other side. I still wouldn't scan the crowd beyond him.

Saddle leather creaked as I settled myself and waited. The announcer bantered some more with the barrelman. The night before, it had all been pretty funny, but I couldn't crack a smile tonight.

The number one chute finally flew open, and the rodeo began. The first event, always bareback riding, went pretty well. I picked up a couple of riders. Jay took a couple. Three or four outstanding rides really got the crowd into it.

Jay and I left the arena through the exit gate to change horses after the bareback event. Old Marvin stood in the corridor, holding my fresh mount. Marvin had been a fixture behind the scenes at Montana rodeos for years, and he'd done his share of steer wrestling before that.

"Thanks, Marv," I said, then I rubbed Snuffy's neck. "Hey there, big fella. You ready to go?"

Jay's pretty young girlfriend was holding his second horse. The bay gelding wasn't big or flashy like the paint mare, but it had done all right the previous night. I changed rides by sliding over from one saddle to the other without touching the ground. Jay dismounted to kiss his girl before he got on the bay. I used to do that with Esther.

Together, Jay and I rode back toward the arena, where we waited behind the gate until the calf roping finished. The rodeo queen and princesses could herd the little doggies out. They didn't need pickup men for that.

I looked over at Jay, who had a lipstick smudge on his cheek. "Feeling good, Jay?" I asked.

He looked back at me, surprised. "Sure, Jimmy Lloyd. I feel okay. How about you?"

"Never better."

I looked over the big gate in front of us. The stands were packed and loud. I found Esther right where Kamal had said she would be. It never got hard to spot her with that blond hair shining like a Fourth of July sparkler. Kamal sat between her and Alice. They were all laughing and eating popcorn. Thor and Jane were in the row below with Brownie and some gal who, sure enough, had big tits. Except for Brownie's gal, they all wore Saturday-night cowboy hats.

"You ready?" Jay broke into my wandering thoughts.

The announcer finished stoking the crowd for the saddle bronc riding to come, and the gate swung open in front of us.

"Always," I replied, looking straight ahead.

We cantered out to our separate spots by the wall before turning around to watch the chutes.

BRONCO BUSTING HAD been my event back when I'd competed, as limber and loose as old campfire ashes. Bull riders got the TV press because folks thought that was more dangerous, but for my money, sitting on top of a wild saddle bronc was just as bad. Horses jumped higher and were smarter, and bronc riders didn't get to grip on with their legs like bull riders did. Bronco busting was all about balance. Bronc riders shifted from side to side, front to back, all the while wishing their ass cheeks could clamp tight enough to stick in the saddle. I still missed it sometimes.

I wasn't familiar with the rodeo contractor or his bucking horses, so every pickup turned into a new learning experience. Jay and I didn't have a whole lot to do at first, though. The first four cowboys washed out before their eight seconds, ending up sprawled on the arena floor with copious amounts of grit in their teeth. The fifth rider coming up was Sam Coskins. Sammy Boy had learned to ride at his dad's place out of Miles City. He was a good one with a knack for keeping his butt Velcroed down. I figured he might win this go-round.

The horse he drew turned out to be a blue roan stud named Blue Comet. He had been causing a ruckus earlier in the afternoon when I went behind the stands to check out the rough stock milling around in their pens. He wouldn't stand still and had tossed his head over and over. I didn't know what had crisscrossed Blue's synapses, but he showed the same unfocused anger that I'd seen in big cities, where crazy street people punched brick walls and raged against life. The big boy kicked at the fencing, bared his teeth, and generally kept the other broncs away.

Some cowboys were back there, too, staring through the rails, each man looking for the horse he would be trying to ride later.

"Hey, Jimmy Lloyd. Going to be pulling me off tonight?"

I turned around to see a serious-faced Sam Coskins watching Blue Comet over my shoulder.

"Can't you get your girlfriend to do that?" I replied, grinning at him. "On the other hand, *if* your scrawny ass hangs on long enough tonight, I *might* come by and give you a lift down if that's what you mean. How you doing, Sammy?"

He smiled in spite of himself. "Afraid I don't have a buckle bunny here. I guess I'll have to settle on you."

"I'll be there."

He looked back into the pen and pointed his chin at the agitated blue roan. "What do you think of that one?"

"That wild-assed one? I tell you what. He's not going to make much money for this contractor. He'll burn himself out before the season's over with all his bobbing and weaving."

"Maybe so," Sam answered. "But I'm just worrying about tonight."

"That's the one you got?" I stepped closer to the railing and studied the stamping horse. "I can see one thing right now. He's half crazy. No telling what he's liable to do once you get on him."

Sam nodded. "That's pretty much the way I read him, too." He reached into his mouth to pull out a wad of dip and fling it on the ground. "I hate these unpredictable ones."

Blue Comet stopped the nervous pacing at that moment and faced Sam and me. Horses didn't scare me, but the air got real eerie right then. Stock-still, he stared hard-eyed at us. His nostrils flared, and he snorted before he put his backside to us, the ultimate equine show of disrespect and hostility.

"I'll tell you something else, too, Sammy," I said. "He's crazy, but I think he's smart."

"Yeah, I was afraid of that." He straightened his hat and started to amble away. "See you in the arena," he said over his shoulder.

HOURS LATER, I COULD barely see Sam's black hat among all the cowboys bunched at the chute, giving him last-second advice. Sam couldn't hear them. I'd been there myself, and I knew his attention was all on Blue Comet. He nodded, and the chute gate opened.

The horse busted out, humpbacked and jumping. He was a kicker, all right, one of those that popped his hind legs rearward every time he got airborne. Sam's head snapped back and forth while he flailed his left hand high up over his shoulder. Those two gave the fans and judges a spectacular ride. I pushed off the wall well before the eight-second horn. Blue Comet stayed in the middle of the arena, still kicking the air. Sam dropped the rope rein and grabbed the front of the saddle, clinging to it like a trick monkey on a sheep-herding border collie.

Blue Comet grunted and squalled in rage at having a man still on his back. The angry, pounding horse made the ground shake. Even on top of Snuffy, I could feel it. He started jumping toward the far end of the arena. Jay came up on their right side before I could get to them. The bronc actually turned toward Jay, punching his hind legs high at me when I rode up on the left. He kicked out, and unshod hooves flashed past my head. Snuffy jerked hard left and tried to get next to Blue Comet. Sam's head rolled to my side, looking and hoping for me to come alongside. He wanted to jump, but I wasn't there yet. I got close enough to see Sam's wide eyes, but then the Comet turned away and kicked again.

The damn horse wouldn't stay in a straight line like we wanted him to. He fought it, always turning to Jay's side, leaving Snuffy and me on the tail end in a game of crack the whip. Sam finally gave up on me and reached his right arm out to grab at Jay. When Sammy lunged out of the saddle, the whole thing played out in slow motion. Like a horse possessed, Blue Comet juked left toward me and faked all of us out, men and horses alike. Sam rolled off into thin air as Blue Comet put space between himself and Jay's gelding. Then the bronc's hind feet caught the cowboy's torso in midair, and I heard the crack of broken bone. Sam flopped end over end to land hard five yards away on the packed dirt. He lay on his back, kicking feebly.

I caught Blue's bridle to get him back to the exit gate. The bronc kept bucking, but the effort was half-hearted. He'd lost all the fury he had shown before. The gate opened, and he followed me through with no problem. Even away from the arena, I could hear Sam's moans along with the wail of the crowd. I turned him loose, and Blue trotted away down the aisle toward the holding pens, through for the night. EMTs already knelt over Sam when I got back under the lights. He rolled slowly from side to side, not making a sound anymore—until they slid him onto a litter. Then he tried to scream.

Jay walked his horse over to me. He pushed his hat up and wiped a sleeve across his face. "That was a tough one," he said without looking at me.

"Yeah, it was."

The announcer earned his money with patter. He even had the crowd cheering when the ambulance drove out of the dirt arena with poor Sammy inside. The judges gave Sam a score of eighty-two, and he won that night's go-round. I doubt he much cared just then, though.

Jay watched the flashing lights on the ambulance as it left. "What just happened there, Jimmy Lloyd? We screw up?"

"Don't know. Hard to say," I answered. "But that son-of-a-bitch roan is *loco* crazy. He doesn't act like normal horses do. He's going to be one to watch out for."

"Yeah, I reckon you're right. Hope Sam makes it okay."

"I hope so, too. Looked like he had some broken ribs. That's never good. Who knows what else?"

The two of us sat on top of our mounts in silence, waiting without listening while the announcer swapped jokes with the barrelman. I wondered if Jay knew I'd lied. I knew exactly what had happened, and I *had* screwed up. Big time. Sam didn't get busted up and almost killed because Blue Comet was crazy. It happened because I'd flinched. When the bronco kicked at my face, I lost my nerve. Snuffy had been game all right, but I'd tightened up on the reins and held him back. Blue Comet had spun away from Jay because the pickup man who should have held him in check wasn't there.

WHEN THE SHOW FINALLY ended after an uneventful session of bullriding, the whole gang trooped down to the stalls in back, where I was unsaddling Crabby and Snuffy. My friends were in a better mood than I was. Sam Coskins was still on my mind.

"Oh, Jimmy Lloyd, you were great, as usual!" Alice ran up to me ahead of the others and threw her arms around my neck. She whispered in my ear, "Shake it off, Jimmy. It wasn't your fault. That stuff just happens." The rest of them gathered around as she let go and stepped back.

They were smiling at me like I'd been elected president. Esther hung back a little. She knew. More than anyone else, Esther knew how much it hurt when I failed one of my cowboys, no matter that

I had done my best. She had always stayed right beside me all night after those very bad times. *Wish she could do that now.*

Kamal's eyes were bright with excitement, and he practically gushed. "You are a magnificent rider, Jimmy Lloyd! That is a hard thing you do, and I was very excited to watch it."

I looked down and toed the dirt. "Yeah, well... thanks. It didn't all go so good, though."

"Yeah, that was a tough deal about Sammy Coskins," Brownie said, shaking his head. "You hear how he's doing?"

"I heard he went to surgery in Billings. They think a rib perforated his lung and maybe some other stuff," I answered, feeling like shit.

Esther bit her knuckle, a gesture of hers I'd forgotten. "Is he at Deaconess?" she asked.

"I think so, yeah."

"I'll check on him in the morning. I'm on shift tomorrow."

I met her eyes. "That's good. That's good. Would you let me know how he's doing?"

"Sure."

"Thanks, Queenie. It'd mean a lot."

She looked at me with sad eyes. "I know, Jimmy... I remember."

Brownie spoke up, jovial again. "Hey, I want you to meet someone." He took hold of Double D's arm and just about dragged her forward. "Wanda, meet Jimmy Lloyd McGowan—the best pickup man in the business—well, you saw him in there, didn't you?"

"Yes, I did." Wanda had a bold eye, which she ran over me like I was up for auction. "I'm pleased to meet you, Jimmy Lloyd." She extended her hand.

I gripped it lightly and shook. "Same here, Wanda."

She squeezed back, holding a little longer than she should have. *Brownie's got himself a live one, all right.*

"All right, Jimmy Lloyd. I'll be seeing you tomorrow." Jay had untacked his horses and come over to check out the ladies. Though he'd spoken to me, he was really studying Wanda.

"Sure, Jay. Hey, let me walk with you a little bit." I turned back to the others and touched my hat brim. "Excuse me a second, guys. I'll be right back." I put an arm over Jay's shoulders as we walked away together. I talked soft so only he heard me in the crowd of people around us. "Jay, what happened to Sammy tonight was my fault. I let you and him both down, and I want you to know I won't ever do that again."

The young cowboy stopped short and looked at me, startled. "*Your* fault? Hell no, it wasn't your fault. I was the one that couldn't keep that horse straight. It was me that missed him when he jumped. It wasn't your fault, Jimmy Lloyd. You're one of the best."

I sighed. "I'm glad you think so, Jay, but I know what I know." I slapped him on the back. "Go and get some sleep. The Sunday matinee always comes early."

I went back to Kamal and the others. They were still milling around at Snuffy's stall, waiting for me apparently. Brownie stuck his hand out. "Guess we gotta be going, Jimmy Lloyd. Time to get these folks home."

I shook his hand then all the men's. "Sure. Drive safe. Thanks for coming out, you guys."

"You betcha. You know we wouldn't miss it," Thor said.

They waved and left. I watched them walk past the line of stalls then turn at the end and go out of sight. The arena staff had already shut off a lot of the lights after the show, so it got hard to tell, but I thought Esther might have looked back at the corner.

I HAD MY POST-PERFORMANCE routine to carry out. Most of the cowboys didn't have such an elaborate routine as I did, but that never bothered me. I started by changing clothes before I tended to the horses. Crabby and Snuffy waited patiently in their stalls for me to come back, heads poking out over the dutch doors, soft brown eyes watching for me. They nickered while I brushed each one down and rubbed sweat off with old burlap. After I checked their feet, I threw a little hay into the stalls. Jay and the others had been long gone by the time I finished. "Good night, boys," I said to the pair as I left. They just munched the hay contentedly.

The route back to my truck took me through the encampment again. Most of the campers were dark, but a few still had lights burning. As I walked past in the dark, I could hear TVs tuned in to late-night comedy shows. It felt odd, and I resented it, realizing people were laughing inside those trailers, not knowing or caring that I was passing by, brooding under a black cloud of my own making. In all the time when I competed in rodeo, no pickup man had ever let *me* down.

I drove home with the window cracked, listening to the wind's whistle and thinking. Dunker had been a lot older than I was when he gave up rodeoing, but he always told me, "You quit when you don't think you can do it anymore, when you don't love it anymore."

I had lost my grip, and a good cowboy had gotten hurt bad because of it. *Maybe it's time for me to pack it in, too.*

The next morning, after a near-sleepless night, I dragged myself out of bed at seven to feed the horses. When I came back in from the barn, I saw the light blinking on my answering machine. I hit the button, and a familiar voice came on. "Hey. This is Esther. Just came on shift and wanted to let you know that Sammy Coskins is going to be okay. I can't say anything more. I shouldn't have even said that much. It's HIPAA regulations, you know." There was a pause, long enough that I thought maybe she'd hung up, before she spoke again. "Jimmy, I'm so sorry this happened. I know how much hurt you have when one of your riders gets injured. I wish I could've been there for you last night. I really do... I've got to go make rounds. Bye, Jimmy."

I played that tape over and over about seven times.

Chapter Eighteen

Late June

I closed the rear doors on the slant load trailer. "Okay, horses loaded. That should be it. You got anything else to bring?"

Kamal shook his head. "No. I have packed everything you told me. I think I am good to go." He looked excited about finally going on the trip he had been hearing about for months.

We got in Ol' Brown and slammed the doors. The back-seat area had been jammed with ice chests, sleeping bags, fly rod cases, and my shotgun case. Kamal's gear was mixed in with mine, but his still looked and smelled new. I had taken him to Cabela's to stock up on gear for the trip.

He'd really liked their gun displays and seemed amazed that anybody could buy one. He'd stared at the blued and nickel-plated pistols under the glass countertops. Then his eyes drifted over the rifles on the wall behind them. "Americans can buy any of these?"

"Well, not if they have a criminal record or if they're certifiably crazy, but otherwise, of course we can."

He gazed at a black AR-15, looking distracted by some inner thought. "So then all Americans are armed?"

I laughed. "No, not by a long shot. It's a personal choice. Some people don't want to have guns around, but here in Montana, I think most do."

"Yes, I have heard that." He gave me a quick sideways look. "How many do you have?"

I slapped him on the shoulder. "Like the governor said once, 'More than I need, not as many as I'd like.'"

"He said that?"

"Yeah. Something like that. Come on, we need to get you some packer boots." I led him away, and we spent the next hour getting Kamal ready for the woods.

At the checkout counter, he'd paid cash for everything, peeling Grants and Benjamins out of his wallet like it was Monopoly money.

A week later, at long last, we were on our way, loaded with all that brand-new gear of Kamal's and pulling horses in the summer heat toward Absarokee and beyond. Kamal looked like he belonged in an L.L. Bean catalog picture, and his heavy outdoor shirt still had store-bought creases in it. He gazed out the window at the Yellowstone River as we crossed the bridge in Columbus.

"Did you bring toilet paper with you?" I asked him.

He looked startled by the question. "No. I did not think of that."

I smiled at the windshield. "Not to worry. I brought extra. If you think of anything we mighta forgot, I'll be making one last stop in Fishtail a few miles ahead. It'll be our last chance at civilization."

"Maybe some beef jerky?"

"Sounds good."

Forty-five minutes later, we pulled in at the Fishtail General Store. Brownie's Ford was already parked there on the highway shoulder, two horses waiting patiently in the trailer behind it. I recognized Brownie's little dun mare, and the big black next to it, standing at least sixteen hands, was Jerry's gelding. We found Brownie inside, holding a bag of groceries and getting an ice cream bar out of the freezer.

"Hey, hoss. You all set?" he said.

"Oh yeah, we are hot to trot and full of snot," I answered.

Kamal laughed, that tired old line being new to him. He and I prowled the aisles of the ancient store, tromping on weathered boards that had seen generations of locals and outdoorsmen come through, stocking up for the outback.

"Hello there, Buttercup." Jerry came up behind us, carrying a grocery sack. He squeezed Kamal's shoulder and spun him around none too gently. "Have you been missing me, little buddy?"

Kamal jerked back out of the grip, and his face darkened. "No. I have not." He backed away another step.

Jerry seemed to think Kamal's reaction was the funniest thing since the Three Stooges. His shoulders heaved in a silent laugh. "Aw now, that's not true," he wheezed. "You been thinking about me, ain't ya?"

I stepped between them. "All right, Jerry. Cut out the bullshit. We got a week still to go here. Let's all try to get along for at least that long." I put the flat of my hand on Kamal's chest and felt the tension in him. "It's all right, Kamal. Jerry just likes to run his mouth off every once in a while. No harm done." I faced Jerry. "Right, Jerry?"

The big man studied me for a second, and I guess he saw I meant it. He hefted the bag. "Yeah, you're right, Jimbo. No harm done. Besides, you're right—we still got a week yet to get acquainted. Right, little buddy?" He winked at Kamal and turned away.

Kamal and I watched him leave the store. "I don't like him," Kamal said as his eyes followed Jerry's back through the dirty plate-glass window. "Why do you even have him for a friend?"

I scratched my ear and shrugged. "I can't exactly say. To be perfectly honest, I don't like Jerry much myself. He's just one of the fellas, though. Always has been." I shrugged again. "Let's get our stuff. We got to be going."

Kamal picked up his jerky and snacks. I got some Solarcaine lotion and, on impulse, an Ace bandage. We met up with Brownie again at the cash register and walked out with him. Jerry was already sitting in Brownie's truck.

"Looks like it's going to be a beautiful day," I said.

Brownie took a deep breath and cracked his back. He turned his head, taking in the Beartooth Mountains, sharp as tacks all around us against a deep and clear blue sky. "Yeah, it does. Real pretty out here." For Brownie, that was as poetic as it got, so we got into our vehicles. He waved his ice cream out the window at us while he eased his truck and trailer onto the highway again. I followed close behind.

I'd never seen the Beartooths on a bad day, but on that particular day, they shined up exceptionally well. It was the stuff John Denver wrote songs about. The Stillwater Canyon constricted from Fishtail on, and long, sparsely vegetated slopes came down almost to the roadway on one side while the river ran fast and white on the other. Boulders as big as bedrooms perched haphazardly up and down the steep hillsides. People said glaciers had dropped them there when they melted eons ago.

Kamal stared openmouthed. "Do people live here?"

"Oh, sure." I pointed to a small cabin across the river. "There's a few folks scattered about out here. Mostly, it's the ones that want to be left alone. Some of these are fishing and hunting camps."

"They are lucky people," he said.

"I agree. Mind you, it does get dicey out here in the winters. Snow gets pretty high. Hard to make a living in these parts unless you work at the Stillwater platinum mine." I gestured ahead as a small industrial complex and parking lot came into view, looking out of place and ugly against the landscape. Two whitetails bounded across the pavement a hundred yards in front of us. "There's some of your payback, though."

"Yes."

We passed the mine then a gated hillside covered with resort homes and cabins. It all looked out of place in a valley that the Crow Indians from two hundred years ago would still recognize. True wilderness lay just beyond us in every direction. Kamal gaped like a college boy in his first titty bar. Of course, he *was* a college boy.

Arriving at the trailhead, I drove aside to the trailer parking lot and pulled in alongside Dunker's rig. Brownie parked on the other side, by CK's truck. Kamal and I got out and shook hands all around. A dozen cars and SUVs were lined up over in the main lot. Hikers gathered over there in cargo shorts with trekking poles and goofy floppy hats that looked like Japanese tourists' headgear. Some of them gawked at our bunch. All of us except Kamal openly packed or were strapping on a firearm, and it wasn't hunting season. We probably looked like Butch Cassidy's gang.

Thor arrived fifteen minutes later, with Deputy Dawg Travis. His diesel was dragging a twenty-four-foot stock trailer crowded with two horses and six pack mules.

"Where you been, Thor?"

"Shut up and help me get these beasts loaded."

Loading the mules took us over an hour, and Thor was particular about the job. Nothing moved until he checked out each pack and sized up how it sat on the mule's back. He retied almost everybody's knots, including mine. Finally, he yanked on the last ice chest, jiggling it back and forth in the pannier to see how it fit. Satisfied, he nodded. "Okay, boys. What's the holdup? Lock your trucks and let's go."

We mounted and started through the main parking lot, Dunker leading, as always. Six of us pulled mules.

A pretty hiker gal asked Dunker to stop so she could take our picture, and he obliged. I would have, too. She was a redheaded looker. Her boyfriend sulked at their car while she snapped a few pictures of us with her little phone. She patted Dunker's horse and squinted up at him. "Where are you guys going?"

"To Yellowstone Park," CK said, second in line and lying his ass off.

"Yellowstone! O-o-oh, I wish I could go with you!"

"So do I, ma'am," Thor said.

Her return smile could have been Mona Lisa's. The rest of us behind Dunker looked at each other.

Then the boyfriend got antsy. "Come on, Cindy. We shouldn't hold them up any longer."

Probably knew what that smile meant.

"Oh, don't keep your shorts knotted up so much, Larry." She strolled back toward him. "Bye, boys," she cooed over her shoulder.

"Are you sure, miss?" CK called. "I can walk and let you ride in my saddle."

We hooted, and Larry didn't like that one bit. I could feel his glare on our backs as we rode by in single file, wild bachelor bulls tempting his prime young cow. I wish I could have listened in on Larry and Cindy's conversation after we left.

Chapter Nineteen

As soon as we hit the trailhead, we entered the roaring Stillwater gorge, where the shaded air smelled of evergreens. The spring snowmelt had come and gone, but enough gray-green water still flumed through the narrow canyon to produce whitewater that no kayaker could have survived. The current jammed whole tree trunks tight against boulders jutting up from the riverbed, before sweeping around and through. Here and there, back eddies held sticks in near-perpetual bondage as flotsam circling round and round before finally breaking free. High rock walls on both sides amplified every sound, and we would have had to shout at each other over the pounding surf-like noise.

A beaten trail clung to the steep bluff along the right bank as we rode upstream. It was safe and wide, high enough to keep us out of the spray below, but slipping from the trail meant a long fall onto the wet rocks. I kept a close watch on Snuffy as he took in the sights and sounds. Our animals, all pack-trip veterans, stayed wide-eyed and edgy for a bit until, eventually, the river became white noise to them.

That part of the canyon was called the Stillwater highway because so many folks liked to walk it. Right away, we began meeting or overtaking hikers. Some were day tourists in hiking boots, but some looked like hardcore backpackers. Out of mutual respect, the people on foot stepped aside to let us pass, and we went wide around them where we could. Everybody smiled and raised a hand. Our bunch looked pretty dramatic against the backdrop of mountains and foaming river, and we knew it. We stopped for another round of pictures for a family from Iowa.

I glanced behind me and saw Kamal posing like a pro. "Pretty here, isn't it?" I yelled.

He grinned from ear to ear and nodded while a little farm kid patted Sweet Ginger's nose.

After a couple of miles, we emerged from the cramped canyon into wide, forested slopes. There, the Stillwater flowed smoothly and silently, finally living up to its name. Wild potentilla bushes with bright little yellow blossoms like miniature sunflowers grew in clusters around every meadow we passed. In another mile, we would be able to see Lake Sioux Charlie, which was actually just a great big wide spot in the river where the current slowed. An unofficial, but popular, campground popped up each summer in the timber along the shoreline. Bright blue, red, and yellow nylon tents added splashes of color there.

Past the lake, the hikers and campers thinned out to none. We pushed on for three more miles before turning away from the beaten trail and switchbacking a thousand feet up in elevation on a steep, little-used path. The horses were blowing hard by the time a grassy clearing came into view—we'd camped there a couple of years before, but the spot rarely saw humans. I dismounted and loosened the cinch so Snuffy could catch his breath then led him across the rocky meadow into the far tree line. I could make out the faint impression where a tent had been pitched there in the shade within the last month or so. They had been proper backwoods campers who left no other trace of their presence, though.

We set about making camp, offloading the big wall tent from one of the mules. Unrolling and pitching the canvas went pretty quickly. As it turned out, Kamal knew a little something about putting up a tent.

"Hey, Kamal," Brownie called. "You pitch these things in the desert all your life?"

Kamal just shrugged as he hammered a tent peg into the hard ground. "Yes, but my life hasn't been nearly as long as yours." He smiled.

Thor laughed. "I'd have to say that point goes to Kamal."

Once the tent was erected and tight, we cleared an area in front of it for a fire pit. Jerry and Thor went into the trees with a shovel and pickax over each shoulder to dig a straddle pit latrine. The rest of us strung picket lines and a rope corral in the trees for the horses and mules. I used a tin can to scoop oats into Snuffy's feedbag. He munched contentedly while I unsaddled him and rubbed down his back with a burlap bag. Taking a pair of binoculars from my saddlebag, I led him out of the trees into the meadow we had crossed and hobbled him so he could graze. The clearing was high enough to offer a good view of the mountains around us. I started glassing the other side of the Stillwater valley.

"Are you looking for something, Jimmy Lloyd?"

I turned to see Kamal had followed me out from camp with his own pair of binoculars. "Nothing in particular," I answered, looking back through the glass. "You see those brown specks there on the other side? Just to the left of that big burnt-out patch?" I pointed to an area about three quarters of a mile across the way.

"I see the burned area."

"Look just to the left. Use your binocs... See 'em?"

I watched Kamal sweep slowly over the area I had indicated. Suddenly, his mouth dropped open behind his binoculars. "I see them! Eight—nine of them! They are elk?"

"You got it."

The small herd moved across the face of the far slope, tearing at the new grasses and brush that had replaced the old-growth forest destroyed by the fire. Like a jealous guardian, a bull sporting a magnificent rack browsed a little higher up the slope from his cows.

Like Larry at the trailhead, I thought. *Except nobody better mess with this old guy's harem.* The bunch slowly disappeared into thicker growth as they continued grazing, oblivious to us watching them.

Kamal lowered his optics. "That bull is a noble animal. I wish I could see them closer."

"You probably will, Kamal. Or maybe some others. We'll be here for a few days, and these mountains are full of elk." We returned to the camp just as Jerry and Thor came back from digging.

"I hope you dug it far enough away so I don't catch a flash of your big white ass when you squat," Dunker said to Jerry.

"Yeah, it's ugly enough already with those tight jeans straining to cover it," Travis said. "I'd hate to see it bare-assed."

"In your dreams, Buttercup." Jerry grunted. He was in too good a mood up in the clear air of the Beartooths to get offended. "We put it about sixty yards thataway." He pointed into the forest down a gentle slope. "We marked the trail with red ribbon so it's easy enough even for an old man like you to find, Dunker."

"Well, that's good, 'cause I gotta take a leak." Dunker started backtracking down the path Jerry and Thor indicated, thus ending that conversation.

Everybody was supposed to take a turn at cooking. The first night, Brownie had the honors, and Kamal made himself Brownie's apprentice. We gathered up armloads of fallen branches and downed timber to stack near the fire site. Kamal watched Brownie arrange the kindling before placing bigger sticks on top. A little wisp of smoke spiraled through the loose lattice when a match lit the dry leaves beneath the wood, then the fire caught and crackled. I set out ice chests so we could sit in a circle around the fire.

Following directions from Brownie, Kamal wrapped eight potatoes in foil and set them in the small bed of coals forming inside the fire ring of rocks. Brownie chopped onions then massaged them and Tony Chachere's seasoning into a loaf of ground chuck. He formed patties and plopped them on a cast-iron griddle over the flames. They started sizzling in seconds. Little by little, the rest of us began to sit down on the chests to watch and smell the proceedings. Suddenly, I felt famished.

Nightfall always came on fast in the mountains. When I looked up from the fire, darkness had settled around us, and bright stars speared the valley with their pinpoint lights. I could hear some of the horses already picketed moving slightly in the trees nearby. The temperature was shirtsleeve perfect. Cold would come later, but I had to smile at Kamal, who had on a heavy insulated coat with a vest under it. The kid was always cold.

"Okay, boys. I think she's ready." Brownie started flipping the hamburger patties onto a tin tray. "Kamal, get the butter out of that ice chest, please."

We scrambled for paper plates and plastic utensils. Brownie put two patties on each plate we held out to him. The potatoes were forked and snatched out of the coals to be sliced open and slathered with butter until it ran over the sides. An entire loaf of white bread disappeared in about a minute. The only sound was chewing and the spiff of opening beer cans.

"Not bad grub, Brownie," I said, and the others agreed, mumbling their assent with full mouths.

"Well, thanks, fellas. It's a good thing you liked it. Meat and potatoes is about all I can cook... well, maybe except for this." Brownie leaned forward with a pair of tongs to slide a tin pan off the griddle. He lifted the foil cover to display an apple pie crisscrossed with strips of melted cheese bubbling like a lava pit. The cinnamon smell was wonderful.

"Whoa! Brownie, when'd you do *that*?" exclaimed CK. "I didn't see you slicing any apples."

"That's 'cause I didn't slice 'em. Kamal did."

"Kamal?"

"Yep. I told him how, and he did most of it while you guys were getting wood." Brownie smiled at Kamal. "Just consider it our dessert gift to you guys."

"And a fine gift it is," Travis said. "Now cut that bad boy up, and let's eat it."

The pie was scorched a little on the bottom crust, but otherwise delicious. Even Jerry commented on it. Pleased and embarrassed, Kamal looked down at his plate while we complimented him on his culinary surprise.

"Thank you," he said quietly.

Our bellies filled, we sat around the dying fire and planned the next day. Dunker agreed to watch the camp and prep the evening meal. The rest of us would scatter and go fishing. If everything went right, we would be eating fried trout the next night.

I walked out through the trees to bring Snuffy back to the picket line for the night. He nickered when I approached in the dark. I rubbed his nose and gave him a horse treat before I started leading him back toward camp. Snuffy's ears flicked ahead, and I saw the outline of a figure approaching.

"That you, Kamal?" I asked.

"Yes. Is that you, Jimmy Lloyd?"

"Checking on Sweet? She's right here next to us."

"Okay." Kamal fumbled his way toward me. He found Sweet Ginger and stroked her neck. "It's very peaceful here."

"Yeah, it is, isn't it? I guess that's why we all like to come up here. The fishing's just an excuse."

He raised his head. "Are the stars always like this?"

I looked up and stared past the treetops into the night sky. Deep space sparkled with a million twinkling lights, and the Milky Way soared across it, bigger and better than the Great White Way of New

York City. "They are up here. You can't see them so much in town. Even at my place, there's too many lights close by to see stars this clear." I gave Snuffy another pellet. "Haven't you ever seen them like this before?"

"Oh, yes, in the desert... This is the closest thing I have ever seen to a desert night."

"It must be beautiful there," I said.

"Yes. Yes, it is." Kamal quieted again for a minute. "But this is better."

I knew I was looking into some private part of Kamal just then. It felt uncomfortable, so I popped him on the shoulder. "C'mon. Let's go roll out our bedrolls in the tent before all the good spaces are gone."

As we walked back to the campfire, Kamal said softly behind me, "This has been a very good day. I wish it could stay this way always."

Chapter Twenty

"Rise and shine, punkin heads. You're gonna be burning daylight pretty soon." Dunker's voice boomed in through the closed tent flap.

I unzipped my sleeping bag and sat up. All around me, men groaned to their feet, scratching at armpits and asses. I looked at my watch. Five o'clock. Slipping on camp moccasins, I stumbled out into the darkness, wearing nothing else but underwear and a denim jacket. Dunker already had a fire going, so I squatted to warm myself there.

"Morning, Dunker," I said, rubbing my scalp. I pointed at the black coffeepot he had set in the coals. "That ready?"

"Should be. Help yourself."

I picked up a tin cup. As I poured the steaming liquid, a loud fart ripped through the tent behind me.

Howls of outrage followed immediately.

"Dammit, Jerry, show some respect! You got other people in here, you know," CK yelled. He and Thor threw aside the flaps and hustled out. "That was the stinkiest thing I've ever experienced," CK said, shaking his head.

"It wasn't natural," Thor said.

Travis came out blowing his nose. "I think Jerry must have just shit his pants."

Kamal and Brownie were close behind, and Kamal was fully dressed and carrying his boots. I suspected he'd slept in his clothes.

Jerry appeared at the tent's entrance, grinning. "Gee, what's the matter, boys? A little night air get to you?"

"Jerry, you are one lowlife sick son of a bitch—that's what's the matter. If I wanna breathe brown air, I'll move to town." CK bristled with indignation.

Jerry hitched his shoulders and grinned again. "Well, everybody has an opinion. If you guys will excuse me, I'm going to get dressed now." He closed the flaps.

Nobody wanted to make the long trek to the slit trench in our drawers, so we huddled around the fire, drinking coffee and spitting until Jerry emerged from the tent, whistling. By that time, everybody except CK was laughing about the whole thing. We entered the tent, making exaggerated fanning motions.

"Don't you fart like that out here by this fire," Dunker warned Jerry.

"Not a chance. I couldn't cut another one like that if I tried," he answered, reaching for the coffee. "At least, not before I eat."

SUNRISE CAUGHT US SITTING on the ice chests, eating Dunker's concoction of scrambled eggs and pork sausage. Kamal picked out the meat without comment. We started another pot of coffee while we got ready. Thor and I decided to ride back down to Lake Sioux Charlie and take Kamal with us to show him how to fly fish. The rest of the crew wanted to go farther up in the mountains to some of the little alpine lakes that dotted the Beartooth Range. We gathered up our gear and horses and separated for the day, agreeing to be back at camp before sunset.

At the lake, we kept our feet dry by staying on the shoreline since nobody had packed waders. I showed Kamal the basic technique of fly casting: rod up, back, pause, forward, then drop. "You don't want to slap it down on the water. Just let the line roll out easy like this," I said as I laid down a pretty fair cast. "You see that?"

"Yes."

I soon discovered that seeing it and doing it were two different things for Kamal. The poor fellow flailed with his rod over and over, barely getting anything right. He lashed the line against the water's surface then managed to snag the only little bush within reach on a backcast. Thor also tried to talk him through the motions. Together, the two of us only came up with a clumsy, irritated young Arab untangling a massive bird's nest in his line.

"This is why you want to fish? Isn't it supposed to be pleasant?" Kamal groused through gritted teeth as he picked at the jumbled mess that spilled down to his feet.

Thor bit his lip and discreetly moved away to fish on his own.

"You'll get it, Kamal. It's foreign to you right now. You just need a little practice, that's all," I said.

Kamal took a deep breath and let it out slowly. "You're right, Jimmy Lloyd. I need to practice this, but you and Thor are good casters. I am only keeping you from doing what you came to do."

"Hey, that's no problem," I said. "Thor and I don't mind."

Farther along the shoreline, Thor shot me a look. He'd heard me, but I wasn't so sure he would have said that himself. Thor could be serious about his fishing.

Kamal kept his gaze on the tangle in his hands. "I will stay here and practice what you showed me. Why don't you move away so you can catch some fish? I'll be all right." He raised his eyes to mine. "I need to do this alone."

He had a point. He didn't need someone jabbering in his ear. Too much thinking just messed up fly fishing. "Okay. That's probably a good idea," I answered, pointing in the opposite direction from Thor, where a spit of half-submerged rocks stuck out into the lake about forty yards away. "I'll just go to that little point there. Holler if you need me." I walked away to start casting. The trout were starting to rise; ripples spotted the lake's surface.

I heard a splash. Thor had hooked one. He played it a little bit then netted it at the water's edge. It looked to be about a nine- or ten-inch brown trout, and he held it up before placing it in his creel.

"Nice one," I yelled.

"Congratulations, Thor," Kamal said.

Thor grinned, and Kamal went right back to casting. After about fifteen minutes of trying, Kamal actually started to lay the fly out pretty decently. I missed a strike watching him, but I didn't mind. He seemed to be enjoying himself.

"Whoop!" Kamal finally had one on his line. The rod tip barely bent as the line swirled rapidly around in the water. "What do I do with it?" he asked excitedly. He started to back away from the lake, pulling the line out with him.

"Whoa, whoa! Don't back up," Thor yelled. "Just reel him in slow. Be careful not to break your leader. Don't lift him out of the water."

"I'll bring the net," I hollered.

Thor and I both hurried over to where Kamal furiously cranked the reel handle, his eyes locked on his line. I knelt to dip the net under the fish. It came out of the water kicking like a wind-up toy. It was another little brownie but shorter than my hand. Kamal was panting as though he'd just finished a mile-long run. Thor and I smiled at each other.

"Well, Kamal, it's not the biggest fish I've ever seen, but it's yours, all right," Thor said.

I pulled out my cell. "Here. Let me get a picture. We'll want to record your first catch in Montana."

Kamal posed solemnly with the wiggling little fish held at shoulder height.

"Okay, now let's put it back in the water before it's out too long," I said.

Kamal's mouth dropped open. "We don't keep it?"

"No, it's too small."

"But aren't we going to eat it?"

"No. Like I said, too small," I replied. "Here, let me show you. Get your hands wet before you handle a fish." I dipped my hands in the lake, and Kamal followed my example. When I removed the hook, I placed the little fish in his hands. "Now just lower him into the water. Be gentle and open up your grip. Let him swim away on his own."

Kamal looked like he could cry when he released his catch. It fluttered for a few seconds between his hands before it flicked its tail and was gone. Kamal stood up, his face such a picture of dejection that it was almost comical. "In Saudi Arabia, we would eat that one," he mumbled.

"Hey, don't worry about it." I gave him a pat on the back. "You got the hang of it now. We'll just catch some big ones from here on."

"Okay, Jimmy Lloyd." He had a little grin. "You're right. This *is* fun."

Thor's one fish turned out to be all we caught that morning. At eleven, we called it a day. We sat on rocks near the horses and watched the lake while eating the sandwiches we'd brought in the saddlebags. A couple of campers with fly rods came by. They hadn't had much luck upstream, either, but everybody agreed it was a beautiful day to be in the mountains. After they walked on, I turned to the others. "It's still pretty early. What do you say we do something?"

"Like what'd you have in mind?" Thor asked.

"Nothing in particular. I was thinking we could ride up the valley a little bit. There's a couple of places we might be able to cross and see what's on the other side."

Thor scratched the back of his neck. "Sounds good to me. We sure as hell aren't doing much good here." He turned to Kamal. "How's that sound to you?"

"Of course," Kamal said. I suspected he was only being polite, because he looked ready to quit.

The three of us got up, tightened cinches, and mounted. I led the others upstream past the turnoff that switchbacked up to camp. A mile beyond that, the path narrowed until I could touch the trees on each side of me. Sunlight sparkled off the river on our left. The forest's pine-needle floor muffled it so much that I sometimes couldn't hear the river at all. On the trail, we followed the tracks of four shod horses. Our other bunch had gone that way earlier.

Suddenly, Snuffy jerked his head up and stopped, ears flicked forward. I leaned down and stroked his neck. "Easy, boy. What is it, big fella?" The old gelding huffed out his nostrils and relaxed. Fifty yards ahead of us, a pair of backpackers appeared around the bend. The young couple stopped short, too, when they spotted us then hurried forward, shouldering their heavy packs. They appeared to be a pair of college kids. The girl wore a crimson University of Montana sweatshirt. We reined up.

"Howdy," the young man said.

"Howdy, yourself," I answered.

"Boy, are we glad to see you guys," he said.

"Oh, yeah? Why's that?"

"Well…" He shared a look with the girl, who rolled her eyes and drew up her shoulders, looking anxious. "I'm pretty sure we just came past some bear shit in the trail back there not too far away."

"You sure it wasn't horse droppings? We've got some friends riding up ahead of us."

"No, I know horse manure when I see it. This was bear; I'm almost certain. It was fresh, too." The kid seemed pretty confident about it.

Thor looked at me then asked the kid, "How fresh?"

"Today, I think."

"Today, huh?" I shifted my weight in the saddle. "Where'd you camp last night?"

"At Hammer Lake. I think we met your friends there when we started hiking out."

"No sign of a bear then?"

He shook his head. "No. Nothing at all until back there in the trail." He glanced at the girl. "It's been great up until now."

"You think it's following you?" Thor asked.

The girl shivered. "We don't know for sure. I just want to get out of here."

"You got bear spray? A firearm?"

They both shook their heads, and the young man held up his walking staff. "This is all we have."

It looked like five feet of stout oak, but it wouldn't do much against a bear. He eyed the pistols Thor and I carried openly. *Sorry, kid. Not a chance.*

"Okay then," I said. "You've got about seven miles to the trailhead, but Sioux Charlie's only four miles behind us. There's plenty of people there. You'll be safe. Here. Take this." I leaned down and handed the guy my can of pepper spray from its belt holster. It claimed to be guaranteed against bears, but I'd never tested it.

"Aren't you going back with us?" the girl asked, her eyes pleading.

"No, not yet, miss. We'll go on up the trail and check it out ourselves. Don't worry, though. If there's a bear around, he'll follow horses over humans." I was lying, but she looked relieved, and that was all I could do for her right then without changing our own plans. "How far ahead is the scat?" I asked.

"A quarter mile—maybe less," the kid answered.

"Okay then. You two head on back. We may catch up to you after we see it for ourselves," I said.

We watched the pair as they hurried along our back trail, anxious to leave all the woodland beauty behind them. They both looked back before they disappeared in the trees.

"Is everything all right? Will they be okay?" Kamal broke the silence after the two were gone. His eyes had widened like the girl's had.

"Oh, I reckon so. A bear won't generally mess with people." Thor shook his head. "It's still crazy though... to come out here with no protection but a big stick."

I touched the revolver on my hip, a long-barreled .44 Ruger big enough to stop any bruin if the shot was placed right. However, I had never fired it from horseback and had no idea what kind of rodeo *that* would start. We checked our back trail and to both sides as we rode on.

The college kid had the distance right. In less than a quarter mile, I knew we were getting close because Snuffy's nostrils flared and he jerked again.

"Easy, boy. Easy..." I dismounted, and the others followed my lead.

We led our reluctant horses on for less than a minute before we saw it. A bear turd nearly always looked like a human one—if that human had a rectum bigger than Andre the Giant's. The log, still soft and damp, lay right in the middle of the trail on top of tracks from the other horses. Yogi had made his deposit sometime after they passed through that morning, maybe five or six hours ago. Flies crawled all over it. The horses snorted, clearly uncomfortable.

I squatted and studied the scat. "You know anything about bear shit?" I asked Thor, who knelt beside me.

"Nope, not really. Just enough to know that's bear shit all right."

"Is it close?" Kamal looked back over his shoulder, as nervous as a cat in a burlap bag.

I stood up to crack my back. "Probably not. No way to tell for sure, though."

"Uh-oh," Thor said. He had pivoted around to take in his surroundings when he got up, and he stood staring at a big ponderosa pine next to the trail.

"What is it?" I asked.

Thor only pointed. The tree had terrible, deep claw marks that raked the bark from eight feet off the ground down to six feet. "Grizzly."

I felt all the blood drain from my face. I hated to think of grizzlies—much more aggressive and dangerous than black bears—being in our vicinity, but a big silvertip had clearly marked his territory here. I peered around at the woods. "I think you're right about that, and maybe that means we should be going."

"Yeah, let's get out of here," Thor replied. "But first, let me mark this so Brownie and them won't miss it on their way back. Don't want them to get surprised." He took some red trail-marking ribbon out of his saddlebag and cut off a length to lay next to the scat, then he tied another piece on the scarred ponderosa while I held his reins.

"Okay," I said. "Let's go catch those campers and walk them back to the lake. I need to get my bear spray back anyway."

We remounted and turned around. The horses stepped out lively, no doubt anxious to leave the grizzly smell behind. I actually had to hold Snuffy back, or he would have run.

When the trail widened a little, Kamal rode up alongside me. "That bear place. It's pretty far from camp, no?"

"Uh, not really. Not for a grizzly. They range for miles."

He pondered on that for a minute. "Do you think it will bother us?"

"Probably not. But he knows we're up here in his mountains. That's for sure." I looked sideways at him. "That scare you?"

He smiled crookedly. "A little."

"Tell you what, Kamal. I've got a Winchester pump twelve gauge back at the tent. It's my camp gun, loaded with slugs. I'll let you carry it if that'll make you feel better."

He nodded. "Yes, it would. Thank you."

"Don't worry about it. I doubt it'll ever come to that. That bear's long gone."

Chapter Twenty-One

The other bunch caught the bear sign on their way back. Knowing for sure that a grizzly hung around the area sobered everybody up, but we weren't panicked about it. Our food supplies already hung at least twelve feet up in the trees, about halfway along the path to the latrine. That night, while chowing down on fish the others had caught, we talked it over and agreed that no one would go off fishing or exploring alone.

"Even a big critter like that wouldn't tangle with a crowd," Brownie said, and we all nodded sagely.

Meanwhile, another situation had been brewing in camp. Jerry clearly didn't care for Kamal and was making a point of avoiding him. The night before, he had moved his bedroll to the other side of the tent once he realized Kamal would be lying next to him. I didn't know if anybody else was noticing, but Kamal sure caught it.

As we were sitting and eating on the second night, Jerry sneered. "Hey, Camel, this better'n that *kosher* crap you'd like to eat but can't?"

Kamal just kept chewing. Without saying a word, I watched the whole thing gathering like a thundercloud. Kamal would have to handle the deal on his own, though.

He dabbed at the side of his mouth with a paper towel before clearing his throat. "It's interesting you would ask that. Kosher food and the food we are allowed to eat are almost identical, except that the Jews actually have stricter rules. In Islam, we follow the *halal* standard. And we love fish, but no pork, of course." He smiled and bit into his filet again, lifting it delicately to his mouth like a crunchy piece of burnt toast.

Jerry gaped for a moment, unsure exactly how he had just been bested, but somehow sensing it.

Travis dug an elbow into him. "Betcha didn't know that, huh, Jerry?" He chuckled, and around the fire, everyone else smiled.

Kamal had won this little exchange, but Jerry was still an avalanche about to slide. I just didn't know when. He eyed Kamal sullenly the rest of the time we sat there.

THE NEXT MORNING, KAMAL and I went with Travis and CK into the Beartooths to a fishing spot that had been pretty good in the past. The air smelled fresh and cool. We rode over the dried bear scat without comment, and even the flies had lost interest in it. Kamal rode with the stock of my shotgun jutting up in the scabbard behind him.

After five miles, we arrived at our chosen stretch of river, a hundred-yard series of riffles and pools, places where trout liked to wait for nymphs and bugs to come floating to them. The water rushed around oven-sized boulders throughout the narrow part. Kamal and CK started casting from the near bank, but Travis and I switched to rubber-soled gym shoes so we could scramble across on the rocks to the other bank. A game trail led downstream, and I followed Travis that way.

He slowed down and turned to me. "What's the story on Kamal? Is he all right?"

The question startled me. "Yeah, he's all right. What makes you ask?"

Travis barely shrugged and pooched his lower lip. "Oh, you know. He comes from over *there*." He waved his hand around vaguely.

"He's a Muslim. It might make some people wonder. What *do* you know about him, really?"

"I'd stake my life on it. He's a good kid. And he wonders just as much about us, believe me." I squared my feet in the trail, suddenly feeling very defensive about Kamal. *Can't he ever catch a break?*

"Okay then, I didn't mean anything by it. I'm a cop. I can't help it sometimes. There's memos at work about some unusual goings-on down south. Lots of cell activity with the bad guys. No details, but I can tell you this—the big boys at DHS are scared shitless that something's gonna blow soon."

"All that may well be," I said, jerking a thumb back toward where Kamal fished. "But I can tell you *that* boy's got nothing to do with anything Homeland Defense might be interested in."

The deputy held up a hand. "Okay, Jimmy Lloyd, you'd know him better than anybody, I guess. It's dropped." He stopped and looked upstream, where Kamal was casting on the opposite bank. "Boy, Jerry sure doesn't like him."

"Jerry's an asshole."

"Agreed. But I do have to say this." He pointed at Kamal, who was jerking to free his line from a tree. "He can't cast worth a shit."

We both laughed.

"Don't tell him that. He's getting kinda sensitive about it," I said. "He'll get the hang of it eventually."

"He is persistent. I'll give him that."

We spread out to start casting. Both of us netted a keeper after fifteen minutes. I'd started to move to a new spot when I heard a loud whoop upstream. CK was doing his version of a rebel yell and pointing at Kamal.

"Haaave mercy!" CK drawled. "Would you look at that?"

Kamal stood with one foot in the water, holding up a twelve-inch rainbow in his net. His grin was as big as a Cadillac's front grill. "Do I put this one back?" he shouted.

"You do that, and I'll make you eat a bacon sandwich tonight," I yelled back. Everybody laughed.

Our quartet caught a few more by noon, but Kamal easily had the catch of the day. Before we started back, I posed him between Travis and CK while he held up his prize. I couldn't tell who had the widest smile.

Back at camp, there were more congratulations for Kamal. Thor had camp and cook duty, so he started prepping all the fish right away. Kamal wanted to help and ended up sitting on an ice chest, cleaning and filleting sixteen pan-sized trout under Thor's watch. By the time I came in from hobbling Snuffy and Sweet, the two chefs had fish sizzling in a cast-iron pan with Tony's seasoning, butter, and lemon juice. Thor wrapped corn on the cob in foil and dropped them in the coals for a few minutes before snatching them out using a pair of sticks as tongs. The meal turned out even better than the one the night before. The boys loved it, and they gobbled at it like wild coyotes, but Jerry didn't say a word about the fish.

WE CAMPED THERE FOR two more nights, doing mostly the same things during the days, exploring and fishing. There had been more elk to watch, and the second evening, wolves howled across the valley. All of us were feeling pretty good by then. My turn for camp duty came on our last full day in the woods. We were set to break camp the next morning.

Kamal asked if I wanted him to stay and help, but I declined his offer. "No, you go ahead, Kamal. There's still a lot more for you to see, but you better be learning some recipes, 'cause next year, *your* ass *is* cooking."

He had the strangest, saddest smile. "You're sure, Jimmy Lloyd?"

"Go on, boy. Get outta here."

I actually enjoyed solitude. After all the others left, I sand-scoured the breakfast pans at the little creek nearby before taking a Texas Aggie bath—I stood next to the water, lathering and wiping with a washcloth and a bar of soap. Then I mixed up a berry pie to bake later in the Dutch oven, gathered a last load of firewood for the evening, and bagged some things to pack out the next morning. I went over to the food-supply trees to lower the dry-ice chest with the steaks in it—our traditional last night's meal. After I set aside the meat to thaw, I got my binoculars and a paperback book and leaned back on a boulder in the meadow near where I had hobbled Snuffy to graze. Instead of thinking about some deep, meaningful things while I sat there, I mostly read Jack Reacher and dozed in the sun.

The guys came back by three in the afternoon. Nobody had fished the last day, just ridden new trails and taken pictures.

"How was it?" I asked.

"Great," Dunker answered. "Saw dozens of elk. One coyote."

They dismounted, tired and happy, although the horses only looked tired. I started getting supper ready while the fellows went about tending their mounts. However, not much time went by before I had a critical audience sitting and watching. The steaks were an inch thick, and everybody had an opinion about grilling.

"Don't char 'em."

"I like mine rare. No, not that rare."

"You're losing a lot of juice there, Jimmy Lloyd."

I pretty much ignored them. They were hungry enough to eat fried toad if that was what I wanted to put down in front of them. The pie cooked in one cast-iron oven, and I roasted big yellow onions with brown sugar and butter in another one. When the eating started, the comments mostly stopped.

"Not bad, Jimmy Lloyd."

"Yeah, not bad."

Dunker pulled out his harmonica. He wasn't all that good, but in that moment, sitting around a fire, the soulful wails he coaxed out of it when he played his old cowboy songs made everything right with the world. I stared into the crackling fire, listening, content with a full belly. It had been a good campout—maybe one of the best. I thought about what Kamal had said our first night out, about wanting it to stay that way all the time, and I wondered why that couldn't be. Actually, I knew why. *Mankind just has a way of screwing up anything good.*

Jerry settled himself down to eat on the chest next to Kamal. When he finished, he set his plate on the ground and wiped his hands on his jeans. He heaved a sigh. "Well, what d'ya think, CJ? You like camping?" He turned to look at Kamal, squinting like a boar hog.

Kamal looked puzzled. "CJ?"

"Yeah, you know—Camel Jockey."

Kamal's eyes flashed. "I do not like that name," he answered softly.

Jerry was treading close to a line he shouldn't cross, but before I said anything, Brownie intervened. "Hey, don't worry about it, Kamal. We all got nicknames." He pointed across at me. "Hell, his name's 'dipshit.'"

"Heeey!" I said, acting offended. "Why you go and tell him about that?" My response produced laughter around the fire, and Kamal eased back a little.

But, always committed to being the turd in the punchbowl, Jerry poked his thumb into Kamal's arm. "So you'd rather be called 'dipshit' then? Huh? Is that it? Dipshit?"

Kamal slapped his hand away. "Stop it!" he snapped.

"What? You can't take it, can you? Dipshit Camel Jockey." Jerry grabbed Kamal's shoulder and shoved. Kamal went sideways, straight onto the ground.

People always figured Jerry was slow. He was heavy in the middle all right, but I'd seen him rope. That big man could scramble out of a saddle and get to a calf as fast as any lean cowboy. Before anyone could move to stop him, Jerry jumped up like a cat and rolled onto Kamal, pinning him by the shoulders. He kneed the youth's legs apart and put his massive weight on top of him.

Brownie said, "I wouldn't be doing that if I was you."

"Get off him, Jerry!" I yelled.

"Let him up, Jerry. I mean it," Dunker said.

"Maybe you should stop being an asshole, Jerry," Travis chimed in.

Jerry didn't seem to hear any of us. He started simulating sex with Kamal, dry-humping him and panting in his face. "Hey, maybe you like this, huh, Camel Jockey? Isn't this how you do it in sand land?"

Travis and I got there in about two steps. Just as I put my hand on Jerry's shoulder to pull him off, he howled and jumped back, almost knocking me into the fire.

"Yeow!" he squealed. "The son of a bitch cut me!" He pulled up his shirt. A trickle of blood oozed from a tiny puncture wound on his left side.

I spun around to Kamal. He was up, standing next to the ice chest, breathing hard and holding out a little dagger with a red handle. None of us had seen where it came from.

"You all right?" I said to him.

He only stared at Jerry. His eyes zeroed on the other man's red face.

"Kamal, look at me." I put a hand up in front of him, and it broke the spell. "You all right?" I repeated when he looked at me.

He lowered the knife. "Yes," he said so quietly that I almost couldn't hear him.

Around the fire, the others sat openmouthed.

"What the fuck! Is *he* all right? What about me? Look at this!" Jerry screeched as he pointed to the wound in his side. To me, it ranked somewhere between a paper cut and a barbed-wire puncture. He covered it with his hand.

Travis bent to look. "Here, let me see it. Move your hand." He studied it for a minute. "It's gonna be okay. Barely a prick. Looks like a big tick bite. You got your tetanus shot, didn't you?"

"That's not the point! The son of a bitch cut me. That's armed assault," he said, looking at Travis.

"Well what'd you expect, you dumb shit?" Brownie said. "You wallowing around on him half your size like you was a walrus fucking a football. You had that coming, and you know it."

"Looked like self-defense to me," CK said.

"Yeah. Nothing to see here," Travis added. When the lawman said that, Jerry deflated.

"All right then. Put some ointment on it and a Band-Aid," Dunker said. "Let that be the end of it. You two shake hands."

A mumbled chorus agreed with Dunker.

"I ain't shaking hands. That was a sneaky A-rab trick. A sand nigger trick," Jerry said through clenched teeth. "I was just playing with him."

Thor chimed in with what I was already thinking. "So what? You were a fat bully. Lucky for you, you had all that lard on you, or Kamal woulda really gutted you up."

"I doubt that," Jerry muttered. "Fucking sand nigger."

"Okay, that's it," I growled. "I'm about to come over there and stomp a mudhole where your ass ought to be, fat man. I won't need a knife to do it, either." I took one step, and a hand touched my arm. Thor.

"Don't do it, Jimbo," he said. "Not worth it."

Travis had my other arm. "Listen to him, Jimmy Lloyd. Let's don't make this worse than it is."

I relaxed, but still seething inside, I jabbed my chin at Jerry. "This asshole needs to apologize."

Jerry had backed away at first, his eyes wide. Seeing me stop, he blustered, "Ain't no way I'm apologizing for just playing with him." He looked over at Kamal. "If he wasn't such a sand—"

"Don't say it, Jerry," I cut in. "You finish that, and no one's holding me back."

"I say they shake hands and call it good. No dishes got broke here," CK said.

"Agreed," Thor said.

Dunker turned to Kamal. "How about it, Kamal? You willing to shake hands?"

Kamal shook his head silently.

"All right then, if that's how you two want it," Dunker said, looking in a fanny pack he carried. "Here, Jerry. You can doctor that scratch with this." He picked out a tube of Neosporin and tossed it to Jerry. "In the meantime, you two stay the hell away from each other."

"Fine by me." Jerry grunted then stood wordlessly off to the side, dabbing ointment on the tiny cut. He lowered his shirt and stalked out of the firelight to sulk in the dark.

Brownie stood up to reach into the chest he sat on. "Here, Kamal. Have a beer."

"I don't like him," Kamal said.

"Hey look, Jerry'll get over it. You should, too."

Dunker put up his harmonica. The mood had been broken.

Chapter Twenty-Two

With Jerry sitting out there in the dark like a pissed-off Buddha statue, we drank our beers mostly in silence. After a while, Thor got up and made a flashlight-aided trip to the latrine.

"Horses are restless," he said when he got back.

Kamal stood and snapped his coat up to the neck before he headed for the latrine himself.

"Mules, too?" Dunker asked Thor.

"All of 'em."

We shined spotlights toward the picket line. The livestock shuffled around, pulling at the overhead tie lines. Their ears stood up, and they stared back wide-eyed, moving their feet in a nervous jitterbug. Some of them huffed. Our lights cast long, eerie shadows behind them that jumped around in the trees like dark, unhinged giants. I walked out to lay my hand on Snuffy's neck and calm things down, but it didn't do any good. He kept bumping me and shuddering his lips. They all sensed a presence somewhere in the darkness.

"I don't like this," I called back to the camp. "They think something's out there."

"I don't like it, either." Dunker stood with his hands on his hips, peering into the darkness around us. "I think maybe tonight, we better guard the animals. We got enough of us to do it in one-hour shifts."

Jerry walked back into the firelight. "Yeah, that sounds like a good idea. I'll take the first watch." Buckling on his holster, he walked out to the picket line, where I waited. Jerry liked everything big, and the Taurus Raging Bull he toted swung on his hip like a cordless drill with a six-inch barrel.

"Take your light, Jerry," Dunker said.

"Got it."

"You want an ice chest to sit on?" Thor called.

"I'll lean on a tree."

I knew Jerry had taken the first shift just so he wouldn't have to get up during the night and interrupt his sleep.

"Okay, Jerry, you got it," I greeted him when he got to the horses.

"Yeah, I got it, dipshit," he replied. "Just don't you be hard to wake up when your turn comes."

I walked back to the fire, shaking my head. *Just likes being an asshole.*

I gathered up the dishes and utensils and dropped them in a big pot of hot soapy water to soak overnight. Food scraps and paper went in the fire. Dunker doled out our watch assignments for the livestock. I drew the shift from two o'clock to three o'clock. The fellows started to stretch, getting ready for our last night's sleep in the wild.

I saw a light bobbing at a distance in the trees, where Kamal was on his way back from the latrine. "Hey, Dunker, what about Kamal?" I asked. "When's he gonna watch?"

"He goes right after you, Jimmy Lloyd. He's young enough to handle getting up in the blackest part of the night."

Some of us sitting at the fire chuckled. We watched Kamal's light getting closer, waiting to see his face when he got the news. I could see his boots on the path as he shined the light down ahead of him.

Suddenly, I heard a yelp. Kamal's flashlight jerked up and fell to the ground, still shining. A large dark mass blacker than the night around it loomed where Kamal had been walking. It shook and heaved like a massive sack of garbage, accompanied by loud crackling in the brush. A scream pierced the darkness—I barely recognized it as human—followed immediately by a monstrous roar that seared my ears. My blood froze. Nobody moved for several seconds as we listened to the thrashing. Then Kamal screamed again. A light clicked on. CK aimed his powerful spotlight on a scene I hoped I would never see again.

"Holy shit!"

Sixty feet away, a grizzly, frosted in the white light, crouched on all fours, head down, worrying at something beneath it. A pair of blue-jeaned legs stuck out, toes down and flailing at the ground. The bear's guttural noises overpowered whatever sounds Kamal might have been making. Slobber hanging from its jaws, the bear stopped to blink at the light. Unfazed, it bent down again. Its wide head whipped from side to side as it picked Kamal off the ground by his back. Then unexpectedly, it spat him out and swatted him aside. The big male silvertip, shaggy and deadly, stood tall and roared. I swore I could feel the air move when it made that deafening sound. Kamal curled into a tight ball where he'd landed against a bush. That might have worked at first, but the bear had become enraged. He turned to his downed prey again.

I fumbled for my pistol, forgetting that it hung in the tent. Then I froze once more as another form moved at the edge of the light right beside the griz. Jerry stepped into the spotlight's beam, teeth bared. As light and quick as a dancer, he moved with both arms straight out, gripping his big .454 handgun. The bear sensed him at five feet. It spun around in a crouch so fast, it made the spotlight seem like a strobe light, but Jerry had already started to squeeze the trigger. The pistol almost touched the bear's snout as it fired. The flash lit up the trees, and the crack sounded like a lightning strike. Jerry's bullet hit the bear square in the jaw. The heavy slug broke teeth and bone and tore through neck tissue before it lodged in the body. The shot would kill for sure, but the bear reared up again, trying to roar through a mangled mouth and throat. Blood sprayed over Jerry.

"Jerry, get out of there!" Dunker's voice was clear in the chaos.

The bear swayed, batting weakly like a punch-drunk fighter. It tried to lunge at Jerry, who stepped back, tripped on a root and fell backward. He fired upward as the grizzly came down and covered him, muffling the sound and flash. The bear seemed to collapse all over him. Jerry became buried under a seven-hundred-pound, quivering mass of hair. But then the giant head lolled to one side, and the movement stopped.

Everyone jerked into action. The others went ahead cautiously, holding out their handguns while CK kept a shaky grip on the spotlight. I ran into the tent and picked up the Winchester. Shucking a shell into the chamber, I hurried back out.

"Jerry, you all right?" Brownie called out. "Answer me, guy!"

They were standing around the carcass when I caught up. The bear was as dead as Judas. No sign of Jerry, though. Travis and Brownie reached down to lift the legs on one side, but suddenly, a massive shoulder twitched. Both of them jumped back. The carcass moved again, and Jerry's head appeared from under its side as he tried to wiggle out. He had so much blood and fur all over his face, I doubted even his mother would have let him in her house.

He struggled against the weight on top of him and gasped for air. "Get this... off me!" he wheezed. "Off!" His bulging eyes could have been in a cartoon strip.

We hustled to roll the bear off. Under the bloody mess that smeared him, he looked pale and shaken. He sat up and brushed the fur from his face with trembling hands. "Thanks," he panted. Then he looked at the bear. "Gaaah!" he screamed, scrabbling back on heels and hands.

"Whoa, whoa. It's okay, Jerry. It's okay." Travis put a hand on Jerry's shoulder. "The bear's dead. You killed it. You shot it, remember?"

Jerry blinked and looked up at us all for the first time. "Yeah, I remember... I just..." He shook his head. "Sorry, fellas. I guess I lost it there for a second." He grinned to himself and shook his head again.

"That's okay, big guy," Dunker said, reaching down to pull Jerry to his feet. "That was a helluva thing you just did."

I looked away into the darkness. "Kamal!" I called, hurrying around the carcass to the original spot of the attack. Flashlight beams followed me, and I found him, still hugging his knees, next to the bush where the bear knocked him. He trembled violently. I thought at first, he was about to do a Jerry-style crab walk away from me, but he didn't move otherwise.

"You okay?" I picked up Kamal's flashlight and knelt beside him, looking for injuries. His heavy coat had been shredded, and rip marks opened up the back and right side, but I didn't find blood until I looked at Kamal's side. The bear had raked its claws along his ribcage. The blood ran down, soaking his jeans. Apparently, the bear had shaken him with only the coat in its teeth since I saw no puncture wounds anywhere. Grizzlies usually liked to get a mouth grip on their prey's heads. Maybe this one hadn't had the time to take that bite. "You okay?" I asked again.

Kamal nodded, his hands still shaking. "I thought... I thought I was dead." He gulped and shut his eyes. "I thought the jinn were dragging me to hell." He shuddered. "Not faithful. I have not been faithful enough." He muttered something under his breath in Arabic.

Thor squatted beside us. "He in shock?" he asked me, taking one of Kamal's trembling hands. "What's he saying?"

"No, not shock," I answered. "Just shook up some. Can't say as I blame him."

"Not a bit." Thor gently placed a hand on Kamal's head. "Hey, boy. You all right?" He spoke softly like he would to a skittish colt. "Kamal, look at me."

Kamal's eyes opened. "What happened?" His gaze flicked around until it found the dead grizzly nearby with the other guys around it. He stiffened and tried to get up, wincing at the pain in his side. Thor and I held him down.

"Easy, Kamal. You're all right now," I said. "There was a bear, a pretty good-sized grizzly. But it's dead now. You're all right."

I didn't think he heard me. He kept staring at the mound of fur. "There was hair in my mouth. So much hair... I was choking," he said, speaking barely above a whisper. He drew a deep breath and looked at me as if he just realized I was there. "What happened?"

"There was a bear," I answered. "We'll tell you more about it later. Right now, we got to get you into some better light. You need doctoring." I turned to Thor. "Help me get him up."

Kamal gritted his teeth to stifle a cry when we picked him up. Thor and I carried him back to the camp, seated and cradled in our arms. At the fire, we set him on an ice chest next to Jerry. Dunker laid a big first-aid pouch open on the ground between them. Jerry had his shirt off, and Dunker looked him over. I started peeling what was left of Kamal's clothes from his torso.

"Ach!" He arched and jerked even though I tried to be gentle around the bloody parts. Every one of us had treated cuts and breaks before, sometimes on ourselves, so we didn't puke at what we saw.

Jerry and Kamal were two of the luckiest people on planet Earth that night. Jerry didn't have a scratch. The only blood we could find on him had come from the bear. He was bruised from his fall and from the grizzly landing on him, but that seemed to be all. Kamal hadn't been quite as fortunate. A set of ugly claw marks bled on his right side. However, the thick, layered clothing he'd been wearing had absorbed most of the damage. The bleeding tracks weren't deep; no ribs were exposed. Nothing seemed broken.

"You two sons of bitches must be living right," Dunker said as he peered at Kamal's side. "Never heard of two people surviving a griz attack so well." He turned to Travis. "Hand me that ointment tube and some of those big gauze patches. We got to stop this bleeding." He bent down to apply the ointment. "This'll sting a little, but nothing compared to what you're going to feel later."

CK held the lantern closer as Dunker began to dab white cream on the cuts. He taped dressings on Kamal's side. I remembered the Ace bandage from the Fishtail general store and retrieved it from my pack.

Dunker raised an eyebrow when I laid it next to him. "You know this was going to happen?" he grunted.

I shook my head. "Nope, I'm just a Boy Scout."

"Well, good for you."

He wrapped Kamal's torso with the Ace. The bleeding soaked some of the pads but stopped.

Jerry, his shirt on again, stood and watched Kamal's treatment. "He gonna be all right?"

Dunker glanced over his shoulder at him. "Jerry, you go take a couple of painkillers and sit down. It's going to hit you in a little while, big boy."

I went into the tent and took a dirty shirt and pair of jeans out of Kamal's bag. Jerry sat quietly while I helped Kamal replace his tattered and bloody clothes. Then together, Dunker and I eased him over to a camp stool, where he sat, head down, his forearms resting on his thighs.

Afterward, I joined Brownie and Thor at the bear's carcass. For a minute, we just stared in silence. It had been rolled onto one side, as if still hibernating.

"Hell of a deal," Brownie said. He looked out into the dark woods around us. "I don't guess there's any more out there."

I shined my light toward the horses. Their ears were up. They watched us with flared nostrils, looking wary but not panicked. "Probably not, but we oughta still stand watch tonight irregardless."

"Yeah."

I picked up the Winchester from where I had set it when I found Kamal. "Let's walk this and see what happened."

Together, the three of us went to the spot where Kamal had been attacked. It didn't take Sherlock Holmes to figure it out. We had screwed up royally. Our food supplies were safely out of a bear's reach, all right. However, we'd hung the grub right beside the path we used going to and from the slit trench. We found claw marks on the tree holding the meat chest. The griz had been trying to get to it, but he was too big to climb very well. No wonder the horses and mules had been so spooked. The bear had prowled around only about eighty feet away from their picket line. And then here came Kamal.

Thor stood quietly in the path, his head bowed.

I stood alongside him and looked where he kept staring at nothing. "Something wrong?"

He gave me a hooded glance. "I walked from the shitter through this very spot just a few minutes before Kamal did." He paused to look at stars shining down through the treetops. "It makes you wonder why some things happen the way they do. You know what I mean?"

"Not exactly."

Thor looked at me earnestly. "It could have been me under that bear is what I'm saying, and I'm wondering why it wasn't."

I had no answers. *You can't account for every roll of the dice.*

Thor wagged his head side to side. "And who'da thought Jerry would be the one coming through when it all hit the fan? I sure wouldn't have. Would you?"

Chapter Twenty-Three

We sat or stood around the fire in silence. CK threw on more wood, making it flare up enough to throw light over the whole camp. I could tell Kamal was hurting some, but he wouldn't say anything. He just gritted his teeth and stared at the flames while sweat popped out on his face. I hoped the big dose of ibuprofen that Dunker had given him would kick in soon. The bear carcass lay just beyond the firelight's reach.

"Okay, boys, we got us a problem here." Dunker sat on an ice chest, checking the coffeepot over the fire; he always made coffee when he wanted to think. "The way I see it is, we better get this thing reported to the wildlife people pretty soon, or we'll be in trouble with the law. Grizzlies are a protected species. Illegal to shoot one."

"Shouldn't be a problem with Fish and Wildlife," Brownie said. "They can't get mad over a case of self-defense."

"They're upset some anytime a griz is killed, but they won't do much here once they check it out," Travis chimed in. "But I'd have to report it either way."

"Aw hell, go ahead and tell 'em, Barney Fife. I ain't worried about it." Jerry popped a Bud Light with a shaky hand, probably needing beer more than coffee at that moment.

"Yeah. Clear case of self-defense. If Jerry hadn't jumped in like he did, we'd be packing out our boy Kamal here in a meat bag." CK had a way of clarifying things when he used that drawl of his.

"That's what I figured, too," Dunker said. "I just needed to hear everybody get on board with it. We all agreed?"

We all nodded quietly.

Dunker looked around the fire then checked his watch. "No use trying to call anybody tonight. I'll give the game wardens a call in the morning after they have their first cup of coffee. No cell phone cover out here, but I got satellite phone in my saddlebag... Speaking of coffee..." He took the coffeepot off the grill to pour a cupful.

Travis said, "Let me have a chat with them, too, Dunker. I know some of those fellas at the Lake Elmo office. Might help."

"Sure thing."

"No, you mustn't!" Kamal blurted out.

I had been watching him throughout the conversation. Apparently forgetting his pain, he'd come alert as the others talked, his eyes darting from one speaker to another. He hadn't nodded with the rest of us when Dunker called for our agreement to contact the authorities. He clasped his hands tightly in his lap and rocked back and forth as if ready to burst.

"What's the matter, Kamal? You okay?" I asked.

"You mustn't call the police."

"Fish and game wardens aren't exactly the police, Kamal. They enforce the laws concerning wildlife—hunting and fishing regulations mostly," I said. "It's okay, though. We didn't do anything wrong here. You were attacked, and Jerry defended you. Open and shut."

"But they will investigate me, won't they?"

"Not really," Travis answered. "You didn't do anything wrong. You worried they're going to send you back to Saudi Arabia for getting jumped by a bear?" He grinned. "They won't. You'll just get your name in the papers for being the dumbass that walked into a bear trap."

Kamal actually looked more worried. His eyes opened wide. "They mustn't put me in the press." He moaned and put his face in his hands.

"Hey, don't worry about it," Travis said. "If you're on legal status here in the US, you got no problem." The deputy lowered his voice. "Kamal, you *are* legal, aren't you?"

Kamal nodded, still keeping his face covered. "Yes." He looked up. "It is that... I can't be publicized... My family... they wouldn't understand."

Dunker spoke up about as kindly as I'd ever heard him. "Kamal, we don't have much choice about this. We *have* to report putting down a grizzly. There's no way around that." He glanced at Travis. "I tell you what, though... Travis has a little juice with the local game wardens. Maybe he can get them to leave your name out of this. You could try to do that, couldn't you, Travis?"

Travis bent down and picked up the coffeepot. "Sure, I can try. No promises, though."

"There, Kamal. That make you feel better?" Dunker sipped steaming brew from a tin cup.

The lad grinned weakly. "A little, yes. Thank you."

Jerry stood up abruptly. "Better go finish my watch. Might be another one."

"Whoa, Jerry. You sure you're feeling up to it?" I said. "I can cover the rest of your shift."

"Oh, yeah, I can do it." Jerry stopped and cleared his throat. "I need to sit out there and think by that dead son of a bitch."

"That was a helluva deal, Jerry," Thor said. "I guess you could use some time out, eh?"

He paused. "Just tell me one thing—how'd you get over there so fast? We was all standing here, still holding our peckers out when you come out of the dark like Batman. How'd you do that?"

Jerry faced the fire, still holding his beer. "Aw... hell if I know. I was just watching him walk back..." He gestured toward Kamal. "And I saw it jump him from behind." He sipped from the can. "I ran over without thinking about it. Too dumb to be scared, I guess—not like right now." He held out the beer can, trembling slightly in his hand. "Looks like I still got some adrenaline pumping."

He turned and walked away in the darkness toward the dead bear, stopping to pick up an empty ice chest. We could see the big man's outline as he shined his flashlight around. He placed the ice chest near the bear, sat down, and played the light over its body.

Kamal stood up. "May I borrow your Winchester, Jimmy Lloyd?"

"Well, sure. You going to bed with it?"

"No, but I need to go out there." He pointed to where Jerry sat.

I reached for the shotgun lying across a saddle behind me. "Be careful. It's loaded with slugs and ready."

"I will be careful. Thank you."

I watched Kamal walk out to where Jerry sat. The two of them were out of earshot, but I could see Kamal lay down the gun when he got down on one knee next to Jerry. He began to talk, moving his hands a lot while Jerry mostly just shook his head and kept his light on the bear. After a minute, Jerry looked sideways at Kamal. He stopped shaking his head and seemed to be listening. Then, he nodded slowly. Kamal extended his hand. Jerry gripped it, and they shook. Suddenly, Kamal was standing and hugging Jerry with his good left arm. Jerry stood to gently return the embrace. They stayed like that for a short while before breaking apart. Both men wiped at their faces with the backs of their hands.

"Wow," CK said quietly.

"Who knew?" Thor said. "Jerry has a heart."

I just shook my head, amazed.

THE NEXT MORNING, EVERYONE chipped in to rustle up our last camp breakfast. Dunker fished out his satellite phone, a plastic brick with a numerical keyboard and a six-inch antenna. We never went into the wilderness unless somebody packed one. Dunker and

Travis dialed the nearest state Fish and Wildlife and Parks office in Red Lodge, about fifty miles away. From the snatches I could hear of their conversation, it didn't seem like we were going to have too much of a hassle. Travis talked with them for a few minutes, laughing at some inside story. When they signed off, Dunker stood up.

"Boys, the wardens are gonna meet us at the trailhead. They got to get their horses trailered first so they should be getting there about the same time as us. They'll want to see the carcass and make an investigation on site. I don't think we'll have any problem, though." He looked directly at Kamal. "Fish and Wildlife is a pretty reasonable bunch."

"Who's coming?" Brownie asked.

"Theron Henderson and Joe Weston," Travis answered. "I know them. They'll be okay."

"Yeah, them two are all right," Thor said.

I knew them, too. Joe Weston had been a semi-regular at the Drifters since his divorce. I didn't know of anything bad about them, and if they were hard cases, I would have heard it.

"I'll put in a word to them, too, Kamal," I added. "Shouldn't be a problem."

Dunker clapped twice. "All right, boys. We got people to see. Let's eat and then get this camp packed up."

We started filling our plates. I sat down beside Kamal, who was looking a little pale. Trying to sleep during the night had been agony for him, partly because he couldn't lie down on those wounded ribs of his. I had heard him thrashing around in the tent as he sat up in the dark, trying to endure the throbbing pain.

"How you feeling, buddy?" I asked.

He grimaced at his food. "It hurts a little, but I will be all right." He set his plate aside. "I do not think I can eat this right now. My stomach…"

"Hey, nobody said you *have* to eat," I said. "But you should try to a little bit. Your body probably needs nourishment after the punishment it's taken. How about you take a bite of the toast while I check your bandages?"

Kamal seemed to think about that. "Okay."

"Can you unbutton your shirt?"

Kamal fumbled with the buttons. I tried to gently lift the shirt off his shoulders, but he stiffened. It was sticking in a couple of places where dried blood plastered it to his bandages.

"Eat your toast," I said while I surveyed his back and ribs. The wounds were covered, but blood had soaked through the gauze and tape. His whole bare torso was covered with crusted blood, yellow-blue bruises, and a fluid that gleamed like pus. I drew in my breath. "Dunker, you want to take a look at this?"

Jerry walked over with Dunker and squatted to look at Kamal's back.

The big man whistled low and long. "That's got to hurt." He leaned around to look Kamal in the eye. "You sure you're doing all right?"

"Yes. Thank you." Kamal seemed to be holding his breath, only letting it out in short gasps when he talked.

Dunker studied the wounds. "Kamal, I'm not going to lie to you. These cuts look pretty bad, what I can see of them, and there's not much I can do for you out here. You got to get to a doctor pretty quick."

"Should we change his bandages?" Jerry asked, concerned about someone else maybe for the first time in his life.

Dunker shook his head. "No, we'd just make it worse." He peered closer at an uncovered gash. "We should put a little more ointment on these exposed parts, though. We're going to be fighting infection here."

"I'll do it," Jerry said.

WE FINISHED BREAKING camp. Thor and I packed Kamal's gear and saddled Sweet. Dunker gave him a couple more big ibuprofen tablets, but the bruises alone would make the two-hour trip back to the trailhead a bitch for him. When we mounted up, Jerry practically lifted Kamal into the saddle. I caught CK's eye, and he raised his eyebrows in mock surprise. We had never seen the big man be so tender before.

As we filed away across the meadow, the dead bear was out of sight back in the timber, but I knew its fur would be riffling in the soft breeze that rustled the trees guarding the carcass.

I rode behind Kamal. It was painful to watch him flinch almost every time Sweet Ginger took a step. He tried to compensate for the bumping by standing in his stirrups until he got too weak to even do that. I heard him whimper a few times, but I'm not sure I would have held up as well. That young man was rawhide tough.

The Fish and Wildlife people were at the trailhead, their bumper pull with the Montana state seal on it sitting next to my rig. A warden wearing a clean straw cowboy hat backed a paint gelding out of their trailer as we rode up.

"Howdy, boys," the second one called out. He was buckling the back cinch on his gray horse's saddle. "Heard you guys had yourselves quite an adventure in the woods. That so?"

"Yeah, I'm afraid it is." Dunker swung down from the saddle. He dropped his reins and reached out to shake the man's hand. "How you doing, Theron?"

"Fine as frog hair. Living the dream. How 'bout yourself?" Theron Henderson nodded over his shoulder toward his blond-haired partner. "Dunker, I believe you already know Joe Weston?"

"Oh, yeah, we've met a couple of times. How's it going, Joe?"

Joe Weston, younger and shorter than Henderson, looked up over his horse's bare back. He grinned, showing bits of snuff in his teeth. "Morning, Dunker. *I'm* doing all right, but how in the hell did you get yourself tied up with *that* piece of shit?" He pointed a gloved hand at Travis. "Couldn't you've found yourself a better cowboy companion than this?"

Travis slid out of his saddle and strode around the rump of Joe's horse. "Smile when you say 'piece of shit,' warden," he growled in Joe Weston's face.

"I did."

Both men burst out laughing.

Travis said, "Good to see you, Joe. You staying out of trouble?"

"Well, apparently, I'm doing a better job of it than you are." Weston scanned the rest of us. Everyone had dismounted except Kamal, who still sat on top of Sweet with his eyes closed, his breath rasping through clenched teeth. "That boy's hurt. He the one that was jumped?"

"Yeah," Dunker said. "That's Kamal. He needs to get out of here quick to a doctor."

"Life threatening?" Theron asked. "You want us to call a medevac?"

"Probably not. He doesn't want to make it into a big deal, but he does need to get going right away."

"I can see that all right," Theron replied.

The two wildlife men watched Jerry and Thor gently lower Kamal to the ground. He could barely stand, even with their help. His head lolled down on his chest.

"Okay," Joe said. "You guys better get him on the road. I'll radio the hospital at Columbus that you're coming." He walked to the cab of the state truck.

"Meantime, Joe and I need to see the bear and where it happened," Theron said. "We need to interview the shooter and at least a couple of eyewitnesses if possible."

"No problem there," I said. "We all saw it."

"I'm the shooter," Jerry said.

Theron eyed Jerry for a second and nodded. He turned to me. "Hey, Jimmy Lloyd. Didn't see you there at first."

"I've been told I don't stand out in a crowd."

We sorted out who would take Kamal to Columbus and who would go back with the game wardens. I decided to stay with the wardens to see if I could help smooth things out for Kamal. Brownie was to hurry our injured young man to the hospital. He loaded his own horse and Sweet Ginger into his trailer. We laid Kamal down in the backseat while CK rode shotgun to watch over him. The old Ford kicked out gravel in the parking lot as Brownie sped away. We watched them disappear around a curve in the tree-lined road.

Chapter Twenty-Four

The mules and CK's horse were put away in Thor's trailer. He would stay with them while the rest of us went back into the wilderness with the two wardens. A pair of hikers getting gear out of a car gaped at us as we rode by on the way to the trail. Henderson's and Weston's badges and pressed khaki shirts contrasted pretty sharply with the rest of us, and those people probably wondered why the law would be taking us back into the wilderness instead of to jail. We certainly looked like a dirty bunch of scofflaws.

The Stillwater smashed itself into foam just like before, only it didn't seem as marvelous as it had before. Fatigue took me way beyond being impressed by fast-moving water. The horses weren't too happy about a return up the river, either. To them, getting back to the trailers meant work was over, and they didn't like the extra trip one bit. Even Snuffy lost his bounce and balked at being turned around. Dunker led the way again. I stayed right behind him, and the two wardens followed me. Jerry and CK played tail gunner.

"Where'd you say all this happened, Jimmy Lloyd?" Theron hollered to be heard against the pounding water.

"Sunlight Meadows campsite," I shouted over my shoulder.

"Sunlight, huh? That's real nice country, all right."

"Yeah."

We didn't talk a whole lot after that. A couple of campers walking out said hello, but that pretty much summed up all our conversations. Our party passed Sioux Charlie and reached relative quiet at the switchback trail that would take us up to the campsite. Dunker reined up.

"Let's let the horses blow a little before we start climbing," he said, patting his mount's neck. "These fellas been working hard all week."

We bunched up without dismounting. Theron stared down at the ground then looked up and down the beaten path. Hikers' footprints were all over, mixed with some of our old horseshoe tracks.

Theron leveled his gaze at Dunker. "You guys were here in these woods five days, and none of you had any idea there was a grizzly around?"

In the silence that followed, Joe Weston fingered a huge wad of chew out of his mouth. He flicked it down hard so that it smacked on some dry leaves like a beaver tail.

Dunker said, "Hell, boys, there's *always* grizzlies in the Beartooths. You know that." He scratched his chin. "But the fact of the matter is... we *did* find fresh bear scat on this very trail a little over a mile that way." He pointed upstream along the main trail we were about to leave.

"When was that?" Joe asked.

Dunker looked around at me. "Oh, 'bout two, three days ago. That sound right, Jimmy Lloyd?"

"Three days," I answered.

"You didn't maybe give any thought to being a little more careful after that?" Theron wasn't smiling. "You stayed out here three more days?"

"Theron, we didn't do anything stupid, so quit trying to say we did," Travis countered. "You think we should just up and leave Dodge every time we step in a pile of bear shit?"

Joe waved a hand at him. "Okay, Travis my man. Nobody's saying anything like that. We're just trying to find out how everything went down."

"We have to do this by the book," Theron added. "You know how it is. Everybody gets excited over a grizzly shooting. The feds will want to investigate, too. Even the governor is going to read this report."

"Well, if it's all that important, let's don't keep the governor waiting," I said.

"I agree, Jimmy Lloyd. Let's go," Dunker said. He lightly touched heels to his horse, and we started to plod the crooked trail up the mountainside.

THE CAMPSITE APPEARED undisturbed. Cold, soaked ashes in the center of a beaten-down area were the only obvious signs of our recent presence. In a month, no one would know we had been there. All of us dismounted and walked down the latrine trail to the bear.

Coyotes hadn't gotten there yet. The night before, we'd spread the body out on its stomach to see its size, and it still lay that way, untouched except for the flies. They swarmed over a bucketful of congealed blood covering the left side of the mangled head and matting fur everywhere. What was left of the lower jaw hung together in shattered pieces splayed out in the dirt. The dry tongue lolled to the side, looking like a piece of liver. The grizzly's eyes glared back at us as if angry we had returned.

Joe Weston whistled. "That's a pretty big boy. Male, eh?"

Theron bent down to study the head. "Damn good shot. Right down the throat. It'll do if you can't hit the brain." He looked closer. "Not wearing a collar. How'd we miss tagging a big one like this?" He started clicking pictures with his cell phone.

"No telling." Weston shifted his wad to the other cheek. "Let's roll him so we can confirm gender and get some measurements." He reached for a giant paw and grunted. "Going to be a job, though. He's stiff as a board."

Turning that bear over was like flipping a seven-hundred-pound sheet of plywood, and it took all six of us to do it. Rigor mortis had set in big time. The carcass crashed, sprawled out and belly up, onto the small bushes nearby. The flies swarmed up in a black cloud around us. A putrid smell came up with them. Theron took more pictures.

"Yep. It's a male." Thor stated the obvious. The silvertip's manhood was on full display with all four of his limbs stretched out stiffly as if he were posing for a bruin porn shoot.

"Whoa. What's this?" Theron leaned closer, peering at the underbelly. He reached down, spreading the thick fur with his fingers. A long red object protruded from the carcass just above the groin area. "What the hell?" He swung his head around to look at us. "You guys know anything about this?"

I studied the thing half buried in hair. "I think that's Kamal's knife. Pull it out, Theron."

He grabbed the red handle and yanked. The thin blade came out easily, even buried hilt deep in the body. Theron held it point up. "Is this what you thought it was?"

"Yeah, that belongs to Kamal," I answered.

"Kamal? He's that kid that was jumped by this bear? The one hurt so bad?"

"That's him."

Weston shook his head. "Well, how the hell did he manage to stick this thing in the griz, especially down that low?"

"The bear was all over him. I guess that's just the spot where he could reach," Jerry answered. "He kept it in his boot."

"His *boot*?" Theron seemed incredulous.

"Yeah, his boot. He's pretty quick with it." Jerry laughed outright. "No wonder the bear jumped up so pissed and knocked the boy away. That little blade stings pretty good."

"I guess so," Theron said.

I held my breath, afraid he would ask Jerry how he knew about that knife's sting. Instead, he studied the small dagger with a straight double-edged blade that ended in a symmetrical point. "It seems like a little toy, though. I sure wouldn't carry this for my knife in the woods."

"Oh, he's got another one, a nice bowie," I said.

Theron eyed me. "So why does he carry this one in his boot?" He looked around at all of us. "Who is this Kamal character anyway?"

"Kamal al Dossari. He's a student at MSU-B," I answered.

"From where?"

"Saudi Arabia."

"Saudi Arabia, huh?" Theron tapped the blade lightly in the palm of his hand. "So what do you know about him?"

Every head turned in my direction.

"He's a good kid," I said. "He rents from me. Pays on time. No trouble at all."

Theron looked back at the dead bear then drew a breath. "Okay, no matter to me, I guess. The feds'll be wanting to talk to him, though. Here—you can give this back to your friend." He started to hand me the knife but stopped. "No wait. Let me get a picture of it." The warden snapped a shot of the little red-handled dagger lying next to where Kamal had punched it into the attacking bear's gut.

"Did you say the feds are going to want to interview Kamal?" I asked.

"Oh sure, you betcha." Theron gave me the knife.

"Well, can't we skip that part? He doesn't want to get into any trouble over this."

Joe Weston was shaking his head even before I finished. "Not our call, Jimmy Lloyd." He nodded at the carcass. "*Ursus arctos horribilis* is a threatened species. US Fish and Wildlife gets involved every time. In fact, we already notified them before we left our office. We got to. I'm sure they'll be sending a team out from Billings today."

"Why do that?" Travis asked. "Your state reports aren't good enough?"

Joe shrugged. "Not to them, I guess. We'll take some preliminary measurements—estimate age and weight—but the feds will haul this big boy outta here and back to a vet clinic."

"A vet clinic? But he's dead!"

"Sure he is, but they want exact stats on him. The biologists will do a necropsy—check his stomach contents, age him by his premolars, check for rabies, DNA—that sort of thing."

Jerry chewed thoughtfully on a twig. "Can I have his hide? I'm the one who shot him."

Both wardens laughed.

"Now that's a good one," Theron said. "No, my friend. No one's getting this hide except the feds. They tell us they tan 'em and preserve 'em for research." He shared a look with Weston. "But somehow, they all end up on some office floors of the big shots in DC."

"Doesn't seem right," Jerry said. "I shot him." He threw the twig down.

"Now you see why Mississippi seceded," CK said. "Didn't treat us right, neither."

THERON HENDERSON AND Joe Weston spent an hour reconstructing what had happened with the bear. They pulled out notebooks and laboriously wrote down our statements. Together, we walked the trail to the latrine site, looking at tracks, broken brush, and the claw marks on trees where we had hung the food chests. The wardens wrote up everything they saw. They inspected Jerry's big-bore revolver and noted the brass from the two fired shells still nested in the cylinder.

"Nice gun," Theron said.

"Did the job," Jerry answered.

Finally, it all ended, and the State of Montana seemed satisfied. Everyone walked back to where the horses were tied. As the others started to mount, I undid the entrenching tool I kept strapped next to the shotgun's scabbard.

Travis noticed I wasn't getting up on Snuffy. "What are you doing, Jimmy Lloyd?"

"Going back to fill in the shitter trench," I answered. In our hurry to get Kamal to a doctor, we'd missed filling in the latrine we had used for five days—an inexcusable breach of camping etiquette. "You fellows go on ahead. I can do it. I'll try and catch up to you." I turned to go toward that beaten path.

"You need help?" Jerry asked.

"I only got this one shovel."

"That's okay. I got a trowel I can use. I'm riding back in your truck anyway."

"Suit yourself."

As Jerry got down and tied his horse again, Theron reined up beside us. "Sorry we can't wait for you two. Joe and I got to be at the trailhead so we can guide the feds back here. No telling when they'll be showing up, but they're coming for sure."

"No problem, Theron. We'll be fine." I paused for a heartbeat. "We appreciate you and Joe's help on this thing. Appreciate your professionalism."

He waved a hand. "Aw shucks, Jimmy Lloyd. Don't embarrass me like that. In this job, the two of us aren't used to getting thanked very often."

I smiled. "Well, I'll say it again, then. Thanks." I reached up and shook hands with Theron then walked over to Joe and did the same.

The four of them started back across the meadow. Dunker stopped and turned around. "Hey, we're going to stop at the hospital in Columbus. We'll probably be there for a while, so why don't you catch us there?"

"Sounds good." I looked at Jerry. "That all right with you?"

He shrugged. "Fine by me."

We waved and started down the latrine trail. Jerry and I made quick work of scooping and shoveling loose dirt over the contents of the latrine. The only problem was the flies that seemed to resent our taking away their treats. They flew around us constantly until we got it all buried. Once the mound was used up, we tamped the soil down before raking leaves and pieces of brush over the spot. I picked up the last roll of toilet paper, and we walked back toward our horses. Without really deciding to, Jerry and I stopped by the bear's carcass. The latrine flies had relocated there, and their buzzing broke the silence between us. We stood back and stared at it.

I glanced at Jerry. "That really was quite a deal, Jerry," I said softly. "I don't know if I could have run up to that grizzly. It was a ballsy thing you did."

Jerry just pursed his lips. For a minute, I thought he wasn't going to answer me. Then he cleared his throat, never taking his eyes from the dead bear.

"Sure you would have, Jimmy Lloyd. That boy's your friend. You would've done the exact same thing if you'd had time to get your shit together." He turned to face me. "I know you well enough to know that."

"Maybe that's true... but Kamal's not a friend of yours. Why'd you do it?"

He looked back at the carcass. When he spoke again, he sounded distracted. "That's a funny thing, you know? The kid was thanking me last night over and over. Said I saved his life, which I did." Jerry chuckled. "You know, that Kamal's not such a bad kid. He said that I saved him even though he hated me. Said he would never forget it. He loves me now." He shook his head slowly. "Hell, the truth is, I wasn't thinking about it was him under that bear. It happened so fast, I just ran over without thinking at all."

Jerry walked up to the body and bent down, grasping a front paw. Ignoring the swarm of flies, he took out his hunting knife.

"What are you doing, Jerry?"

He pretended not to hear me. With quick swipes, he severed first one, then two, of the bear's front claws. He straightened up and held them aloft, a pair of four-inch curved scimitars protruding out between the fingers of his fist.

"I figure I ought to get a little something for shooting him. Fuck 'em if they can't take a joke."

We continued on to the horses. I strapped my entrenching tool back onto the saddle bag. Jerry was already mounted when I swung up on Snuffy.

I looked over at him. "Just tell me one thing, Jerry. Would you have done that if you *had* remembered it was Kamal?"

Jerry pushed his hat back and looked me in the eye. "Well now, that's the funny thing, Jimmy Lloyd—I think I would have."

THE WARDENS WERE STILL at the trailhead, waiting for the feds. Jerry and I said goodbye to them again while we loaded our horses. About thirty minutes down the road, we met a US Fish and Wildlife truck pulling a four-horse trailer. Theron and Joe wouldn't be getting home until well after dark.

The Columbus hospital looked like a 4-H show at the fairgrounds with all the horse trailers in the parking lot. I parked mine alongside the others. Jerry and I found the guys sitting and standing around in Kamal's room. The star attraction himself was sleeping like a passed-out drunk, an IV dripping into his arm. Clean white bandages covered his torso. He looked younger and smaller in that roll-around bed.

"He's going to be fine. Took a few stitches," Dunker told us. "Doc says he's doing okay, but he was real lucky. He said he's seen some that didn't come out so good after a griz attack."

"He been sleeping long?"

"Ever since we got here."

Brownie pointed at the IV bag. "It's something they got in that bag. Knocked him right out."

"All right, you men. It's time to go," a raspy feminine voice said behind me.

The nurse had walked into the room, and she didn't look happy. Streaks of gray ran in her hair, and about thirty extra pounds sat on her hips, but I also noticed laugh lines creasing her face. "I already told you once that there's too many visitors for your friend to handle. He's had too much excitement already, and now there's more of you." Her voice softened. "Your friend's going to be fine. He just needs to rest. Let him sleep now. I'll tell him you were all here and you can see him tomorrow."

"How long's he going to be in here?" Jerry asked.

"Up to the doctor—a couple of days at least. Now go on. Get out of here with all that manure on your boots." The old gal smiled to show she didn't mean anything by it.

We shuffled down the hall and into the lobby.

"Well, I guess that's good news," I said.

"Yeah, he's doing a lot better now that the news people are gone," CK answered.

"News people?"

"Yeah, you missed it, Jimmy Lloyd. Both channels had their cameras out here, wanting to interview him."

"You're shitting me. Did they see him?"

"Nope. The hospital wouldn't let 'em. The nurse said Kamal was still pretty upset about it. They did some video. You know—where the pretty gal stands at the entrance and talks about how a young foreign student 'cheated death' in the wilderness and all that bullshit. They got Henderson's and Weston's names, too."

"How did they even know about it?"

CK raised his hands in helpless surrender. "Between the state office, the feds, the hospital... Who knows how this stuff gets out?"

I had to drop my head and smile in spite of myself. "Boy, Kamal's sure not gonna like that."

Chapter Twenty-Five

The Billings Gazette did a big spread on the bear attack, front page and all. Kamal never did talk to any of them, but the news people managed to get a picture of him anyway, bandaged up and sleeping in his bed. He looked pretty grim, so it didn't surprise me that he had to stay there almost a week. Dunker sat with him the most during that time since the rest of us had to get on back to making a living. At work, I found some wag in the control room had written "Grizzly Adams" on my hard hat and "Davy Crockett" on CK's. That place was a card deck chock-full of jokers.

On my first day off, Kamal called to say he was being released, and I drove to Columbus to bring him home. I found him sitting in a wheelchair at the entrance. I never thought to get him a fresh set of clothes, so he had on the same funky stuff he'd been wearing when he came in, bloodstains and all. His color was back, though, and his face lit up when he saw Ol' Brown pull in under the front portico. A matronly volunteer rolled him to the passenger door.

"Well now, how do you do, boy?" I hollered out the window.

He grinned at me. "Pretty good, Jimmy Lloyd." He turned to the attendant. "May I get out now?"

She nodded and smiled. "Of course you can. Good luck, young man. I hope you keep improving."

"Thank you. I will." He stood, holding a plastic bag full of odds and ends from the hospital, and climbed stiffly into the truck. I realized he was weaker than he looked by the way he slouched in the seat.

"Buckle up."

He clicked the belt together as we pulled out of the hospital area. "They wouldn't let me walk to the front. I had to sit in that wheelchair."

"Yeah, that's part of the deal. They don't want you to fall down on the way out and then sue them for not taking good care of you."

"The lady was very nice."

"I expect so. Those folks that volunteer at hospitals are good people."

Kamal stared at the floorboards. "Everyone here is a good person," he murmured, saying it so low, I almost missed it.

"Well, not *everyone*." I chuckled. "You talking about Americans? Some of us are assholes, you know."

"Yes, I know that, but even those like Jerry can be a friend." He shook his head. "I did not expect this."

The glum expression on Kamal's face made me laugh. "Really? So then why'd you come to Montana, Kamal, if you thought all of us would be assholes?"

He just kept looking at the floorboards.

Before leaving for Columbus, I had called Esther to see if she would check in on him once I got him settled at home. She agreed, much to my great unsurprise. But it did startle me a little to see her sitting on Kamal's front porch when we came down the long driveway. She must have just finished her day shift since she was still wearing her hospital scrubs.

Florence Nightingale couldn't have looked more beautiful.

"Hello, boys. How are you feeling, Kamal?" She bounced out to the truck and opened the passenger door. "Okay, let me help you."

Kamal slid to the ground and would have collapsed, but Esther caught him under his arms. I came around to help, and together, we got him inside.

She shooed me away. "Go on, Jimmy Lloyd. I can handle it from here."

"You sure? What if this hard-headed fool gives you trouble?" I inclined my head toward Kamal, who had dropped into a padded chair.

She looked sideways at him. "Oh, he wouldn't dare. I'm a trained professional, you know."

"Yeah, I guess you got that right."

Esther glanced down at Kamal, who looked about to fall out of his chair. "Hey, c'mon, young man. You don't need to rest on the floor. Let me get you to your bed." She took Kamal by his armpits again, helped him to his feet, then led him in a stumbling gait toward the back room. "Can you wait here a few minutes until I get him tucked in?" she said over her shoulder.

"Sure thing." I went out on the front porch and took a seat on a log bench Esther and I had stained together some years back. I ran a hand over the still-smooth surface. That finish had held up pretty well—better than Esther and I had. After a few minutes, the screen door opened behind me, and Esther came out.

"How's he doing?" I asked.

She put a finger to her lips. "He's sleeping."

"Good. He needs to rest." I patted the seat beside me. "Hey, Queenie, remember this old bench?"

"Sure do. You spent days sawing and sanding on that thing." She smiled a little at the memory but didn't sit down.

"Those were the days, huh?"

Esther leaned down to stroke the bench. "Yes, I suppose they were."

"So how is Kamal really?" I stood up.

"He's going to be fine. Just needs to rest and recover and purge the drugs out of his system for now."

"You sure? Won't he need pain meds or something?"

"Sure, for a little while longer, but he's about weaned off them." She smiled gently. "You won't have to fret about him, Jimmy. Kamal's my friend too." She laid a hand on my forearm and looked directly into my eyes. "I'll make sure to take good care of him for both of us."

"I know you will, Queenie... You've never let me down." I placed my other hand over hers. "Not like I've done you."

She pulled her hand back and looked away. "I've got to get inside and make some soup for when Kamal gets up. You can go on, Jimmy. We'll be fine."

"Sure." I walked out to Ol' Brown.

"Jimmy Lloyd?" I turned around.

Esther leaned against one of the porch posts, her arms crossed across her chest.

"Yeah."

"Remember the first time I sat down on that bench?"

The corners of my mouth twitched up. "Why, yes, as a matter of fact, I do." Esther had sat on it before the polyurethane finish dried. The bench stuck to her bottom when she stood up and ruined one of her favorite pairs of jeans. "But I was swore to secrecy on that matter." I raised my right hand. "And I have never said a word about it to a soul."

She interlocked her hands into a tight fist in front of her with both index fingers pointing at me. "That's exactly right, and you *still* better not *ever* tell anybody, either."

"You know I won't, Queenie." I leaned back to spread my arms along the top of the truck bed and sighed as I rolled my eyes. "But I sure am sorry I wasn't allowed to preserve that pretty shape on the seat." Esther had insisted I refinish the bench top, even though I wanted to leave her imprint there as an example of a pure heart.

Esther smiled to herself and shook her head slowly. "You sure made me laugh back then, Jimmy Lloyd."

"I know." I studied the roofline of the house. "You think you ever could again?"

She straightened and took a deep breath. "I don't know. Not yet." She looked at the yard off to the side. "You better go. I've got a patient to take care of."

I drove off, thinking that Kamal was a luckier man than me in some ways.

FOR THE NEXT COUPLE of weeks, Kamal probably thought he was getting a preview of the seventy-two beauties he could expect when he hit paradise. Not that they were brown-eyed virgins, but Esther, Alice, and Jane must have waited on him hand and foot. I lost count of all their trips past my house, bringing him fried chicken and casseroles. Sometimes, I would sit out on the back deck, sunning with my shirt off, but they still never offered me any. Finally, Alice and Jane did stop by one afternoon on their way in.

"Nice pecs, Jimmy Lloyd," Alice called out from her car.

"It's all for you, sugar."

I slipped on a T-shirt as I ambled out to them. "How's our boy doing?"

"He's doing fine. Getting his stitches out tomorrow when Esther takes him in. But, hey, don't be playing dumb with us, cowboy." Jane laughed. "Kamal already ratted you out. We know you go back to his house and clean up whatever he doesn't eat himself."

I acted real hurt. "Aw now, you ladies got me all wrong. I just take him his mail is all. Speaking of which..." I pulled several flyers and one envelope out of my back pocket. "I got to be delivering this to him in a little bit." I rapped the mail on the car's roof. "What'd you bring him today?"

"Chicken enchiladas," Alice answered.

"Enchiladas, huh? I hope you didn't put too much seasoning in them—for Kamal's sake, you know. His stomach's still a little tender."

Alice smiled like a sunrise. "Up yours, Jimmy Lloyd. Eat like a man. And you might as well come on back there now so you're not scavenging leftovers like a coyote." We all laughed, and I could still hear them cackling as they drove away. Her enchiladas were delicious, and she knew it, no matter how much I might rag on her about the seasoning.

Enchiladas were best hot, so I got in the truck right away. Kamal already had a second plate set out for me on the kitchen table when I knocked and walked in. A pitcher of iced tea sat beside it. Alice and Jane were sitting at the table with him.

"Hello, Jimmy Lloyd. Help yourself. It's very good." He pointed a fork at the pan still two-thirds full of Alice's prize Mexican entrée drizzled with cheese.

"Well, I don't mind if I do," I answered as I drew up a chair. "Here's your mail." I laid it across the table next to him. For the next couple of minutes, I got too busy loading up my plate and eating to pay much attention to Kamal or anyone else. When I did finally look up at him, he had a squirrelly expression on his face as if his whole life savings had just been wiped out in a surefire investment plan from Nigeria. He had stopped eating and held that one letter open in his hand. When he realized I was watching, he folded it quickly and picked up his fork again.

"These are good, aren't they?" he mumbled around a mouthful of enchilada.

"Yeah, Alice's grub is the best," I replied before glancing at her. "Don't take that to your head, lady. Just a slip of the tongue."

"Well then. You don't have to eat it." She reached across the table for my plate and started to slide it away.

I gripped it tightly and tried to give her a repentant look. "Uh, wait a minute. Let's talk about this. Did I say 'slip of the tongue'? I meant 'I want to slip it on my tongue.'"

"Hoooo, that's pretty lame, Jimmy Lloyd. I woulda thought you could think of something better than *that*," Alice replied, but she did wink and push the plate back. Everybody smiled, except Kamal.

I cocked an eyebrow at him. "Is there something wrong? You get some bad news?" I indicated the letter as he stuck it in his shirt pocket.

"Oh no, no bad news at all." But Kamal wouldn't meet my eyes. "I don't think I have told you much about my family, have I?"

"As a matter of fact, you haven't. I don't believe I ever asked."

"No, you have not. You don't ask about things at all, Jimmy Lloyd." He drew a deep breath. "I have some cousins. They will be coming to visit me."

"From Denver?"

Kamal's head snapped back. "How did you...? What do you know about...?" He put his hand over the pocket with the letter.

That response seemed all out of proportion, but I let it pass. I pointed at the empty envelope on the table. "Wasn't hard to figure. No return address, but I saw the postmark."

You would have thought that envelope had suddenly appeared out of nowhere, the way Kamal looked at it. "Oh, I see. Yes, of course." Something in the far hills must have caught his attention then because he kept staring out the window while he talked. He leaned back and cleared his throat. "Yes, they are in Denver, but they would like to come to school here as I do. I have told them about this university."

"Well, okay. You expect they'll stay here with you?"

"Yes, if that's okay. They won't stay long." Kamal answered hurriedly, like a man running out of breath.

"Sure thing. No problem with houseguests. Just don't let 'em go wild and crazy on me. How many cousins you got?"

"I have many cousins, but there will be three or four coming here."

"You don't know for sure who's coming?"

"Four. Four will be staying here."

"Well, that's fine with me. Hell, don't get so nervous about it, Kamal. I don't mind. In fact, I'll be glad to meet some relatives of yours. I got some stories for them. When do they get here?"

"They don't say for sure—two or three weeks, I think." Kamal rubbed his eyebrows with a thumb and forefinger. His enchiladas sat forgotten.

"Well fine and dandy. Bring 'em on."

I finished off my plate and took seconds while the gals and I chatted. Kamal stayed lost in his own thoughts. Finally, I got up. "Excuse me, folks. Nature calls."

I walked back to the bathroom. I tried not to tinkle too loud since the walls in that little house were pretty thin. After I washed and started drying my hands, I could hear Jane talking in the kitchen, and I stopped to listen.

"Why don't you want Jimmy to meet your cousins?" she was asking, clearly surprised.

"It might be better if he did not. Jimmy Lloyd, he is very... I don't know how to say this. My cousins are... older. They are different from me, and he would not understand."

"Understand? Understand what? What's to understand?" That came from Alice.

"My cousins are very set in their beliefs. I don't think he would like them. It would just be better if they did not meet at all in the time they are here."

"Kamal, I think I see what you're saying, but why are you telling us all this?" Jane asked.

"Because I cannot say these things to Jimmy Lloyd. Would you tell him for me?"

I had never been pissed at Kamal until that moment. My face got hot, and I opened the bathroom door. "They won't have to," I said loudly.

Their conversation stopped, and when I walked into the kitchen, they all stared at me, openmouthed. Kamal looked miserable. His foot tapped a mile a minute under the table.

"Is there something else you want me to know, Kamal? Or have I heard enough already?"

"Jimmy Lloyd, I-I did not mean for you to hear—"

"Oh no, that's okay. In fact, it's even better this way. Now you don't have to ask my friends to deliver your chickenshit message for you."

"No no, you don't understand—"

"Maybe I do *understand,* me and you being such good friends and all. You don't want me to meet any of your family. Probably I'm too coarse. Is that it? Too crude for your kin? Well, don't worry about me giving them a bad impression of you. I'll be careful not to interfere with your visiting." I started for the door. "See you around."

"Jimmy Lloyd, wait! It's not like that."

"Oh, I think it is, Kamal. I think it is." I walked out to Ol' Brown and yanked the door open.

Kamal came out on the porch. "Jimmy Lloyd, please. I should explain better..."

"You explained it just fine, Kamal. I think I got it now. See ya."

I drove back up to my house, kicking up dust behind me. In the rearview mirror, I could see Kamal standing and watching me.

Chapter Twenty-Six

August

For the next couple of weeks, Alice and Jane stopped on their way to see Kamal with their food delivery, and they tried to convince me to go suck up to him.

"Come on, Jimmy Lloyd," Alice would say. "Ride back there with us. He didn't mean anything by what he said. You're taking it way too hard."

"No thank you, ladies."

Esther even put in a word once when she came with them. Ordinarily, I would walk on eggshells to stay away from her bad side, but not for this one. I tried to explain the best way I could that anytime someone was embarrassed to be seen with me, I would spare them that indignity. She didn't buy it, though.

"You can be so stubborn, Jimmy. So pigheaded. Kamal is sorry he ever spoke to you like that. He's told me several times."

"Funny, he's never said any of that to me. I guess he just likes to talk to you gals."

Esther's face clouded. She turned to walk back to the gravel drive, where Jane waited. Before getting in, she looked at me over the top of the car. "You know he misses you, don't you?"

"Does he?" I waved. "Have a good afternoon, Queenie."

They drove on back to Kamal's place, and I went inside, feeling like shit. Esther was right, of course. They all were. I was one arrogant son of a bitch who would never be caught standing around with flowers and valentines, trying to make up with anyone. I suppose Esther knew that about me better than anybody. I popped a beer and settled in the recliner, zombie-watching Oprah because I couldn't bother changing the channel. I heard Jane's car leaving about twenty minutes later. I didn't get up, and they didn't stop.

ABOUT A WEEK LATER, I sat in the afternoon shade of the front porch, polishing a pair of my show boots for a rodeo the next night in White Sulphur Springs. Out on the highway, a white panel truck went by. I wouldn't have noticed it except that the vehicle was traveling well below the speed limit. It braked right after passing the turnoff to my house. I watched it come around at the next wide spot down the road. The vehicle returned, moving even more slowly, then stopped at the mailbox. As it turned onto my long drive, I put the shoe brush down.

I assumed it was a lost delivery truck. Four Hispanic-looking men sat abreast in the broad cab, jostling against each other as the heavy vehicle bucked from side to side on the rutted roadway. It stopped beside my house. A cloud of blue-gray cigarette smoke wafted out when the driver rolled down his window.

"Can I help you?" I asked, stepping off the porch to walk out to the truck.

"This is where Kamal al Dossari lives?" the driver asked politely, with decent-enough English. He smiled weakly as if unsure of himself. I realized these men were Middle Eastern, not Hispanic.

"Not here. He rents from me, though." I pointed toward the back. "The house is down that way. You'll see it when you top that rise."

"Thank you." The driver took his foot off the brake, letting the truck ease forward.

"Hey, wait a minute," I called. "Are you Kamal's cousins?"

The truck stopped. I saw the driver exchange a quick look with the others before he looked back down at me.

"Yes, he is our cousin. Thank you. Goodbye." The vehicle started to roll again.

"Wait, wait!" I hopped up on the high running board to speak directly into the cab. "Would you give him a message for me? Tell him Jimmy Lloyd wants to talk to him. Would you tell him that? Ask him to stop by the house sometime." I leaned back, still holding on to the cab's frame, because up close, the combination of smoke and dank man sweat was overpowering, even with their AC going. Four pairs of eyes—none of them too friendly—regarded me silently beneath baseball caps. I smiled at the four. "That's me. I'm Jimmy Lloyd McGowan. Pleased to meet you fellows." When no one responded, I stepped down, but I tried again.

"Looks like you guys brought your own furniture. You need any help unloading? I got a couple of hours before work."

They studied me like a stamp under a magnifying glass. The short, darker dude next to the driver answered for them all. "No. Thank you very much. We will do it. Goodbye."

The driver rolled up his window as the white truck started off for real. I stood, watching them go and scratching my head, not believing what I had just done. I hoped Kamal would appreciate my offer to talk and come to see me. The cousins disappeared over the rise. *They're sure not like Kamal. I guess us Americans don't have a monopoly on being assholes after all.* I laughed to myself and went back to finish my boots.

I SPENT THE WEEKEND in White Sulfur Springs, working that rodeo with Bugeye Tommy. Kamal never did stop by to talk when I got back, and after a few days, I regretted ever even making the effort to reconnect with him. *I suppose his cousins* are *all he needs anyway, blood being thicker than water and all.*

Occasionally, I saw a pair of them going by in his Honda, although he rode with them. At first, I would wave or lift a finger to them if I was outside, but they always looked the other way as if they hadn't seen me.

Since they didn't introduce themselves, I gave them names in my head. The one driving the truck had to be Mario Andretti. The dark little guy was Shorty. The other two I thought of as Dandy Don and Dufus for no particular reason except that the Dandy was the best looking one of the bunch. He combed his hair back like Elvis. Dufus just looked funny. Shorty seemed to be the head honcho. He sat shotgun no matter who else rode in Kamal's car.

Chad came by looking for work, and I sent him back to continue painting the barn at the rent house.

"You know where the stuff is, don'tcha?" I asked him. "The paint and brushes are in the front tool room. Ladders's hanging around the side."

"I got it. You coming, too?"

I shook my head. "Nope, not today. I got some things to do here."

"Okay, Jimmy Lloyd. I'll get started. Gonna be slow though by myself." He started walking toward the back.

The truth was, I didn't want to chance running into Kamal since he apparently still didn't want to see me. Then again, I couldn't help myself. "Hey, Chad..."

He stopped and turned back to me.

"Go ahead and see if Kamal will give you a hand. I can pay him, too. Same as usual," I said.

"Yeah, okay, I will." He brightened up at the prospect of working with Kamal. He strode up the rise, twin braids swinging down his back.

Four hours later, he was back, splattered with red paint, and not so chipper. I met him on the deck with a wad of cash in my hand.

"I got 'bout half of one wall done," he said.

"Good man," I answered, peeling off forty bucks and an extra five. I handed him the money. "What do I owe Kamal?"

"Nothing."

"He didn't help you?"

"Didn't show."

I slowly refolded the extra bills and shoved them in my front pocket. "You talked to him?"

"Nope, never saw him."

"That's odd," I said.

Chad looked aside and spit over the railing. "They all odd back there."

I reached for the back screen door. "Come on in, Crow Warrior. Let's grab a Coke, and I'll give you a ride home."

"Thanks, White Eyes."

IT ANNOYED THE HELL out of me when the Drifters crowd kept bugging me about Kamal.

"Where's that young man, Jimmy Lloyd? You never bring him around anymore."

"He's a grown boy now, Alice. He can drive himself if he wants." I took a sip of beer. "Besides, you know the whole deal. He doesn't like us gringos anymore."

"No, Jimmy, I don't think so. *You're* the one who's mad."

The band started up a cover of an Ian Tyson song, *Alberta's Child*. Alice gave me an inviting look. I loved that song, but I couldn't dance right then. I felt mean like the Grinch stealing Christmas, and I really didn't care.

Thor sat with Jane at my right elbow. He eyed me. "Hey, I get it, Jimmy Lloyd. That boy dumped on you." He looked at Jane. "A man doesn't forget stuff like that. Cowboy pride won't let him."

"Oh, cowboy pride, my ass!" she retorted. "You men all act like little boys in a schoolyard."

"I agree one hundred percent," Alice said. "You all need to let it go."

Brownie and Double-D Wanda came back to the table just then, breathing hard from their bout of two-stepping. "What's the fuss about?" she asked.

"Oh, the guys are still pissed at Kamal 'cause he said something *ugly* to Jimmy Lloyd," Alice answered. "I guess he feels disrespected, and that's why he's making a boo-boo lip." She shaped her mouth into a little pout.

Brownie shot a knowing look at me and headed for the restroom. He sure wanted no part of our conversation.

"It ain't all that easy, Alice." Dunker had been sitting quietly with his wife, Jill, just listening until then. "Maybe it's one thing to not be liked, but it's another thing altogether for someone to act *ashamed* of you. That's pretty tough, you know, and that's what I'm hearing our young friend did."

"Now that's just baloney, Dunker! Kamal only asked Jimmy Lloyd to not rush in on his kinfolk like a bull in a china shop—like he usually does."

"Oh, really now?" Dunker leaned back and settled one arm around the back of Jill's chair. "Let me ask you something." He gestured with his free hand at Thor and Jane sitting across from him. "Supposing Thor's mama was to call him up one day and says she's coming to Billings for a visit. Then supposing Thor says to Jane, 'Honey, my mother's coming for a few days. Would you kindly stay away from the house so she won't see you? You wouldn't like her anyway, darling.' Now what do you suppose Jane's reaction to that would be?"

"I can tell you that right now. I'd scratch his eyes out." Jane laughed and popped Thor on the arm. "But I've already met his mom."

"But that's different, Dunker!" Alice insisted. "That would be a real insult. But here, all you guys are just big nut sacks of testosterone, walking around, looking for something to get jacked up over."

Dunker cocked his hat back. "Well, now you might have a point about that last part, I agree." He leaned forward slightly. "But is this *really* all that different? Kamal doesn't want Jimmy Lloyd to meet his family. Maybe he's embarrassed by his new American friend. Maybe he's embarrassed by me, too—all of us." He gestured around the table. "Tell the truth now. Wouldn't you help Jane scratch Thor's eyes out if he ever hinted she wasn't good enough to meet his mother?" He looked sideways at Jill. "I know *she* would," he said, squeezing Jill's shoulders and pulling her closer.

"Damned straight, I would," she said. Jill only stood about five feet and three inches, and her long braid was more gray than brunette, but not one of us sitting there doubted that she could do it.

Alice dropped her stare. "I see your point, I suppose. But still..." She pivoted to me. "I'll admit Kamal was wrong to say that stuff about you, but can't you be a bigger man anyway? Why don't you just go and sit down with him? Work it out between you and him? Kamal told us he's sorry he ever hurt your feelings. It was a mistake."

Nobody knew I'd already asked Kamal to come talk with me. I guess the fact that he hadn't responded was why this whole thing really chapped me. Maybe his family hadn't even relayed the message, but he still could have come on his own. I slapped my hand on the table. "All right, I tell you what. Why don't *you* go and be friends with him? You go and buddy up to him and his kin, 'cause I'm sure not."

Alice and Jane looked at each other then at Wanda.

"We just might do that," Jane said.

"Fine by me," I answered.

"And I'm going to ask Esther to go with us," Alice added.

"Even better."

The drive home seemed longer than usual when I left the Drifters that night. Silver-edged clouds drifted overhead, and the moon played peekaboo with me when I finally got out of Billings to hit the last short stretch of highway. I glumly listened to the tires whine in the dark.

At the house, I opened the front door and walked straight through to the kitchen to take the last can of Bud Light from the fridge. I went out on the back deck, where I could hear the night noises, mostly coyotes yipping at that evasive moon. Usually, that put me in a good mood, but not tonight. I sat down in a deck chair, popped open the beer, and did some pondering.

The gals were right. Alice, Jane—all of them. Of course the fellows were backing me on this Kamal thing, but the fact was I had been a complete buttwipe, overreacted, as usual, and was too stubborn to admit it. I sighed and took a sip. *I'll fix this in the morning.* I stood up to pour the rest of the can out over the railing. *No more trying to contact him through those asshole cousins. I'll go see him tomorrow myself.*

Chapter Twenty-Seven

The next morning, I rattled back to the rent house in Ol' Brown. Kamal was standing on the front porch before I could get the truck's door open. His smile seemed weak, like his insides were hurting, as he raised a hand in greeting. "Hello, Mr. McGowan."

"*Mr. McGowan?*" I said, sliding out of the truck. "Hell, we're not *that* mad, are we?" I walked up to him and reached out to shake his hand. "How you been getting along, Kamal?"

His smile brightened a little, but he wouldn't meet my eyes. His handshake was also weak. "I'm fine. You are well, too?"

"Good as I can be." A curtain flickered in one of the front windows behind Kamal. I indicated the porch steps between us. "Step down here, and let's sit and talk."

He hesitated and glanced back at the door. "Okay."

We sat staring straight ahead, like two awkward teenagers with a chaperone, before I cleared my throat. "Just wanted you to know that I realize I've been sort of a jerk these last few weeks." I turned to face him. "I flew off the handle when I shouldn't have, and I'm sorry about that."

Kamal kept his head bowed, looking down at his hands gripped between his knees. "That's okay, Jimmy Lloyd. I should not have insulted you that day."

"Aw hell no, boy." I slapped him on the back. "I freely admit I can be a jackass sometimes. I wouldn't want any of my family around me, either."

"Yes. That's true."

"Wha—"

Then I saw Kamal's little possum grin as he punched my shoulder.

"You jerkwad," I said, laughing. "How about it? Friends again?" I stuck out my hand once more.

"Friends still." He took my hand firmly this time and shook it hard.

"Tell you what I'll do, Kamal." I glanced back at the window and lowered my voice. "I'll just keep leaving you alone to visit with your cousins, and once they leave, me and you'll just take up where we left off. In fact, I got an elk-hunting trip coming up this fall. How's that sound to you? You ever been on a bow hunt?"

"No, I have not. That would be good." Kamal's voice was saying the right stuff, but his face went glum again.

"Okay then. I'll get back to you once they're gone. When are they leaving anyway?"

He shuffled his feet. "Uh, I'm not—"

The screen door popped open. "Kamal!" Shorty stood in the doorway. "There is more work to do." He glared at me for no reason I could think of. "You can talk to Mr. McGowan another time."

An electric cattle prod in the ass wouldn't have made Kamal jump up any more quickly from those porch steps.

I rose a little more slowly. "That's fine. I was just about to go anyway." I walked to the truck and opened the door. "I'll be seeing you, Kamal."

"Yes." Kamal stood next to Shorty on the porch, almost a head taller than his cousin but looking completely cowed by him.

As I started to crank the engine, Kamal broke away and ran out to the truck's window. "Thank you for coming, Jimmy Lloyd." He glanced over his shoulder at Shorty. "It was good of you. I have missed talking to you and Chad."

"No problem. I'll be sure to tell Chad, too."

Kamal practically sprinted back past Shorty and into the house. As I drove home, I wondered what Shorty's problem could be. I felt sure he had listened in on my conversation with Kamal. *So what's he so torqued about? I didn't said anything wrong.*

That's when the whole thing popped me right across the bridge of my nose. *I* wasn't the asshole. *They* were. Kamal had tried to keep me away from his family because of their attitudes, not mine. I smiled to myself. *Well, this is something new.* Ol' Brown eased to a stop at the house, but I sat there for a minute, thinking. I hadn't been making the situation too comfortable for Kamal, but I could make it all up to him once the others left.

We'll bag us an elk, Kamal. Promise. I stepped out of the truck and walked into the house, feeling better than I had in weeks.

COMING HOME FROM WORK a few days later, I stopped at my mailbox out on the highway. After I shuffled through the junk mail, I noticed Jane's car sitting up at my house. *This can't be a good thing.*

Four doors popped open when I pulled up and parked alongside it. The whole girl crew had come calling: Jane, Esther, Alice, and Double-D Wanda, all wearing frowns like they had just stopped by after a wake.

"Hello, ladies."

"Jimmy Lloyd, we got to talk," Alice said. "Can we come in?"

"Sure, you can. When have you ever had to ask?"

The four trooped in behind me and settled down on my sofa and chairs. I brought out another chair from the kitchen for myself while Wanda took in the ribbons and belt buckles displayed on my rodeo wall.

I sat and propped an ankle on one knee. "Well, ladies, what can I do for you?"

Esther must have been the designated spokesperson, because everybody looked at her. "Jimmy, it's about Kamal..."

I had figured as much, so I held up a hand. "Queenie, I appreciate all of you coming out here to see me, but I've already made it up to that boy. Kamal and I are friends again. True buddies. I'm just gonna lay low for a while until his kinfolk leave. So if your intent is to get me to change my mind, it's already a done deal, and I'm afraid you've wasted your time." I uncrossed my legs and started to rise. "Now would you gals like some iced tea or—"

"It's not that, Jimmy. There's something else wrong!" Esther leaned forward with wide, intent eyes. "Back at the rent house. Something's going on."

"Things go on all the time, Queenie. What the hell are you talking about?"

Esther looked around at the others. Alice held her palm out, giving her the floor again.

"We went back there to see Kamal today."

"All of you?"

"Yes."

"So what's the problem? Didn't he tell you that we're going steady again? I gave him my class ring, and he's giving me an oil well. Everything is beautiful." I held my arms out dramatically.

"Jimmy, for once, just listen. For once. This is serious."

I settled back in the chair. "Go on."

"You're right. We did go back there to see if we could help patch things up between you two. Alice even took a platter of chocolate chip cookies to barter with." Esther glanced at Alice and grinned a little. She also fidgeted with the turquoise ring she always favored, more rattled than I'd seen her in a long time. "The problem was... Kamal didn't come to the door."

"Well, maybe he wasn't home."

"No, no that's not it. His car was there. One of his 'cousins'"—Esther made quotation marks with her fingers—"answered. Jimmy, it was so creepy. The guy wouldn't even open the door all the way at first."

I shrugged. "I got to say, so far I don't see any problem. Any man would be intimidated by you four."

"Just *listen*, Jimmy Lloyd. There's more," Jane interjected. "He said Kamal was out, but he couldn't have been. His car and that big white truck were both parked right there."

"And then the guy didn't want to take the platter when I tried to leave the cookies for Kamal," Alice added. "He just smiled and waved me off. I must have looked like a fish, standing there with my mouth open. He finally said I could leave them on the porch chair."

"That's when he told us to not come back. He said we weren't allowed there," Jane said.

"He can't do that, can he?" Wanda asked. "I mean... you own the house, Jimmy Lloyd. Can't you kick them out or something?"

I could feel my face getting hot. "I certainly would like to, but I don't think it's all that easy to do. I can't just say for Kamal and them to get out because I don't like the way one of them thinks."

Esther leaned forward. "Wanda didn't mean Kamal. I'm positive he's not the cause of this. Just tell those others to leave. Can't you at least do that?"

I shook my head. "Kamal pays his rent steady, and as long as his cash has dry ink on it, I have to let him and his guests stay." I pulled on an earlobe while I thought for a second. "Which one of them talked to you, anyway? Did you see any of the other cousins?"

"Oh yeah, you betcha we did," Alice replied, nodding emphatically. "That was the *really* creepy part. When we turned around to go, the other three had come up in the yard between us and the car. We all got a little scared right then."

All the gals nodded and looked at each other.

"Here's what's scary," Alice continued. "Nobody saw it except me, but the guy at the door made a little motion with his hands like he was shooing chickens. He was telling them to step aside. I don't think they intended to let us out of there if he hadn't done that. I really don't."

"Was that doorman the one darker than the rest of them?"

"Big time darker," Wanda said. "Like he spent way too much time at the tanning salon."

I stood up. "All right, ladies. I think I get the big picture here. I don't believe I can evict any one of them yet, but I tell you what—I'll talk to Travis first and see what the law allows. Then, no matter what he tells me, I *will* go and have a few words with Kamal about the conduct of his cousins."

"There's still one other thing, Jimmy," Esther said.

I raised an eyebrow at her. "What else?"

"Sweet Ginger. I only saw her from a distance in the back corral, but she's caked with mud and looking thin. Kamal's not taking care of her like he used to, and I'm about to come take her back."

"Whoa, Queenie. It might be better if I do that for you. I'll just move her up here with my horses like before."

"Thank you, Jimmy. I thought you might offer." Esther looked at me in a way she hadn't in a long time. We were silent for a few seconds, and it felt like we were alone, but I didn't know what else to say.

"Okay. We're done here," Wanda blurted. "You two can get a room later. We got to go."

Esther started for the door with the other women. She turned back just before going out. "Thanks for patching things with Kamal, Jimmy Lloyd. I know you have a good heart. Promise me you'll check on him right away."

"I will, Queenie. I promise. And I'll go get Sweet, too. Just let me talk to Travis first." I walked over to her and put my hand out. We only touched fingertips, but that touch jumped in me like a bolt of energy from God. Then the screen door swung shut behind her. She walked down the steps to the car and got in. I followed her onto the porch.

Jane yelled out the car window as she backed away, "Tomorrow's Friday, Jimmy Lloyd. You coming to dance with us?"

Esther looked at me from the back seat and gave me a barely perceivable nod.

"I suppose I could, ladies," I replied from the porch. "Got to leave early, though. I'm helping Thor Saturday."

"Yes, you are," Jane called back. "I'll make sure you both get home early."

They laughed and waved. I watched them drive off, replaying that little nod of Esther's. Was she saying she would be at the Drifters tomorrow night, too? *Don't be stupid, Jimmy Lloyd. You're hanging your hat way too high up on the wall.*

The gals' story unsettled me more than I had wanted to let on, especially the part about Sweet. Kamal loved that horse, and for him to neglect her meant something really must have gone sideways back there at that little house.

Just as I'd expected, Travis didn't tell me anything useful or good when I called him.

"Sorry, bud, but you can't throw anyone out on the street without going through the whole due process. I bet I've served dozens of eviction notices myself, and none of them were easy on the landlord. And let me tell you, some of those tenants had done stuff way worse than anything you've told me about in this case."

"Yeah, I pretty much figured that," I replied.

"Well, you could go at it from another angle. Have they broken any of the terms of your lease?"

"Don't have a lease. Never needed one before."

Travis laughed. "No lease? Dude, you are really hosed. Are you even putting that rent money on your income tax?"

"Hell, you know I'm not."

"Well, there's your problem." He chuckled, and I knew he was shaking his head. "If they wanna make a stink about getting kicked out on the sidewalk, then you, my boy, could be in big-time trouble with the IRS. Hell, they might even send *me* to arrest *your* sorry ass." He laughed out loud at the thought.

"Yeah, well, thanks for caring, Travis."

"Hey, Jimmy Lloyd, don't get mad at *me*. I'm on your side, remember?" He paused. "Tell you what. I'm working the day shift tomorrow. You want me to bring the cruiser out there? I could have the blue lights winking, ask to see their papers—stuff like that. Might scare them a little. How would that be?"

I thought about it for a second. "Naw, thanks anyway, though. I don't want to get Kamal all riled up. I don't think he's the problem."

"You still like that kid, don'tcha?"

"Yeah. Underneath all this bullshit, I still think he's an okay guy. It's that family of his that's starting to bother me."

"All right then, Jimmy Lloyd. Sorry I couldn't give you any better news."

"No problem, Travis. Catch you later."

Chapter Twenty-Eight

I was beat from work and still sore from the rodeo, so I slept in late Friday morning and didn't get up until seven thirty, when the sun was already bright and getting hot. I ate breakfast on the back deck then padded around the house in my socks for another hour, waiting for Chad White Horse to come by as I'd asked. The barn still needed painting.

I stayed busy doing a little housecleaning, a little laundry, a little bill paying. Finally, I decided he wasn't going to show, and it was getting late. *Time to go see Kamal and his kinfolk.* I pulled my boots on.

A colony of prairie dogs had moved in on the northwest corner of my pasture weeks before. They would eventually dig enough holes to be a danger to the livestock If I didn't take care of it soon, so I figured it might be a good time to pick off a few. I got out the Henry .22 and a brick of long rifle bullets, intending to go do some eradicating after my little chat with Kamal. I laid the Henry and ammo on the back seat before I climbed in Ol' Brown.

Everything looked normal, even serene, when I came over the rise and down the slope to the rent house. Kamal's Honda was parked in front of the house, and his cousins' big delivery truck had been left over by the barn. I parked next to the car and got down. Nobody answered when I rapped on the screen door.

I pounded louder. "Hello? Anybody home?" I called. "Kamal, you in there?" I opened the screen and put my ear to the wooden door. Nothing.

"What do you want?"

I jumped. When I turned around, I recognized the van's driver, Mario Andretti. He stood on the ground next to the corner of the porch, apparently having come from somewhere behind the house.

"Oh, hello. Didn't hear you come up," I said. "Hate to bother you, but I wanted to see Kamal."

"He is not here. Is there a problem?" A second voice spoke. Shorty stood at the opposite end of the porch. He must have come up quietly on the other side of the house. Both men had their shirts off and were sweating profusely as if they had been working out in the heat before I interrupted them.

"No. No problem. I just wanted to talk to him about the mare and some other stuff. So where is he anyway? His car's right here." I gestured to the parked vehicle.

"He is gone," Shorty said.

"I know. You said that, but where'd he go without his car?"

"He went to see his family. We took him to the airport."

"What? When?"

He rolled his eyes to the side, mentally calculating. "It was a week ago."

Dufus, also without a shirt, joined Shorty beside the porch. *Why do I feel like they deliberately want me standing between them?* I knew there had to be a fourth guy somewhere. I looked over my shoulder before I spoke. "He didn't say anything to me about it. He go back to Saudi Arabia?"

Shorty rolled his eyes again. "Yes."

"He's coming back?"

The darkest cousin lowered his gaze then glanced at the man beside him. "Yes, he will return. He *likes* it here, Mr. Jimmy Lloyd."

He was lying, and I knew it. I challenged the lie with my stare, but he wouldn't look away.

"Fair enough then." I stepped off the porch and turned toward Sweet's corral.

"Stop! Where are you going?"

"To check on the horse," I said over my shoulder.

"You can't go back there."

That really pissed me off. I spun around to face Shorty. "Don't you be telling me where I can't go, sir," I answered angrily. "This is *my property*. Kamal rents this house, but the barn and corrals belong to me. Now, if you boys will excuse me, I'm going to go see about the welfare of that mare." I was so mad, I might have been shaking.

"Wait. I will come with you." Shorty hurried out toward me. That was when I caught Dandy Don standing farther back against the house where I couldn't have seen him from the porch. Bare chested like the others, he held one hand behind his back—a Wild West posture I didn't like. I turned, and Shorty had to trot to catch up with me.

"The horse is fine," he puffed as he fell in step beside me.

"I'll just see about that." The back of my neck crawled, feeling the stares of the other cousins. I felt sure that Dandy alongside the house was packing in his back waistband, where his hand rested. *Oh well, in for a dime, in for a dollar.* I walked on, trying to look confident.

Once around the corner of the barn, I drew up short at the corral, shocked by what I saw. Sweet stood at the far railing, listless, her head drooping almost to the ground, her coat caked with mud. I could see ribs through the matted hair. She looked like she hadn't been fed in days. The door to her inside stall had been shut, so she wouldn't have been able to get out of the rain. I stepped closer and leaned on the rail.

"Sweet? Hello, baby. Come here, girl." I called to her softly, and she didn't seem to hear me at first. "Come see me, Sweet," I called again.

The mare swayed then swung her head ponderously in my direction. She nickered weakly and walked toward me slowly like an old man.

Shorty glanced at my face anxiously. "See? She is okay."

I reached up to stroke Sweet's face before I probed a finger into the side of her mouth in the gap where the bit would lie. Her tongue was dry. I strode over to the water trough next to the barn—bone-dry empty.

"What the hell is this?" I whirled back to Shorty, my fists clenched. I could feel my jaw tighten. "You couldn't even find the time to turn on her water?" I grabbed the cold-weather faucet handle at the fence and gave it a quick yank. Cool water pounded on the bottom of the galvanized container, sounding like Niagara Falls hitting an empty oil drum.

Sweet Ginger's ears shot up, and she went quickly to the trough to bury her nose in the shallow swirling water. I watched her taking in great gulps for a half minute before I turned off the water. She would get sick drinking too much at once.

I looked at Shorty. "I ought to kick your ass."

Shorty straightened his shoulders with his chin raised. I truly wished he would take a swing at me, but he only stared at me with unconcealed hostility. If a look could have done bodily harm, I would have gone into pain right then and there. I turned away to head for the barn door.

"Stop!" he called behind me. "Where are you going now?"

"She needs hay. This horse hasn't been fed in a week." I reached the door and started to slide it open.

Shorty caught up and put his hand out to stop me. "You can't go in there. It is an invasion of privacy."

So now he belongs to the ACLU? I didn't care. "I believe I already explained to you once that I can go where I want here. The horse has her hay rack in the inside stall, and I'm going to feed her in there. Now, out of my way." I jerked open the door.

The interior of the barn was dark, so I stopped just inside to let my eyes adjust. Shorty stepped in and stood silently behind me. The center aisle was lined with stacks of wooden crates, most of them shaped like little four-foot-long coffins with rope handles on the ends. It smelled like a grease gun had exploded in there.

"What's all this shit?" I asked angrily.

"Tools."

I looked at him over my shoulder. "Tools? You selling tools here? What kinda tools you sell from a barn?"

"It is equipment for oil drilling."

"Well, that's just Jim Dandy. I guess you boys would know about drilling for oil, all right. You know I ought to charge you extra for this storage." I walked through the crates toward Sweet's stall, but one of the stacks had been placed against its gate. I turned around to face Shorty. "Damn it all! Look at this! I can't even get to the stall to feed her with all this crap here in the way." I grabbed the rope of the top crate and tugged. It felt like trying to pull an anvil. "Damn," I grunted. "Help me get these moved."

Shorty had already hurried next to me. Without a word, he took the handle on the other end and helped me swing the heavy load down. Something clinked inside. The crates had been stacked four high, and it didn't take long to clear a pathway to the box stall.

I looked at him. "Kamal didn't tell you guys to take care of this horse?"

He tried for an innocent expression, but it didn't sit well on his face. "He said nothing to us about her."

You're covering something up, you lying sack of shit. I threaded my way through more boxes to the back of the barn where Sweet's hay was stored, my new helper staying Velcroed to my side. Something had been set near the back door with a tarp thrown over it. I jerked a thumb at it. "More tools, I suppose."

"Yes."

Shorty was still sweating hard, and even in the dim light, I could see he was nervous. His face twitched like he had swallowed too much Ex-Lax while he watched me split out two pats of hay from a loose bale. Any more than that wouldn't have been good for Sweet, considering the shape she was in. Once I had the hay in her feedbox, I unlatched the outer stall door and let her come in. Shorty watched every move.

Sweet Ginger stumbled through the door. Up close, I could run my hands over her back and side, feeling every rib. She appeared to be in even worse condition than I had thought. I brushed clods of dried mud off her coat.

"Poor baby," I crooned in her ear. "Good girl. Everything's going to be all right now."

It was a sorry sight to watch how Sweet devoured that hay, almost choking on it. I didn't think she would have lived another day if I hadn't checked on her. She would have just lain down that evening and never gotten back up. *And these assholes probably wouldn't have even noticed.* I exited the stall and closed the Dutch door gate behind me.

"She will be okay now. Everything is fine," Shorty said, nodding. He stepped back and aside as though he wanted me to pass by.

Instead, I put my hands on my hips and lowered my face until my nose stopped inches away from Shorty's. "I'm going to go hook up my trailer and haul that horse out of this hellhole you've put her in, and *then...* I'm calling the sheriff on your asses for animal abuse. Start packing your bags right now, because you're out of here. I don't care if you're in jail or if they fly your asses back to Saudi A-fucking-rabia. Either way, you're gone—all of you."

Shorty's hard stare met and matched my own. So much hate passed through that space between us that I was surprised the air didn't crackle. Then, slowly he started to smile—the cruel smile of a brutal man who'd just realized he had the upper hand. "Of course. We will leave as you wish," he said, speaking as if he were soothing a baby. "We don't want to cause any disturbance here. There is no need to call the police."

"Too late for that, bub." Suddenly, I didn't feel nearly as sure of myself as I tried to sound. I could see Shorty's calmness was papering over a tightly wound spring. It gave me the same feeling I got standing too close to a coiled rattlesnake. A chill melted down my back. I needed to leave before the chute busted wide open.

"As you say then," Shorty said softly. That feral smile never changed as he turned to lead me from the barn. Mario and Dufus waited just outside.

I blinked in the bright sunlight. *Where's the dude with the gun?* I elbowed through the waiting pair and started walking for the truck, my scalp tingling with alarm. Behind me, Shorty was speaking low and fast to his kinsmen at the barn door. They answered in excited voices, apparently disagreeing over something. I glanced back then tried to speed up without actually breaking into a run across the dirt barnyard. The three of them started following at a distance.

When I came up to the house, Dandy was sitting in a lawn chair on the porch, holding a newspaper in his lap. He eyed me suspiciously as I approached Ol' Brown. I yanked open the truck door to slide behind the wheel quickly. Sweat dripped into my eyes, and I paused to wipe it with the sleeve of my shirt.

"Mr. McGowan, stop! We should talk about this," Shorty yelled. I looked back at him through the passenger window. He was trotting, the three of them angling to get behind me. As an answer, I fired up the motor and shifted into reverse. The old Dodge rocked on its shocks as I cut the wheel hard to spin it around, facing toward home. Shorty yelled again. Out my side window, I could see him screaming at Dandy on the porch and pointing at me. I couldn't understand what he said in whatever language he used, but I picked up on the intent.

I jammed the shift lever into drive and floored the accelerator. Gravel sprayed the porch. In the mirror, Dandy threw both arms up to shield his face. He jumped to his feet, and a black pistol—some kind of automatic—clattered from the newspaper onto the wooden deck. Ol' Brown rattled and shook across the cattle guard while I hunkered my head down between my shoulders. *What the hell is going on?*

Crack! I'd never been on the muzzle side of a gunshot before, and I didn't like the sound at all. *Crack!* The tailgate clanged when it took the hit. A flurry of shots boomed behind me. Four, maybe five, more bullets pounded into the truck. Suddenly, Ol' Brown lurched to the right, bucking like a rodeo bull and steering like a blind mule. Mohammed Dandy back there had somehow holed both my right-side tires. I kept the pedal down, and the truck lumbered painfully up the gentle rise, fishtailing me away from the shooter, spewing dirt and dust from its shredded radials.

Pop! The windshield spiderwebbed in the center. The bullet for that special effect had shattered the back window and passed right by my ear. I wasn't sure if I'd hollered or not, but I did let go of the wheel to throw myself sideways over the glass-splattered center console. Ol' Brown nose-dived hard into the shallow ditch on the right side of the road to crash and die there. I slammed up against the dash when the truck hit.

Chapter Twenty-Nine

Dazed, I lay there for a second, trying to clear my head. *That idiot shot at me?* My ribs ached like blazes, and my head had taken a rap as if Jacob's Ladder himself had finally gotten me on the ground. Faraway, excited voices gradually worked their way into my consciousness. I shifted a little and raised my head enough to look out the passenger window. The rental house sat about a hundred yards away.

Handsome Dandy Don must have emptied his magazine. He still stood alone on the porch, just holding the pistol down at his side and watching the truck. I didn't see anyone else. That babble of voices came from inside the house. Dandy saw me and turned around to yell something at them. The front screen door banged open, and the other three hurried out, carrying AK-47s. Someone handed an extra one to Dandy.

What kind of wasp's nest have I stumbled into? I couldn't be sure what was happening or why. I only knew it wasn't good. The pain in my ribcage made me gasp when I reached back to open the driver's door. Then it hurt some more when I kicked the door open and slid out backward on my stomach until my feet hit the ground.

Staying low, I couldn't see the cousins anymore, but I could hear them talking over the ticking of the dead motor. Their voices were getting closer. I yanked open Ol' Brown's back door. The Henry .22 had been pitched to the rear floorboards in a jumble with an old coat and rope. Fighting panic, I grabbed it and the brick of long rifle shells next to it.

I sat back against the truck and twisted the rod to open the tubular magazine. My fingers shook as I crammed four tiny rounds into the tube's feed slot. I stopped there to close it up and cock it. The voices stopped abruptly on the other side of the truck. There was no mistaking the sound of a lever action jacking a round into the chamber. I could have counted to ten in the silence that followed.

"Mr. McGowan, are you okay?" That was Shorty's voice.

I braced myself against the rear wheel. Somehow, I knew better than to answer.

"I'm sorry, Mr. McGowan. My cousin got excited. He didn't understand that we have worked out an understanding about the horse. He meant no harm. We will be leaving now. You can come out."

They waited in silence.

I stayed put. *No way, Jose.*

Another barrage of shots zinged through the cab next to me. Had I still been lying in that front seat, I would have reenacted the deaths of Bonnie and Clyde. When the shooting stopped, Shorty gave orders in Arabic, and feet scuffed in the gravel road, traveling to the side. Someone was trying to come around me in the roadway. *No time to think about it now.*

I popped up. Three of the cousins, still shirtless, stood side by side in the road about thirty feet away, holding their weapons at port arms. Mario Andretti had split off and come a bit closer at the side.

It's funny some of the things you notice when you're about to crap yourself. When I pointed my rifle at Mario, his mouth made this little round O. I ignored the Henry's scope and just sighted the barrel and pulled the trigger. A little pop of blood jumped out from his bare shoulder.

I collapsed down behind the truck's bed, recocked, and yelped at the pain in my ribs as I rolled away from the wheel well toward the front. No one heard me for their own gunfire dumping rounds all over where I had just been. Large-caliber bullets tore and whined through the sheet-metal sides to kick up gravel on the road behind me. I prayed they wouldn't hit the gas tank. The last tire blew out, and battered Ol' Brown sagged down in the dirt like a swamped bass boat.

When the shooting stopped, I came up and snapped off a one-handed shot across the hood, pointing at Shorty. I missed him, but the four of them must have run out of ammo and suddenly realized how exposed they were, standing there like Keystone Kops out in the road. They all yelled at once before I heard them slamming gravel running back toward the house as I lay in the ditch behind the truck.

Since bullets had stopped pinging off the engine block, I crawled to peek around the front bumper just in time to see the four cousins scramble up the porch steps and into the house. Mario was holding his shoulder, although the injury didn't seem to be slowing him down any. I slumped down with my back against the front wheel. I took two painful deep breaths. Then three. Then four. I had bruised ribs—maybe a cracked one. *What the hell is going on?* Those Arab boys had just come completely unglued. *Over what? Over me threatening to go after the law?* It hadn't been an empty threat, and Shorty knew it, but still...

I put my hand to my throbbing left temple, and it came away smeared with blood. Probably hit a radio knob when Brown crashed into the ditch. I would live. I smiled to myself in spite of the situation. If those fellows had only known how dinky my gun was against all their firepower...

My smile faded as I realized just how close I had come to getting my shit blown away. I still didn't have enough gun, and it wasn't over yet. Maybe I *wouldn't* live.

I shook a handful of shells into my left palm. The sides of the pickup bed had been so shot up, it was easy for me to find a spot where I could look through a gaping hole and watch the house while I reloaded. My hands still trembled as I poked the little bullets in, making sure the Henry got up to chockablock full, seventeen long rifle rounds.

Nothing moved at the house. But they were watching, sure enough. I would certainly bet on that. Behind me, the roadway gradually climbed for another hundred feet before it crested the rise on the way back to my house. If I could stay in the ditch and keep what was left of the truck between the house and me, I might make it over to some better cover. It seemed like a fine plan, except for the matter of my ribs. I couldn't run, and I couldn't crawl much, certainly not that far up the hill. I considered just staying put to keep them bottled up in the house until I got some help. It was time to call 911.

I patted the shirt pocket where my cell phone had been before the dance started. Empty. No sign of the phone anywhere on the ground nearby, either. Thinking it must have fallen out in the cab, I lay down, gripping the half-opened door's lower edge to ease it out wider.

Three quick shots shattered the quiet. The first round hit the cab; the other two screamed overhead. I ducked for a few seconds, wishing Kamal's cousins hadn't had any extra ammo in the house.

I checked Ol' Brown's floorboard. No cell phone on this side. It had to be on the passenger side. I crawled in, keeping low on the floor, all too aware of the holes in the far door. I couldn't keep counting on all of them being poor shots if they saw me. I probed over the center hump with my outstretched arm. Nothing except my hat.

A man needs a good hat in a firefight. I raised it enough to see the right floorboard. The pain felt like an ice pick twisting between two of my left ribs. My phone lay out of reach, against the passenger door. I had to take short, shallow breaths to climb up on the ruined front seat. Sliding over glass shards and wads of shot-up foam padding, I scooted close enough to pick up the phone. From there, I could look out through the bullet holes. I scanned the house and everything around it. Nothing moved at first, but then I caught a flash of bare torsos running toward the barn to the right. It looked like they intended to outflank or get behind me.

I backed out of the cab like a crawfish. The .22 looked like a kid's toy leaning against what was left of the truck bed, but I snatched it up. Braced against the side of the cab, I settled the scope's crosshairs at nine power on the center of Shorty's back then raised it a bit to allow for the distance. I could see his sweat as he sprinted.

The little gun barked like a Chihuahua when I squeezed the trigger. Nothing else happened. I watched through the optics, but Shorty still ran strong, apparently not feeling a thing. Somehow, I had missed.

Before I had a chance to cuss at myself, the top of the cab exploded into shredded metal as a bullet pounded into it. I hit the ground once more. "Jimmy Lloyd, you idjit." Three of them had been running. That left the fourth one in the house to cover me. I was just lucky none of these fellows appeared to be sharpshooters.

But then I had missed, too, and normally, I could pick off a prairie dog at a hundred yards. The Henry had taken a fall off the back seat in the truck wreck, and that bump must have knocked the scope out of alignment. I didn't have time to re-zero it. If they were trying to get behind me, I had to move fast.

Across the road to my right, a jumble of sandstone slabs heaved up out of the dry ground near Ol' Brown's carcass. On my side of the road, the terrain was mostly smaller chunks and cactus. It would be better to go right and meet them behind good cover, before they expected to see me. All I had to do was get over the roadway without being shot up by the guy sitting in the house. I put on my hat.

Adrenaline was all I had going for me as I skittered across the gravel road to dive into the far ditch, never giving the guy in the house a chance to draw a bead. The adrenaline didn't stop me from grunting hard when I crashed, but I had to keep going. The rocks made it easy to move without being seen as long as I stayed low. The house sitter fired a few blind shots, and sandstone splinters chipped off around me before he decided not to waste good ammo. I crawled slowly up to the high ground. Years earlier, I'd prowled the rocks regularly, looking for rattlers, and I prayed I wouldn't run into any of those diamondbacks. Payback would be a bitch.

Little stones and pebbles scattered under my boots and elbows as I crawled up the gentle slope. It reminded me of stalking antelope.

Lord, my ribs hurt! I had to stop every ten feet or so to grit back that agonizing ice pick in my side. Finally, I reached the slab I wanted. It jutted up like the marble headstone of a prominent banker. About fifty yards away from the road, low enough not to be skylined, and with decent cover in front of me, I felt secure enough to test the waters. Off came the hat again, and I cautiously poked my head around the side. Movement, not the lack of camouflage, alerted an antelope to danger. I figured it would be the same with men.

The house looked quiet. Broken glass glittered on the porch on each side of the door where someone had busted out shooting holes in the windows. I looked to my right, searching for the flanking party. Nothing moved. I strained my ears, holding my labored breath to listen. Still nothing. Three men scrambling through these rocks couldn't be hiding their presence that well. *Where are they?*

I leaned up close against the back of the slab to think as I watched. Four cousins—one in the house and three God only knew where. *And Kamal. Where's Kamal?* He hadn't been one of those three running from the house. *Is he waiting at one of the windows down there? Waiting to shoot his friend, Jimmy Lloyd?*

Sitting there, hiding in the middle of that sunbaked sandstone, I finally had a clear moment of realization. The chute opened, and out jumped the devil. *Cousins, my ass.* Whoever or whatever they were, Kamal wasn't one of them. I couldn't figure out the whole situation, but I was sure of that much. I also suspected things probably weren't going well for him, either.

I did finally feel safe enough to ease back behind the tombstone and take out my cell phone. Before I could dial, a sound like a heavy load being dropped came from the direction of the barn. I peeked around the rock. In the corral, Sweet Ginger had her ears cocked and was watching the area behind the barn that I couldn't see. After a few more noises, then I heard a *whump* like an air cannon shooting a pumpkin about ten miles. Excited cries came from behind the barn. Sweet moved away from the fence. Suddenly, a long burst of automatic fire flared from a window at the house. I ducked as bullets pocked the ground all over the hillside in no particular pattern.

"*Allahu Akbar!*" the shooter yelled. A chorus of voices behind the barn responded.

Have they all lost their minds?

The cries stopped. There was another pumpkin whump shot, then another. They came every few seconds almost like clockwork. I rolled to my hands and knees and slung the rifle over my back. Then I started crawling farther to the right to see just what was going on. The adrenaline had worn away, but the pain had become a continuous hard ache that was bearable if I didn't bang myself on anything again. I threaded my way through the rocks while the house boy occasionally blasted away at the area behind me. It was pretty clear that he had no idea where I was.

Fifty or sixty yards away from the first rock, I found another good spot. Two suitcase-sized slabs leaned together with a little triangle opening at their base. I crawled up to it and lay down to look through. The opening showed me the back of the barn. I needed a few seconds to get a grip on the scene below me.

Shorty bent next to a canted pipe maybe four feet long held up by two metal legs, keeping his eye to a contraption on the side of it. Dufus carried something in two hands. He lugged it to Shorty, who straightened up and started peeling little pieces of yellow paper from one end. Dandy Don was using a crowbar to open rectangular wooden crates that I recognized from inside the barn earlier. Shorty handed the heavy object back and stepped away. Dufus held it for a second at the mouth of the pipe. The object looked like a gigantic bullet with a six-inch broomstick coming out of its back end. He dropped the thing into the pipe, and all three of them stopped to hold their ears. It didn't come immediately, but then smoke and fire flashed up out of the pipe. I heard another, louder, whump. They were crewing a mortar!

Incredulous, I watched as they started over. Shorty was looking through what I realized had to be a sight of some sort. He lined it up with a vertical red-and-white-striped stick nailed to the barn wall. Dufus and Dandy picked up more rounds while Shorty consulted a notebook. He turned a crank and fiddled with something on the tube. They brought him two more shells, and the yellow paper shucking started again.

The mortar tube pointed over my shoulder in the general direction of Billings. I rolled around to look behind me. *Big Sky Country, all right—hardly a cloud in sight.*

I couldn't see the town over the gentle rise, but a small smoky smudge squatted right on the skyline there. Shorty and his boys must have seen it about that time, too. They started yelling "Allahu Akbar" again. It sure made them happy. Mario at the house cut loose into the air with his AK. I guessed he saw it, too.

They bent to continue their work at the tube, and the next round got sent on its way. I cupped my ears to listen. After a long time—much longer than I'd thought it would take—I heard a soft distant boom like faraway thunder.

I started dialing as they fired off another one. It rang several times. "Nine-One-One, what's your emergency?" The lady sounded stressed and rushed. Excited voices babbled in the background.

"Yes, ma'am—" My voice cracked. "I need to report that some people are firing a mortar. I think they're starting some fires in Billings—"

"This about the fire at the refinery? Yes, sir, we know about it. Emergency crews are on their way. Thank you for calling." The line clicked and went dead.

I sat there in disbelief, holding the disconnected phone to my ear. That black smudge on the horizon had grown to cover a good part of the sky over Billings, rising straight up until high northwest winds flattened it and streamed it away down the valley. The smoke appeared to originate from the Concord refinery almost in the middle of town. If that place blew, the explosion would level half the city. I dialed again.

"Nine-One-One, what is your emergency?"

"Did I stutter, miss? I said *mortar*! There's people out here shooting a big-ass mortar at downtown Billings!" I tried to keep my voice calm and low.

"Sir, I can barely hear you. Did you say 'mortar'? Like the army ones?"

"Yeah, that's what I said. There's a crew here on my place, firing off rounds, and it looks like they're shooting at Billings!"

"Are you sure, sir? We already have a situation here."

"Hell, yes, I'm sure! Ma'am, this mortar is what's causing your situation. They're popping off rounds every minute."

The lady was silent for a long moment. "May I have your name and address, sir?"

I gave her the information then pounded the ground in frustration while she read it back to me.

"That's off 87, right?" she asked.

"Yes, ma'am, it is—can you please get some law here soon? I'm sorta pinned down out here."

"Pinned down? Is someone shooting at you, Mr. McGowan?" She sounded alarmed.

"Hell, yes, they're shooting at me. Why'd you think I'm calling you, for God's sake?"

"Okay, Mr. McGowan, I'm trying to get a unit to you right now. Stay on the line please." The line went silent as though she'd covered the mouthpiece. I snuck a peek around the sandstone. Shorty was back to tweaking the mortar sight while Dufus waited with another round.

In a minute, the gal came back on the line. She didn't sound good. "Mr. McGowan, all our available people are tied up right now. Nobody—I mean *nobody*—can get loose. There's a lot of casualties..." Her voice broke for a second. "I promise you, when we get help here from some other counties, I'll send a unit to your location."

"How long will that be?"

She blew out a breath. "I can't say, sir. They're coming, but it won't be soon."

"Well, that's just great, ma'am—just fucking great. There's men here with guns and a mortar—shooting at the town, and I'm not in much of a position to stop them by myself."

"Mr. McGowan, I'm sorry. We just can't help you yet—"

"No, they're not shooting at *me* now. Just listen to me, please. I'm saying that these guys are shooting at the city. If they're hitting that refinery—"

"There's too much going on here, Mr. McGowan. But I won't forget you. I promise you that. You *will* get help if you can just hang on for a while."

"Hang on for a while? Your situation's only going to get worse if you don't get someone up here!"

"I'm so sorry, Mr. McGowan. I have to go now."

"No, lady, you don't under—"

The line went dead again.

So the cops weren't coming. It looked like the way the cards lay on the table now, it would be up to me to play them on my own.

But I needed help. I dialed Dunker. Another round blasted off down at the barn as the phone started ringing.

Chapter Thirty

Dunker answered on the second ring, and he sounded rattled. "Jimmy Lloyd, you at work? What's going on over there?" He must have been in his truck. Its engine rumbled in the background, and I could hear a radio reporter reading off bulletins.

"Why hello, Dunker... It's nice... to talk to you, too," I gasped, panting to get the words out. My ribs were taking potshots at my lungs with each breath. Everything hurt much worse than it had even just moments ago when I'd talked to 911.

"Jimmy, what's going on? You don't sound good. Is that fire at your work?"

"Don't think so... I'm not there, anyway... but I'm... in trouble... at the rent house."

"What? I can't hear you. Say again." The truck radio clicked off. Highway noise took its place.

I paused for breath. It ached so much just to suck in air. "I'm in... deep shit here... Kamal's cousins... Arabs... shooting a... mortar... at town."

"*What?*"

"At barn... It's set up... shooting at... Concord... I think."

"Kamal's shooting a mortar at the Concord refinery?"

"No... *not* Kamal. Doesn't look good here."

"You're hurt?"

"Okay... Ribs hurting... bruised... Pinned down... in rocks by the barn... I need help, Dunker." My adrenaline surge was wearing away fast. I began to see red just from the effort of talking.

"They're shooting at you?"

"Some... mostly doing mortar... got my .22... with me."

"Call the police. I'm on my way."

"Called... Cops busy with fires... Where you at?" A long pause settled in.

"I'm a long way out, Jimmy Lloyd. 'Bout halfway to Hardin, but I'm turning around now." The highway sounds in the phone slowed, and I could hear Dunker's truck bumping as it rocked over rough ground in the median. Dunker grunted with each jolt. When the rattling stopped, the whine of tires on an interstate started up again. "On my way, Jimmy Lloyd." He got quiet for a moment. "Damn, but that's a lot of smoke! I can see it clear from here."

"Yeah... looks bad." I shuddered in a breath. "You packing?"

"Got the Judge with me." Dunker used his concealed carry permit to keep a .45/.410 pistol in his truck.

"Good."

"You betcha, pardner," he replied. "Look, Jimmy Lloyd, I'm still a long ways away from your place. You sit tight. Keep your head down and hold on till I get there, okay?"

Another mortar round thumped and sizzled away into the blue sky. I was shaking my head even before Dunker finished. "Can't wait... They're shootin'... Got to stop 'em now."

He didn't answer at first. I listened to the sounds of his Ford blasting up the highway. "Okay, Jimmy Lloyd. You do what you gotta do there. I'm coming. Let me get off this phone now. I gotta watch the road at this speed."

It felt damn good to know Dunker was coming. "Okay, good."

"You be careful, boy."

"Drive fast."

We clicked off, and I lay on my back for a minute, listening to the mortar fire and trying to get my pain under control. Dunker was at least forty to forty-five minutes out, too far away to help me with this. I finally pushed myself over to crawl back up to the peephole and dragged the Henry around so I could use the scope.

I pulled the little rifle back to inspect the scope and mount. I had missed Shorty clean at a hundred yards, but that drop off the back seat shouldn't have knocked everything out of alignment all that much. *But just how much?* A knot stood out in the freshly painted gray barn wall behind the mortar. Ignoring the men, I poked the barrel out and placed the scope's hairs on that spot and waited. When Dufus dropped a round down the tube, I slowly squeezed the trigger, and the mortar's blast swallowed the Henry's tiny cough. I cocked while keeping the scope trained around the knot, sweeping back and forth, up and down the boards, looking for the impact point. There it was—two feet up and two feet to the left. I slowly lowered the hammer.

I eased back to a sitting position. The effort and pain had me sweating in the sun like a truck-stop hooker. I mopped my face with a crusty handkerchief before loading three bullets to replace the ones I'd shot. The smoke in the sky over Billings looked like a giant black thundercloud. Using my legs to push myself, I crept back to the peephole between the two slabs. It hurt like hell to use my arms.

Things had gone quiet down at the mortar site, and when I looked through the opening, I saw why. Dandy Don and Dufus labored to swing the tube around toward my right while Shorty kept sighting through the optics at that striped stick on the barn wall. He cuffed Dandy on the back of his head and said something. They carefully inched the tube back a little. Shorty started twirling a handle. More than two dozen rounds had gone downrange to the Concord refinery in the last fifteen minutes. It looked like it might be Excalibur Mountain's refinery next—my job site and my friends'.

I slid the rifle barrel through the opening in the rocks, thumbing back the hammer as I peered through the scope. Shorty stood at the mortar with his back to me, about ninety yards away, consulting his notebook, while the other two humped more wooden boxes out from the barn. He was the only one of the three not moving. I put the crosshairs at the nape of his neck then went down two feet and two feet to the right, reckoning with the same Kentucky windage I used to shoot prairie dogs. Shorty was a bigger target than a desert rat all right, but my hands were trembling a little. *Deep breath. Ignore the hurt. Let it out slow. Squeeeeze.* The .22 seemed to crack like a sonic boom in the stillness.

Shorty jerked to his right and clapped a hand to the top of his left shoulder. I'd managed a hit, but not a solid one. He spun around, looking up in my direction. I could see the shock on his face through the scope. His mouth went slack-jawed as his gaze rolled over the rocks around me. The top of his shoulder was bleeding.

I cocked the lever action and centered the crosshairs on his sternum then adjusted a shade more than two feet to the right and down... and squeezed.

Shorty jerked back, tripped over one of the tripod legs, and crashed to the hard-packed ground. I'd hit him in his right pec, but at such range, the Henry wouldn't likely kill a man unless I got lucky with a shot to the eye. He sure jumped up and bolted for the barn door like he hadn't been touched, despite the small red bloom on his chest.

The other two dropped the box they were carrying and dashed after Shorty. I popped off a quick shot at one of them, but he outran the bullet. Or possibly I missed.

The mortar sat unattended and mute. A pair of AKs still leaned against the crates five yards from the wide-open barn door. Dandy had snatched up a third one on his way into safety, but that still meant somebody would have to come busting out if they wanted to get the other two. One of them would likely check out the situation first, like a curious pronghorn. I dialed the scope to a lower power, centered it on the door, and waited.

The barn's interior was too dim to see much, but I could make out a movement at the far side of the door. I zoomed the scope in and dead-reckoned an aim point right on the edge of the doorframe and about head high. I recognized Dandy Don's pompadour as he peeked one eye around the doorframe. When I squeezed the trigger, the bullet splintered the old wood at his nose and drove on. The man fell screaming with both hands to his face and thrashed in the doorway, heels kicking at the ground. I worked the lever, too pumped up to stop, and tried to put another round at the center of his torso. The way he kept on screaming and bumping around, I didn't know if I'd hit him again or not. It was a quick shot.

I was starting to feel better about my odds. *One down, and Shorty's hurt, too.*

Just as I began to congratulate myself on my marksmanship, everything started to go south. A burst of gunfire chattered out from inside the barn, chipping the two rocks over my head. They had found me. I pulled back, but little pieces of sandstone already stung my eyes. Without thinking, I started crawling back the way I had come, blinking away the tears. Two guns were firing, peppering the rocks. One of them must have recovered his rifle. I kept moving until I reached the tombstone-shaped slab again while those two pockmarked the hillside behind me. The sun beat down something fierce. Little cuts bled all over my face, and my ribs hurt again. The man I'd shot in the face still wailed away inside the barn while his buddies stayed more focused on killing me than on helping him.

I slowly leaned around the standing rock. Shorty and Dufus had come out of the barn, all right. The two squatted behind boulders at the base of the slope not more than eighty yards away. They scanned the area in front of them, popping up for a second, firing off a couple of rounds, then dropping down, still looking for me where I had been hiding a couple of minutes ago. I was sorry to see that Shorty, the nearer one, didn't appear to be hurt much.

I had a shot on him, though. Even crouched behind his rock, his head and most of his torso was visible from my side angle. He turned to the other man beside him. Both made hand gestures as though they were getting pumped to move. It took me a few seconds to get my breathing under control, then I slid the barrel out and adjusted a zero on the back of his head.

A slow squeeze. Shorty's head snapped forward, and he was done. His rifle went clattering on the hard ground as he fell face-first toward a shocked Dufus.

Crack! A shot hit the slab next to me and sent rocky shrapnel into my head and torso. I had forgotten about Mario Andretti in the house. His aim had improved some, although I still had the advantage of optics if I could keep remembering to adjust down and right.

Dufus started firing at my position, probably guided by Mario's shot. Crossfire bullets sprayed all around me while I huddled below the rock. *Time to move again.*

Not knowing what else to do, I started crawling back down toward what was left of Ol' Brown. I was growing used to the near-constant burning in my side, but I couldn't forget it entirely. Blood seeped through my ripped shirt.

It would be only a short while now before Dufus and Mario both got themselves up into the rocky ground where I hid, and that would be the end of whatever small leg up my scope had given me over them. Even with just their iron sights, those two assault AKs could easily overwhelm me at a closer range. To make things worse, I was getting weaker, probably from blood loss. *Not much time, hoss.*

I stopped at the last large boulder before reaching the road and the truck. There was no easy way to see over it, so I slipped off my hat to peep around one side at the house. The front window to the right of the door was completely broken out. A rifle barrel lay propped across the windowsill, pointed to the vicinity of the tombstone rock. It fired twice then pulled back into the house. A white patch flashed in the dim interior of the house—a bandage on Mario's chest where I had hit him earlier. The gun quickly protruded from the window again, probably holding a new magazine. The barrel tracked from side to side, looking for me back where I had been.

The man in the window bent forward to put his eye to the sights of the rifle, showing me the profile of his head. While he searched the rocks well to the right of me, I cautiously brought the Henry around to my shoulder. It would be the longest shot yet—well over a hundred yards. The crosshairs centered on his temple then slid down to a spot near the porch floor. *This one has to be true.*

Suddenly, the man's AK spat twice, shooting at sandstone, and his head jumped with the recoil. It almost made me jerk the trigger in surprise, but I caught myself and waited for him to settle again. The aiming site blurred in the scope as sweat and blood ran down the side of my face. I drew in a ragged breath and let it out while I gently pulled the trigger one more time. As the shot connected, he threw a hand up and pitched back into the interior. A chair clattered. His rifle thumped out onto the wooden porch bench that I had built so long ago.

I waited a full minute, watching the little house. Nothing moved. *So now it's one on one.* I was too tired and too hurt to feel like celebrating the new odds. I craved sleep. But Dufus could be anywhere. By then, he probably had an idea where I was, and he should be making his way toward me. I needed to put distance between us. Rising to my feet with hitches and groans, I started to stagger across the road, back toward the truck. If I could just get over to the far side and keep going, I could hide in the rocks and cactus and wait for him to show up.

I didn't hear so much as feel the gunshot behind me. A sledgehammer pounded my left shoulder, spinning me around and knocking me to the gravel roadway. Dufus had caught up to me. I struggled to get up, but the bullet had exploded my shoulder. I lay flat on my back with the sun blazing down in my eyes, fighting shock while blood pooled under me. The little Henry was still in my right hand. I must have closed my eyes because the first sign of his presence was hearing gravel rattling down the path I had been following through the sandstone. I raised my head to see him. Dufus didn't look so funny anymore. He moved cautiously and looked up and down the roadway before he stepped out.

"Hi there," I gasped.

His attention snapped onto me. The AK rifle came up, and his eyes locked on my fluttering eyelids. "You are alone?"

"No... Rangers coming."

He stopped about ten feet away and scanned the area around us, then he looked back at me, grinning a little. "No, you are alone."

I managed a smirk. "Behind you, asshole."

He hesitated a second then actually turned to look. I raised that Henry like a pistol and snapped off a shot that struck him in the side about navel high. He lurched and looked down at the sudden little puncture already oozing blood onto his bare skin. Still on my back, I worked the lever, cocking it one-handed like I was a kid again, playing the Rifleman on TV. As he raised his AK, I got off another shot to his body.

Dufus staggered back and tried to raise his weapon again, but his grip failed. The AK tumbled into the gravel. He turned his back, and I shot him again, hitting a kidney. My adrenaline let me pump bullet after bullet at him while he tried to stumble away. I don't know how many times I fired, much less how many times I might have actually hit the man. I only know he finally fell to his hands and knees. That was when I dropped my good arm and let the faithful little .22 plop to the ground. I could hear him struggling to get up, but I couldn't do anything more about it. Everything blurred.

Dufus must have eventually made it back to his feet. My head lolled to the side, and his scuffed Nikes stepped into focus right next to me. My eyes closed. *Shouldn't be long now.*

I floated in a lazy, bright sea at first before the sun gradually changed to overhead lights. I was sitting on Crabby as we cantered out into an arena. The stands were packed, and Esther was there, too, her hair shining and both hands waving.

Everybody cheered from the bottom of a dozen wells. "Jimmy Lloyd! Jimmy Lloyd! Jimmy Lloooyd…"

Chapter Thirty-One

A soft light glowed somewhere high behind me when I cracked my eyes. I lay on my back, listening to a rhythmic whoosh. Little lit-up numbers swam above my feet in the dimness. Everything ached, especially my head. I tried to sit up, but I couldn't move. My shoulder suddenly hurt like hell, as though a branding iron had been dragged across my neck and chest. The whooshing sound got faster and sharper—my own breathing, hissing inside a mask attached over my nose. Something beeped. I may have heard a voice then, too—a woman's—but I couldn't be sure. I drifted off into that warm sea again. It felt good to just drift.

Somehow, I sensed time had passed. I feebly thrashed my legs, and an angel spoke to me. "Mr. McGowan? Jimmy Lloyd? You're awake?"

I barely opened my eyes enough to see that the light was brighter than before. The angel wore a smock covered with irregular splotches and swirls in red, blue, and yellow. I knew the pattern from somewhere.

"Marge?" I croaked.

She leaned over and touched my forehead. "Sssh, Jimmy Lloyd. Don't try to talk just yet. You're going to be fine." She stepped back and turned to an IV bag hanging nearby. "Sounds like you had quite a time of it out at your place."

I stared at her. Marge was a friend of Esther's. *No, not a friend.* She was Esther's ICU supervisor. I was lying flat on my back in the hospital.

"What...?"

"Sssh. I told you. Just rest now. I'll go tell Dr. Lee you're awake." She patted my hand, hung a clipboard at the foot of my bed, and bustled out, as efficient as a mama hen.

I lay there, and the images started coming. The roadway at the ranch. My little Henry .22 rifle. Something had gone wrong. Something... I jerked as it all flooded back to me. *That mortar! The fires. Someone has to stop it!* Sharp pain dug into my shoulder at the movement, tearing away the fuzziness just as a white-coated doctor strode in.

"Mr. McGowan, good to see you this morning. You're still with us, I see." He greeted me all cheerily, like a used-car salesman. It probably wasn't fair, but I instantly didn't care for him or his chipper mood. He looked at the clipboard. "Everything is looking good. You had a good night's sleep. So how do you feel?" The doctor pulled a penlight from his pocket and shined it in my eyes, one at a time, without saying another word.

My eyes watered, and I blinked. "A little woozy, Doc. What's going on?" Air whooshed out when I tried to talk.

The doctor reached over to slip off the attached mask and hose. "You're in the intensive care unit at Billings Clinic, but you won't be in here for much longer." He glanced up at a monitor off to the side of my bed as Marge came back into the room.

"I'm being released?" Even as doped up and groggy as they had me in that bed, I doubted that was a good idea.

"Oh no, you're far from *that* yet," he answered. "Your vital signs are good, though. We're moving you to a regular bed. We need this space. There're some serious cases here." He shook his head gravely. "We've got burns and major trauma still coming in."

Of course. "Doc, I got to get through to the sheriff's office. There's some serious shit going on. They're shooting at town, the refineries—" My words slurred like I was underwater.

"Don't worry about that, Mr. McGowan. It's all being taken care of." He paused. "Actually, sir, you did it yourself, so I'm told." He turned to Marge. "Get him in a room. No visitors until afternoon, except family. No interviews. Especially no law enforcement." He started for the door then stopped and looked back. "Good luck to you, Mr. McGowan, and thank you for keeping this whole thing from being any worse." He left the room.

Another nurse came in and helped Marge with attaching and detaching wires and tubes.

"Marge, you mind telling me what's been happening? What time is it?" My voice still drawled out like a lazy man's.

She stopped to look at me. "You *don't* know, do you? Dunker brought you in yesterday, and you've been here almost twenty-four hours."

Everything seemed a dreamy haze again, but I managed to ask, "That long, huh? What's going on in town?"

"It's been terrible. Those fires at Concord. So many people dying. We're overwhelmed with burn cases."

"I'm... sorry..." I sighed. "I tried to stop 'em..."

"Oh, you did stop those men. You did." Marge and the other nurse exchanged a glance that I barely saw through my fluttering eyelids. "You might not know it yet, Jimmy Lloyd, but you're a hero."

SUNLIGHT STREAMED IN through a window when I woke up again. A television, its screen dark, protruded from the wall, and an IV still hung like a sagging bat over me. Thor leaned back in a padded chair on one side of the room, his head cocked back against the wall. His mouth hung open, imitating a rain gauge, as he dozed. A roll-around tray sat next to the other side of the bed. I hadn't dreamed anything—I was in the hospital, all right.

"Hey... you awake?" My voice grated like sandpaper on rust.

Thor started and brought his head down to eye me. "Wondered when you was gonna quit fakin' and get up. How you feel, bud?"

"Not too bad, considering." I reached up with my right arm to feel the dull ache in the other shoulder. The bandages wrapped tightly around my chest and shoulder were as stiff as starched drawers. "Mind telling me what happened?" I rasped.

"We sorta thought you might be the one to be tellin' *us*, Jimmy Lloyd." He got up and came to the bedside. "There's a whole bunch of folks outside, wanting to talk to you, but the docs are saying *not yet*." He stopped for a moment. "Truth is, I'm not supposed to be in here, either. None of us is. But we got us an inside connection." He winked.

"Thirsty."

"Yeah, she said you would be. Here you go, hoss." Thor poured water from a pitcher on the roll-around. Ice chips clinked into the plastic cup. He dropped a bent straw in and held the cup in front of my face.

Nothing else had ever tasted as good as that ice water on my tongue. I gulped about half of it before I had to stop, gasping and short of breath.

"Whoa. Easy now." He chuckled. "Too much of a good thing can be a bad thing, you know."

"Thanks." I gazed around the room, starting to get my bearings. "So what happened?"

"Well, like I said, you'll have to fill in a lot of gaps, Jimmy Lloyd, but near as we can figure, you had a tussle with those four Arab fellows. Appears they were bona fide terrorists. You capped two of 'em good. Another one was in ICU next to where you was, but he probably won't make it, either, so I hear. Head shot in the temple. The last one's going to live even though he's hurt bad. Barn splinters in both eyes." Thor grinned, and his mustache tips spread like bird wings.

"You popped that one next to you six times all around. What'd you do? Make him dance?"

"Something like that. Didn't have much time to think about it." I took a deep breath, checking out my ribs. "So how'd I get here?"

"Dunker showed up just about the time you passed out. You lost a lot of blood, Jimmy Lloyd. A whole lot of blood..." Thor shook his head. "That guy you was dancing with was lying almost on top of you. Looks like he snapped his neck when he fell and hit the ground... unless you reached over and snapped it for him. You remember that?" Thor shot me a sly look.

I shook my head slowly. "No way, Jose. Last thing I knew, he was standing by my head in the road, and I thought I was the one going to die. He musta crashed pretty hard." I stopped and looked at the wall for a long time. "It appears I'm the one still breathing. Makes me happy." I took another sip of water.

"Me, too, Jimmy Lloyd. Makes all of us pretty cheerful."

Thor set the plastic water cup on the roll-around. "So anyways, Dunker threw you in the back seat of his truck and brought you in. Says you owe him for new upholstery."

"He got the cousins?"

"No, he didn't fool with any of them. That Dunker's a smart old codger. He already called Travis on his personal cell. Knew he wouldn't get through any official channels. When Concord blew, half the town caught on fire. Cops and EMTs busy everywhere. I was at the downtown Shipton's store, and it was nothing but smoke and sirens all around. They thought they was gonna have to evacuate the hospitals for a while, but that scare's over. I hear there's dozens killed and dozens more they ain't found yet."

"Travis came?"

"Yes, he sure did. Told his boss he knew where the fires were coming from, and he jumped and left." He shook his head again. "Coulda lost his job over that, but he believed you and Dunker. He got out to your place right behind Dunker and took over. Called out everybody but the National Guard that wasn't fighting the fires. They found the splintered-eye one flopping around in the barn like he was a fish out of water. The FBI is out there at your place right now. Been there ever since it all came down."

I lay there quietly. Things had happened too fast for me to follow. I needed to digest. One thing nagged at me. "Kamal?"

Thor looked straight at me. "There's a fresh grave out behind the barn. Looks shallow, and they're gonna dig it up. Looks like that boy wasn't as far deep in this thing as the others. We'll know for sure pretty soon."

I closed my eyes. "Okay, Thor. Thanks." I felt him touch my good shoulder.

"I'll be back later, hoss."

I opened my eyes again as he left. Thor's "inside connection" touched his arm when he passed her standing in the doorway. She wore a smock with those red, blue, and yellow splotches. A stethoscope hung around her neck, and tears streaked her face. She came over and squeezed my hand for a long time. "Hello, Jimmy."

"Hi, Queenie."

"Let's talk."

I SPENT THE NEXT COUPLE of days mostly flat in that bed, although I stayed pretty busy dealing with the delegations standing in line to see me. I guess I felt like the pope. The FBI came in—two men in short sleeves, not like the ones in the movies, where they wear suits. That disappointed me a little. I never did remember their names, so I thought of them as Joe Friday and Magnum. They mostly asked me about the four mortar men. How did I know them? What did I know about them? My gunfight didn't seem to interest them, and they appeared to like my version of things okay enough. After all, it was the truth, and I'd never been that good of a liar anyway. The interview went on for a half hour the first day, until a doctor came in and said I had to rest. I was glad to see him.

"Wait a minute," I said when the two agents got up to go. "You haven't asked me anything about Kamal."

They glanced at each other before Magnum answered. "We'll get to that tomorrow, Mr. McGowan. You've already given us plenty of information to work with."

I snorted. "Bullshit."

"Excuse me?"

"I haven't told you much of anything useful. Even I know that," I said. "What about Kamal? He was in that grave, wasn't he?"

They shared a glance. "How did you know about that?"

"Stuff gets around. So it was him?"

Friday cleared his throat. "Yes, uh, the remains we found appear to be those of a young man of Arabic descent. We're still waiting on a positive ID from forensics."

I closed my eyes. "How did he die?"

A long silence filled the room. I sensed a decision being made between the two before Friday spoke. "His throat was cut, and it was very severe. Someone almost took his head off."

I raised a hand to cover my eyes. "Thank you."

They left quietly and closed the door behind them.

"Mr. McGowan?"

I had forgotten about the doctor standing there the last minute or so.

"Are you all right? Would you like a sedative?"

"No thanks, Doc. I'll be fine."

"Very well, then. Just let the nurses know if you change your mind. I'll leave the authorization with them. I know this must be stressful for you."

"Thanks, Doc."

When I heard him leave, I opened my eyes and stared at the ceiling. *Kamal, what the hell were you doing? How'd you ever get into this?* I hadn't cried since my dad died. I didn't even shed much of a tear when Esther divorced me, but right then, I cried. Great wet tears rolled down the sides of my face. I grieved for Kamal, and I wasn't ashamed of it. I grieved for his death and for whatever part I must have played in it. I shouldn't have let myself get so mad at Kamal. I should have tried harder to talk to him. Maybe I could have gotten him out of there. *Maybe, maybe... Maybe if I was a rat, I could scratch my ass in the dirt. Maybe, maybe, maybe...*

Chapter Thirty-Two

A lot of stuff came out over the next few days. The FBI and Homeland Security talked to me some more until it was pretty clear I couldn't tell them much about how the terrorists had operated. They didn't let me in on any inside stuff ahead of the news, but they did tell me that the guy in ICU with the head wound had died and that the blinded guy, Dandy Don, was awake and singing. Maybe they waterboarded him. I didn't ask.

Dunker came to see me on my third morning in the hospital. He had his hat off when he stuck his head around the half-opened door to the hallway. His hair had thinned and grayed considerably over the years, but I hadn't noticed so much before. "Well, well, I see you're living the life of Riley in here." He stepped into the room and took a seat in the padded chair. "How you doing, Jimmy Lloyd?"

"Pretty fair, I guess."

We stared at each other for a moment. Dunker crossed an ankle over his knee and set his hat on the other knee.

"I heard you finally got to the hoedown," I said. "Never knew you to be late for a fight before."

Dunker scratched his ear. "I was counting my money."

"Thanks for coming. That was good thinking, calling Travis direct."

"Wasn't much." He shifted his weight and cleared his throat. "The sheriff says you saved the Excalibur refinery singlehanded."

"Wasn't thinking a whole lot about that. Mostly just trying to save my own ass."

"Nothing wrong with that. You sure put a bunch of little holes in all of 'em." He looked up at the blank television then shifted his gaze out the window. "They tell you much about what's going on?"

"Not really, they haven't." I pointed at the TV. "Might as well be wearing a blindfold as to watch the news. They just keep saying the same stories over and over."

Dunker nodded. "You're right about that." He jiggled his boot. "There's a shitload of stuff I don't know, either, but here's what I do know." He uncrossed and leaned forward, hat in both hands. "Turns out there's a whole lot of these groups—cells, they call 'em—scattered pretty near all over the country. They musta smuggled in dozens of those mortars over the Mexican border. This bunch come up from Denver with one. That fellow you didn't kill thinks there was about twenty, just from there alone."

I eyed Dunker quizzically. "How are *you* getting all this? CBS sure isn't talking about it."

He chuckled and settled back in the chair. "No, I guess they ain't. Don't say anything about this, Jimmy Lloyd. You could get some people here in serious trouble."

"Travis?"

"Him and others."

"Others? What others?"

Dunker smiled. "Did you know Jacko was a fed?"

"Jacko! The biker?"

He kept smiling at me. "The one and only. You know me and Jacko go back a ways. He and Ronnie, my youngest boy, been friends since grade school, and he wasn't a bad sort back then. Ronnie and him played on the O-line together at Laurel High. Sometimes Jacko stayed with us when things weren't so good for him at home. We still keep in touch now and then. Jill worries about him all the time."

I shook my head in disbelief. "So what happened to him? Why's he a dirtbag now?"

"Oh, you know the tale. Drugs, the wrong crowd. A good man goes bad."

"That doesn't explain what he's got to do with all this."

Dunker watched the clouds out the window as he talked. "After Jacko killed that fellow some years ago, he got real scared. Told me he knew he'd really shit in his own plate for once. He was facing years in the pen for second degree or manslaughter. Nothing looked good. Then the ATF made him an offer." He turned back to face me. "I was the one convinced him to take it. He's been their man undercover ever since."

"Wow! I'da never figured that."

"No one would. Ronnie doesn't even know. I'm only telling you all this because Jacko dug up so much stuff about the mortars getting here that he's got to come out in the light now. He'll be going into the witness protection program tonight. Probably have to get himself a shave."

"But how would he know anything about mortars coming in?"

"ATF, Jimmy Lloyd. Alcohol, Tobacco, and *Firearms*. Jacko's had his fingers in the gun-smuggling business for years, usually going the other way across into Mexico. Not too long ago, he got rumblings from the California gangs about some heavy weaponry disappearing from armories all over Latin America. Nobody knew it was coming here, though."

"Then that means there's others ready to go."

He nodded. "Probably so. It appears the plan was to have a big fireworks show nationwide on 9/11. You know—cripple the whole American economy in one day. Billings was probably one of their smallest targets." He smiled again and shook his head. "But then here comes this redneck cowboy pickup man threatening to call the law in over a sickly horse. He spooks the shit out of them, so they start their shindig a couple of weeks early." Dunker spread his hands. "The rest is history."

"Who else's been mortared?"

"Nobody yet, and hopefully, not ever." Dunker got real sober. "Some of their planning was pretty slick, I have to say. One bunch in Louisiana had set up in some old abandoned shack in a soybean field right across the Mississippi River from a huge refinery. Another one in Texas put their mortar in a leased barge close to another refinery and some chemical plants. All they had to do was slide back the cargo covers when they was ready."

"You said dozens. Where's the rest of 'em?"

"Oh, I imagine the FBI's going full bore on their trail. People are phoning in all kinds of tips now that the word's out. According to Travis, Homeland Security and the cops been finding firing pits all over in backyards, empty swimming pools, and empty warehouses. East coast, west coast—everywhere. They caught some of the crews—them boys wasn't all Arabs, you know—but I reckon a bunch of 'em will get away. They probably scatter like deer when a white tail goes up."

I settled deeper in my pillow. "Concord?"

"Concord's ruined, Jimmy Lloyd. It's gone. That mortar put at least thirty rounds into it. One of them four boys was some kinda refining engineer, and he had figured it out enough to tell where to shoot to do the most damage. Pipes blew apart. Furnaces blew apart. Burning gas spewed all over, and more fires started from that." Dunker stopped, lowered his head, and massaged his forehead.

"Go on..."

He didn't look up. "They said it turned into one big inferno that spread out to houses and businesses. Hell on earth, and no one could tell it was dropping out of the sky. They're saying there was dozens of deaths, Jimmy Lloyd, but I'm telling you there's hundreds. Ambulances filled up hospitals all across Montana and Wyoming with burned men. Women and kids, too. You could hear sirens and helicopters for hours." He paused. "The bodies they could recover, they had to stack in the West High gym."

I closed my eyes. "Anybody I know?"

He exhaled loudly. "Probably some, you do. Brownie's daughter worked at Concord's front office, and he hasn't heard from her yet." He stopped to rub his eyes. "She's gone—that whole building collapsed and burned to the ground, but Brownie won't believe it yet. He's still hoping she'll turn up at one of the out-of-town hospitals."

I looked at him again. "I met that daughter a few years ago. Angela. She was just a kid then... How's Brownie doing?"

Dunker looked at the floor. "This has just about broke him." He took another deep breath and let it out. "As far as I know, there's nobody else close. Not so far."

"That doesn't really cheer me up."

"No, I don't reckon it would." Dunker rotated his hat in his hands and nodded sadly. "The cops found all kinds of Excalibur refinery maps and diagrams at your rent house, marked up with places to target. No telling how they got them. Those bastards wouldn't have been just guessing at the good spots if they'd ever got off any shots there."

We both stayed silent for a minute. Finally, I had to ask. "What about Kamal? What'd he have to do with all this?"

"You know they killed him. I heard the feds told you that much." Dunker looked me in the eye, and I nodded. "Well, Travis told me some of this, and some of it I'm just guessing at, but it appears the boy's job was only to come and set up the safe house for them. One young Saudi coming into town wouldn't cause a stir, whereas four of them might. Kamal did enroll at MSU-B, but he never went to any classes."

"Those so-called cousins?"

He shook his head. "No kin."

I took a breath. "So why'd they kill him?"

Dunker put a hand on my good shoulder. "According to the survivor that you *didn't* kill, it seems he tried to get them to change the original attack time for when you wouldn't be on shift—you and CK both."

"So we wouldn't be there when..."

Dunker nodded. "That's right. He made the mistake of admitting that was his reason, and their leader butchered him for it."

"Their leader. Shorty?"

"If that's what you call him." Dunker sat back and put his hat on. "I guess Kamal wouldn't have turned out all that bad of a fellow, but he was kinda like Jacko. Got sucked up into something he couldn't handle as a young man, and it killed him. Jacko gets to start over. Kamal doesn't."

"He was a good kid."

He stood up. "I don't disagree." He turned around before he went out the door. "They won't catch all those birds, you know. Some might still be lying low, waiting for another go-round. I don't know about that, but I will tell you this, Jimmy Lloyd. You can let the FBI and those fellows handle it from here on because you already put down all of this particular bunch, including the shithead that killed Kamal. You did us all proud." Dunker walked out of the room, leaving me openmouthed and a little embarrassed.

About an hour later, Chad White Horse appeared in the doorway, as quiet as morning fog, waiting there like he needed an invitation.

I set down my paperback and beckoned to him. "C'mon in, Chad. What the hell brings you up here? You sick or something?"

He grinned and shook his head. "Not me, Jimmy Lloyd. You're the one what's laying up in bed."

"You do make a good point there." I must have grimaced some as I swung my legs down onto the floor.

"You okay?" he asked anxiously.

"Oh yeah, I'm fine. It just smarts sometimes when I try to dance."

"Well, don't dance then. You probably ain't good at it anyway."

"I'll keep that it mind. Have a seat, Crow Warrior."

He sat down in that padded chair that everybody else favored, as well. We stared at each other for a second before he spoke. "How are you doing, White Eyes? Tell me for real."

"I'm fine, Chad. I really am... Thanks for asking."

"That's okay, brother. I just like having you around." He leaned back in the chair and set an ankle across his knee just like Dunker had. I watched his foot jiggling for a long time in silence. Suddenly, I could feel the hairs on my forearms rising.

"I've seen those shoes," I said.

Chad's face went blank. "I guess you have... I wear 'em all the time." He watched me intently. His foot stopped moving, and he put it back on the floor.

"No, it was last week. I was on the ground then, waiting for Dufus to shoot me."

"What're you talking about, Jimmy Lloyd? I think they giving you way too much dope in this hospital." He tried to laugh like a poker player who couldn't cover the bet he'd just made.

"Naw, I'm not juiced today," I answered, still staring at his shoe. "But I was for sure fucked up that day. In fact, I was 'bout passed out where all I could see was a pair of raggedy-assed Nikes in my face." I looked up at Chad's face. "It was you."

Chad White Horse could have been a carved totem pole head for all the expression he showed. He had eyes like dark-brown marbles that stared at nothing. After a long pause, he leaned back. "You was in a bad way, all right. That dude had shot you pretty good." His forefinger ticked softly on the chair's arm. "He was crawling back to his AK when I got to him. Grabbed his ears and popped his neck." He made a twisting motion with both hands. "Easy as doing an old cat."

"You killed him?"

"Didn't have a whole lotta choices there, Jimmy Lloyd. He was about to kill you."

"But... but how'd you *get* there? Where the hell did you *come* from?" I sputtered like an engine choking on too much fuel.

"I heard all the shooting about the time when I walked up to your house. Guess I was a little late that morning. It sounded like someone target practicing for the next war." He rubbed his armpit. "Then I heard that mortar going off. Knew what it was, too. I figured you might be in some real shit back there, so I didn't go straight up the road. I come around through the rocks on the side." He slithered his hand and arm back and forth like a snake. "I seen your old truck all shot up to hell, and then I seen you hiding behind the sandstone with bullets puckering all around your sorry ass. You looked to be in bad shape."

"Yeah, I cracked a couple of ribs."

He nodded. "That's what I heard."

"So you were there all along," I said.

"Not all along. I wasn't but about twenty yards behind you when you was crawling around and dinking at someone with that little popgun of yours, but I couldn't see who you was shooting at or if you was doing any good with it. I found out later that you did." He stuck up a thumb.

"I never saw you."

"You was busy."

"I suppose it did seem that way," I replied.

"When that last one come up in the rocks to find you, I wasn't close enough to stop him shooting you in the back, but I got behind him and picked up a rock while you was talking to him and pitched it hard at his back to draw him off. I was gonna jump the shithead and get his AK, but then you started shooting like a wild man." Chad shook his head, smiling at the memory. "It was crazy the way you was putting out bullets. Some of 'em hit him all right, but I had to drop and hide the way they was whizzing around me, too."

"Wait," I interrupted. "You threw a rock and hit him in the back?"

"Sure did."

"Well, I'll be... *That's* why he turned around. I thought I'd fooled him with some bullshit about a ranger."

Chad laughed. "Yeah, I heard you saying that crap. Guess I helped you a little on that one."

"More than a little, Crow Warrior. A lot more. I owe you my life, man."

He spread his hands. "No big deal, Jimmy Lloyd. I didn't do nothing much."

The silence went on longer until I finally had to ask. "So I got a question... You left after that? Nobody's said anything about you being there, so that means nobody saw you. Why'd you do that?"

Chad studied the floor and shuffled his feet. "I didn't leave you, Jimmy Lloyd, if that's what you're thinking."

"I never thought that. Just wondered why you weren't there when everybody else showed up."

"I was there. But I didn't know if there was any more bad guys left. After I checked on you, I went back in the rocks 'cause I could hear a truck coming. I hid, and I seen it was Dunker. Blue lights come over the hilltop while he was picking you up. I knew you might make it then. Wasn't much else there for me to do, so I skedaddled."

"That doesn't answer anything. You still haven't really said why."

He leaned forward to clasp his hands together. His forehead wrinkled as if deep in thought. "I ain't never killed nobody before, Jimmy Lloyd, and I found out it's not a good feeling. Not like the movies at all. I felt his neck pop between my hands. After that, I just wanted to run. Besides, you know how it is. They catch an Indian killing someone, he goes to Deer Lodge for life. I didn't want to be no grandpa in prison."

"But how'd you get away? There must have been cops all over the place by then."

He winked at me and smiled. "We Crow been hiding from you white boys for two centuries. It wasn't hard."

I had to laugh in spite of myself. "Yeah, I guess you got that right, cuz."

"There's one thing I gotta ask of you, Jimmy Lloyd." Chad's eyes bored into mine.

"You know you got it. Just say what it is," I answered.

"You can't tell no one about this—not even Dunker or anyone. I don't want no one to know I was there or what I did. Hell, I wasn't intending to even tell *you*, White Eyes. I was just gonna check on how you was doing, but you have to see my damn shoes."

"It's just us, Crow Warrior. I'll keep it quiet, but I'll never forget. I owe you big time."

Chad stood up to go. "Naw, you don't have to worry about it. Just be sure you pay me on time. I'm going to charge you an hour's wages for that day." He started for the door.

"Hey, Chad. Can you do me a favor?" I called out.

He stopped. "Maybe. What?"

"Could you check on Sweet Ginger for me? I'm afraid she might get lost in the shuffle."

"Already been doing that, White Eyes. She's getting fat and sassy. No problem." He slapped the doorframe on his way out, and just like that, he was gone.

A day later, I was released from the hospital. Dunker and Jill were going to take me in while I healed up out of the public eye. Roger came to see me that morning before I left.

He found me sitting up and dressed, and stood awkwardly next to my bed. "How're you feeling, Jimmy Lloyd?"

"Oh, all right, I think. The doctors tell me I won't be at work for a couple of months."

Roger nodded like he'd already heard it. "Sure, sure. No hurry on that."

I grinned at him. "I'm not getting fired, huh? This wasn't a rodeo injury, you know."

He laughed. "No, don't worry. That's not going to happen. You just get yourself well before you come back. That's all I want." He fumbled with his cap and looked up at the mute television. "Um, Jimmy Lloyd, have you done any rethinking on that job promotion I talked to you about a while back?"

"The one I turned down?"

"That's the one. You thought any more about it?"

I leaned back against the pillows. "Yes, actually I have, Roger." I indicated the wrapped shoulder. "They're telling me I probably won't be able to use this like I used to. Guess I won't be a pickup man anymore."

"That so?"

"Yeah. Some other things might be changing, too. When did you say Brian's leaving?"

"Brian's retiring in six weeks, but we can hold the job for you if you want."

"I want." It felt funny to hear that come out of my mouth.

Roger looked relieved. "That's great, Jimmy Lloyd. That's good news. I know you'll be great at it." He looked at his watch. "Well, I'm going to go now. I'm sure you have things to do here before you can sign out. I'll be getting in touch with you before you come back to work."

"You betcha, Roger."

He stopped at the door. "What else is changing?"

"Pardon?"

"You said some other things might be changing. What else you got going on?"

"Oh, that." I smiled. "She should be coming in any minute now. I'm her favorite patient."

Dear Reader,

We hope you enjoyed *Dust We Raised*, by Channing Turner. Please consider leaving a review on your favorite book site.

Visit our website[1] to sign up for the Red Adept Publishing Newsletter to be notified of future releases.

---

1. http://bit.ly/SMYH1u

About the Author

A son of the South, Channing Turner grew up in Arkansas and Louisiana before graduating from Louisiana State University in Psychology. He did graduate work in marine biology and became an estuarine biologist along the Texas coast. After retiring from the petrochemical industry where he worked in Louisiana and Montana as a laboratory analyst, he managed the 2010 US Census in Montana and northern Wyoming.

Channing now lives in eastern Washington with his wife, Barb. Channing served in the army and was discharged as an Armor captain. Reading and writing are his sedentary pursuits, but he also enjoys riding his Tennessee Walker in the Blue Mountains of Washington and Oregon.